THE
READYMADES

CONTENTS

La Consistance du visible		13
I	Odin's Eye	14
II	Nine Worlds	21
III	'Don't You Know Anything'	30
IV	Shining One	37
V	Winter	40
VI	What Tourists See	45
Invisible Dark Matter, Weighing Heavy		49
Appendix 1		61
Appendix 2		66
Appendix 3		76
Appendix 4		82
Appendix 5		89
'To Warmann'		99
'Fly to Your Own Heights': Beginnings and Forefathers		100
Notes Towards a Political Context of Our Art		114
Post Sexual Art: LGB and Homosexuality		126
Appendix 6		311

For reasons unknown, the son of a Hungarian parliamentarian, M. Warmann, asphyxiated himself in a boarding-house on Rue Saint-Guillaume.

— *Novels in Three Lines*
('Les Faits-Divers' in Le matin)
by Félix Fénéon, trans. Luc Sante.

And then one night, as the story goes, the gods tried to make a return.

The Serb let the heavy streetdoor close silently behind him, his huge frame dwarfed by the expanse of its opening and went out across the street, his familiar emptiness defined that night by the cold, the lateness of the hour, the empty streets left between still open bars and brothels and sushi restaurants. L'Avenue de l'Opéra had some traffic moving down either side of its length and the streetlights ascending to the Garnier were enough to keep his mood up. He turned right and walked down rue des Petits-Champs, a mote against the detail of storefront and awning, then circled the near-deserted bauble of Place des Victoires. The cold had been so dry in recent days that it reminded him of the cold of the Slavonic winter; more specifically the cheap material of his shirts carried over from boyhood, chafing his pubescent breasts and hysterical nipples. Once they had even burst, bleeding stigmata pressed onto him like some profane favour unwanted.

It was the time of year for the gods to make a return.

The rills of water were captured from one day to the next in ice, their bulging forms caught as they gushed out in the morning's gutter founts, caught like spirits photographed while fleeing before some impending armageddon. Crossing onto rue Etienne Marcel he saw that they were still rapt in their escape. The cold was so total the stalls of the Marché Saint-Honoré had been empty lately and washed down by lunchtime, the slosh and brine freezing as dark started to draw out the city's infinite lights: this Serb, this disbeliever of progress, had to chase an hour or two of daylight, go out and buy some fish at the market from his friend the fishmonger before going back to his bed to continue his erasure of the preceding night. His group had seen two men, huge like sumo wrestlers, punched and pinned to the ground by indifferent Algerian bouncers, their victim's blood the same dark carmine as almost everything he remembers from the scene. It was like their very first days in the city, hardened war refugees meeting anger and violence on every street corner. He was back out eyeing for violence, for some shimmer of erotic assent. He entered the subdued café on rue Montmartre in which they always started their nights and he placed his hands on the metallic bar, bracing himself.

Seita and Saffa joined the men whenever they got tired of the trendier parts of town that they felt it necessary to frequent: Convention, Belleville, Saint Germain and Mabillon even, if fashion dictated so. They liked having kirs with them because it recalled how Russians, homeless from the revolutions, would have been in the long ago and in Paris everyone liked to recall how it was in the long ago. They liked that when fucking there were three men to their two, how as a group they were all equal in their nakedness and could share the broken world the city had destroyed for them alone to pleasure their needs with. They had faith in what it was no longer possible to have faith in. Prenez un kir avec les victimes de la faim was their ironic way of deciding to go across town to the quiet, bland rue Montmartre and have some fun. They were the kind of moped girls, la jeunesse dorée, who read and venerated Catherine Millet and believed her sexual licentiousness was the real thing. They hated Sarkozy but would like to be the girl fucking him. They made animated points in the air with their cigarettes whenever they liked to think about getting what they wanted whenever and wherever they liked. They made the three guys grin indulgently; they made themselves laugh out loud.

They appeared on the other side of the window, catching the disbeliever in profile, elbow bearing his weight, shored up at the bar as if on time for an appointment that had never been made. Through the window it was obvious he was on his own, his friends leaving him in the waiter's preoccupied company. The girls ran the agenda whenever they came along, that much was certain, and the disbeliever, as always, was glad to see them come in from the cold. This night they were both drunk before they even started, the dark cold getting to them, opening up a lewd apathy with routine. They were both excited and talked over each other, slurping at their glasses, Seita's stockinged, strong leg inserted immediately between his legs the better to feel out the stiffening of his prick, the jostling at the bar allowing for desultory groping. They had news of a gathering in the third or maybe ninth, not far from Republique in any case.

– *Le Cabaret des filles d'extase, on va y aller j'espère.*

– *On verra.*

– *Viens vite, viens.*

She grabbed at his crotch the way she always did when she wanted to rise him up out of his stupor. Drink the coffee, she was saying, ignoring the arrival of the round headed one and the sickly intellectual. It was always the same whenever the girls showed up: noisy remonstrations and physical persuasion along the length of the metallic bar. The two girls held themselves so well they could do whatever they wanted, they could walk up and down the bar, knocking pastis flying and do a little routine for the whole café, forcing them all out on the street, hungry for more. The disbeliever played it cool, pleasing himself with their ebullience, letting the blood flow as slowly as it would without them and so driving the two of them mad with childish frustration. The three men grinned and drank their café-calvados like Breton fishermen bolstering themselves to brave the sea and the mundane prospect of gutting infinite scores of fish.

They talked sex dreams and the Belgian parliament's inability to form a government.

– *Viens vite, viens. On est chauds là.*

The club was a surprise, a place for tourists not far from the Cirque d'Hiver, a run down slot in the façades of the rue des Filles du Calvaire that stood for all things tarnished and dead to day. From the crowded hallway he made out the abandoned spectacle and the tiredness of inert tassels: les filles de joie were hyperactive with paychecks and their own bodies fused with the proximity of suited people, all turning into beasts before their ribald bodies. One girl was hooded in a loose robe, a shrieking Saint Theresa. Most remained in their outfits, the room so hot from the red lights and smoke that they sweated anyway, their spandex shorts like black paint ready to run under the heat. A cast of the hungry filled out the baking green room, bottles of yellow widow were popped open and drunk. The waiter from La Connetable lay on the floor, recognisable to most from many febrile dawns, the one man among them who could always afford to orgy. He chattered about poppers and the stupidity of glory holes, smoking a pipe, grinning and giggling and hiccupping, waving to the disbeliever when he saw him by the door. Saffa went over and lay beside him, speaking into his ear gravely as if the bombs were dropping and she had to break the news.

In the middle of night they started to don theatrical props, to mobilise their bodies, stroke each other, warm up. The Serb started to gulp, swallow champagne indiscriminately. There was a new face for everyone and they all quickly had one, a poor Grand Guignol that left the scene a cut-up deformation of some penurious idea of the gods, a secular cartoon of the sacred. Horny and inebriated: faithless. Soon it was a demented cavalcade, a Procession of the Cross that veered out onto the rue des Filles du Calvaire, the rumour of a four-star hotel suite drawing out the reluctant and prudent. The gods were returning: Venetian boys and girls at carnival, on their way to a holy wedding of god and mortal, defiant and doomed. Anonymity a beautiful shade overtaking the street lights, real life and people who were no longer people: they were something much more, something much less. The gods, they were on the return.

There just inside the door were several recidivist sybarites. There across the two huge double beds the disbeliever, the round headed one and several others: les enragés left homeless and without love from the peace and unity of fallen borders. There was Pan, braying like a tortured Montenegrin hill goat, legs bent, a proud rump in the air ready. There in the cramped bathroom skilled practitioners of a certain acceptable self-sedition, recognisable to everyone from television sets giving out deranged smut in sharp focus, cut up bodies reassembled in throwaway print publications. There were cocks awank, laughter and spider-fingers tickling out tears of anguish and release. There was a diapason of pain and beauty; anonymous naked bodies, cheap vin mousseux being poured over cum smeared chests and backs.

There was the pervert, as the papers would later call him, the son of a Hungarian parliamentarian, who had managed to asphyxiate himself: he was the first to go. Amongst the Janus faces deep in the clefts of assholes and pussy, the geometry of abandon plotting their arrangement, his belted neck looked in one direction only and that was at his slit-eye opening, holding the air back for the surge of pleasure he never got to register fully. Nobody had seen his selfish withdrawal, his last stand against a unity he wanted no part of, the truer image of the beyond his to have then forever. The son of a Hungarian parliamentarian, not that anyone knew this, was dead in their midst, his hung head a totem to dissolve and leave the conceits of the world behind – the stunned silence brought their own lives, left behind on the deserted boulevards, back to shadow them and immediately, spontaneously, they fed off the waiter's giggling and continued on with their orgy with renewed rigour.

The gods returned as they can only do in nightmares, and there were termagants and viragos, Seita and Saffa amongst them, roaring profanities in four different languages, drawing blood with their claws. Artemis, Persephone, failing artists and unapologetic businessmen, all the soiled hosts of countless strangers turning the grinding mill wheel of intoxication, the crushed white flour alive with the struggle of wheedling maggots.

And suddenly they all had heavy revolvers in their free hands, capering and twisting into irrepressible contortions, penetrating each other further, fucking profligate.

Suddenly, they were shooting the gods.

LA CONSISTANCE
DU VISIBLE

I — ODIN'S EYE

The shrieks and cries of children playing surfaced inside his head as if the clientele of The Old Navy had metamorphosed and lost their years in the time it had taken him to take a piss in the pay-per-use toilet. A kindergarten playground at eleven in the autumn morning, distracted by their own innocence. A long way off, John decided, from the pre-dawn hubbub of inebriation and beer-food. The tiny place was packed, each of the tables that filled the narrow space over-flowing with the well coiffed and stiff collar Yves Saint-Laurent denizens of the Left Bank. Steak-frites, stale *demis* of Stella Artois and Leffe, carafes of light red wine all threatening to over-rule the order any restaurant hopes it plays out convincingly. John returned to stand at the bar, arm outstretched to steady himself, his feet and legs tired, fingers pinching the foot of his glass. He frowned at the two girls. They called themselves Seita and Saffa and were both now laughing, once more, straight at each other, a closed system of daftness, he told himself.

More drink.

– Une autre, s'il vous plaît, he managed, raising up his empty glass. Plates were raised aloft behind him, thin, wide slabs of meat hanging off them.

The Old Navy, Boulevard Saint-Germain. The tiredness of it all, the deflated sound of the words themselves made him drink, as if all the booze he consumed could protect him from his situation. Just before dawn, that time when it was unseemly to be still in the same bar as the one you started in, but not quite wide-awake daytime either. What was he doing here, he thought, drinking from the new beer, in Paris, in this all-night dump?

– You stay awake, ok? My little Irish boy. Saffa tried to remind him of some reasons to keep going and he smiled blithely at her, moved away from her hand's grasp.

They were an unusual pair: two blonde girls from Marseilles, his friend Jean-Baptiste had introduced him way back at the start of the evening. A different lifetime. A lifetime in one night, nothing but emptiness in the morning after. And he found them attractive, was disarmed and powerless in the face of their evident beauty and the power of it. Their English a ridiculous French drawl that managed in itself to mock the language, as if it somehow wasn't up to their level of silk-lined sophistication. John had expected them to drift off, get called away, hail a taxi, direction Neuilly or anywhere else more refined than clapped-out Saint-Germain. But they hadn't, they had stayed the term drinking him under the table, smoking close on sixty cigarettes, mauling him in the tight corridor at the back of Bar Framboise.

In his time away from the city he had forgotten how strange it could be, how just as you thought its immaculate surfaces gave no leeway, no crack, no worthwhile reflection, no comfort, a hole opened up and you were bathed in your desires once more. A good meal. A good fuck. The pleasure of a new word.

Between him and the girls stood a man who had appeared out of nowhere. They seemed to know each other and John turned around in order to face him, try to act a little social. Had this man been there before? Impossible anymore to remember. He had on a heavy looking sheepskin coat, its collar a wide fan of fur. John wanted to go, to sleep or fuck, just get out of the repetition of drink and shite-talk.

– Irish man you say? The man was facing John now, apparently pleased with what the girls had just told him.

– That's right, John managed. Where're you from?

– Ah, he sighed, I'm from Serbia.

He looked like a pained man, as if something was adrift in the enclosed field of his life, tired eyes dull points of a sorrow that wouldn't let go. John had met a hundred guys during the course of all-nighters, all as random as the next and who were twisted, deranged, out of control and at first glance he guessed this guy to be no different, but this prejudice quickly disappeared once he started to talk.

– You a student or something? An artist maybe? No, let me guess: a writer? Philosopher? He was sneering, his long hair and dark features had been once menacing, terrifying even, to the more well ordered in life. A big fucker, John thought, not someone to get on the wrong side of. But then his roughness (John could only imagine all that had so coarsened a man) now seemed more deploring than anything else. It was hard to say how exactly, just as if too much had been hewn off, something fundamental now lacking.

– Actually, I'm a teacher. At least that's what I do a bit of now and then. But mostly I'm a publisher.

He didn't know why he bothered.

– A publisher? The man brightened, clearly cheered by this information. And what do you publish?

– Oh you know: books. Art books.

He hadn't the energy for enthusiasm.

– Really? I need a publisher! The man smiled, showing large teeth, a bit yellow in the light, but all there. It was hard to know if he was being sincere or not, but there was no doubt smiles belonged, at least once, on his face, this troubled grin at home there like lights on in a house in the dark of wintertime.

– What is it you want to publish?

– Oh, let's just say that it's a long story. It's an attempt at an explanation.

– Explanation?

– Of my art, my history.

The man grinned a mirthless grin that suggested less the light than the surrounding darkness.

– Well sounds just like something I'd be interested in publishing.

– Ah, but there are problems my friend, there are problems.

– What kind of problems?

– I'm distracting myself.

– Distracting yourself?

– With sickening history. With dead art. The end of things.

John laughed at him, full on and instinctively, the guy was doing his best at being lugubrious but the effort, for John so late at night, was comic only. Comic, but also drawing out his curiosity.

– Seriously though, is it an essay, a piece of history, what?

– I had intended mapping the rise of Dada, its move into the Balkans in the '20s, '30s, then its resurfacing in Paris in the form of Nouveau Réalisme in the '50s, '60s, all in an effort to make our own art seem rooted, you know.

– Whose art?

– There was a group of us. From all over.

– A group? Did you have a name?

– LGB. He laughed: Don't worry, I'm not offended that you've never heard of us. Actually we went to Ireland in 2004. Quite a show. But really the beginning of the end. Maybe you saw it?

– No, sadly not.

– A long journey from our time playing soldiers to the bright lights of Dublin and golden halls of an expanded EU.

– Well, I'd really like to read it.

The man grew serious and looked away at a full table receiving plates of steak frites.

– Yes I'd like that too, but as I said, there are problems.

– Just to look at it.

– You're too young to be a publisher. What do you publish?

– I'm looking for stuff just like this, John said ignoring the man's words and out of focus from drink he blinked slowly then, trying to think of something intelligible to say.

– What are you talking about George? Seita interrupted, stop boring poor John with your troubles.

– Yes, said the other one, get a drink and lighten up a bit.

But he just shook his head and slowly his face changed, dropped. He stayed for a while as the girls mauled John, bringing him closer to them, trying to tell a lewd joke that wasn't at all funny.

– Bon, je me casse, Djordje announced after a time, and even the indifferent barman looked at him from behind the counter he spoke so loud, with such definition. I've got to go my Irish friend. The conversation has obviously died and gone…someplace? You look after these girls. Someday perhaps I'd like you to read my manuscript.

– Yes, I'd like to read it. I never caught your name. I'm John. He lifted up his arm, dangling his hand in front of the man's chest.

He smiled, offering his teeth once more, but it was a smile devoid of any mirth, a broken smile.

– Call me George. And yes, perhaps you could help me out. He narrowed his eyes, keeping them on John, their dull points suddenly seeming lucid. I could do with a young publisher like you.

Dark, hoarse laughter.

– You never know.

The man, George, kissed the girls' cheeks and left. The girls turned back limply to face each other as soon as he had stepped away, John on the other hand followed him out the door, saw him turn right and head off up the boulevard.

– Never heard him speak English, Saffa was saying. It's very good, no?

– Poor George, so sad these days.

– Why is he sad?

– Why shouldn't he be?

– Is it what he's writing?

– Probably.

– What is it exactly?

– A history of the group he belonged to, Saffa said, they were really successful for some time. But I think it's killing him, to remember everything like that.

– Sounds interesting.

– Oh it was John, for a time, some years ago, but who knows how difficult it is to find again an art group once it's gone missing?

– Let's go, Seita declared, George suddenly no longer on the girls' minds. Remember your bag. I've paid, so come. I've had enough.

He drank his beer and picked up his shoulder bag, which was coated with specks of ash, and they walked out into the grey disorientating brightness of the dawn. They crossed the street, clamoured into a taxi like hunted animals seeking refuge from the wrathful eye of Odin.

– Rue Beaubourg, s'il vous plaît, Saffa spoke up. I'll get off at Rivoli mes chéris, feeling a bit tired.

– Comme tu veux, Seita said, her hand already firmly between John's legs, which he hardly noticed. He was staring out the window, thinking of the huge man who had shaken his hand, a strange meeting in the dawn, an introduction to such sadness, such trouble. Yes, trouble in a plain, unfortunate guise. Paris wasn't very good at accommodating plain, melancholic trouble. What city was? He knew about that. His hand moved over to Seita's lean leg, the buildings blurring, dissolving out the car window.

– Merde! Saffa was getting out of the car.

John jumped awake, a moment of sleep had overcome him.

– What's wrong?

– Les poubelles. Bin truck. We haven't moved for ten minutes.

The taxi driver raised his arms and offered them his consoling, pursed lips in the rear-view mirror. Other cars were sounding their horns, uselessly. Orange lights roved around the street. Which one? Rue Dauphine he guessed. He paid the fare before extracting himself: ten euro for two hundred metres. Looking from the dark blue sky to the green of the bin truck, the figures of the bin men rushing around it, doing their job, one of the first of the new day, John thought of waste. The millions of cubic metres of rubbish, the beautiful city surrounded by hills of shit, seagulls and domestic vultures and earth-mover drivers their only site-seers.

La Propreté de Paris.

He thought of the opposite, of a shit-smeared city somewhere off in the future, he thought of rubbish. He didn't stop to consider where his ash-speckled bag was.

De: Lubardamx@wanadoo.fr
Envoyé: sam. 08/10/08 20:44
Répondre à: Lubardamx@wanadoo.fr
À: Djordje (djorboj@googlemail.com)

---

djordje,
brother, sorry for not calling round over the weekend.
first off you need to remember you got out man. and none of it was your fault, we were kids in Bosnia. and its not like we went on to kosovo.
youre not there anymore, youre here. in paris! the art market, materialism, progress – fuck all that, you know that better than i do. why shouldn't we live the way we live? we ARE broken men, i give you that, were an army of a few thousand that this shitty city welcomes, as it has always done and who it somehow protects. even if it no longer wants to. were here because you got beaten up and stabbed, we are here because Trifke took us here, were here with the tainted likes of him, with the child soldiers, the rapists, the torturers. but we can still go out in the citys ruins. to the fucking cinema or to a bar. hold our heads high. even in the shop those japs know you, your the old man. its called respect and like it or not you have it.
i dont know what the fuck im talking about.
look I agree, there are problems. i just hate to hear you so fucking miserable.
were in a bit of a dead end. but writing the history of us, of yugoslavian avantgarde, will not help anything. we need to get back involved in an immediate sense, not write about it. maybe go to london. or berlin. in the meantime i wish youd ever fucking cheer up. im going out to play, maybe the girls will come too. i want you to come – well be on rue montmartre for a while – but yeah i can see your just a naval gazing cunt right now. just dont get used to it!
ill call you tomorrow,
L

II — NINE WORLDS

He had been here before, he was sure of that. Métro: Convention, 15th arrondissement. As an Erasmus student he had done a language exchange with Pierric from Concarneau on the wide, gently sloping rue Constadt. John had even been to rue des Morillons itself, at least between the pages of a book. Once, maybe twice, he could recall reading some roman policier by Simenon beginning there, at the city's extensive lost-and-found. When John had lifted his mat outside his door an hour before and found a letter from the Le Service des Objets Trouvés it took him a moment to remember that he had lost his bag, that he had need for such a service.

The sun was out, a slack, slow setting sun of a temperate October. He moved a hand across the back of his neck, relieving the skin of the coarse material grating against it. It would have been nice to be more awake, fresher. The little square was busy: the kiosque à journaux had a little line forming outside it, the afternoon editions carrying the news of J. M. G. Le Clézio's Nobel prize.

Going straight down rue Vaugirard he missed the squeeze of the market and turned left onto rue des Morillons. He stepped through the large arch, unnecessarily asking the policeman who was stationed there for guidance, who in turn unnecessarily asked John for some identification, for the letter itself, as if it was by invitation only at the city's central lost-and-found. Irritation again around the neck, a quickened heartbeat. The policeman pointed to a door further down the courtyard. Anonymous stairs drawn to a large, public dimension, a caged-in elevator. Then, through swing doors into a humming waiting area, a long desk behind which were office workers, their computers, shelves with lost items. He took a ticket and waited for his turn.

– Bonjour madame. He handed over his letter and passport when his number finally came up.

– Bonjour monsieur, a stylish woman twenty years his senior, he found her incredibly attractive, making him for a moment startled by shyness.

Most of the lost items were never collected. Useless, forgettable. Don't be fooled, he told himself, civilisation does not reflect itself in its nine worlds of endless bureaucracy. A trait of some sort of collective autism perhaps, and there exists more to envy a society for than that. He smiled once more as she went to retrieve his bag. For the first time that day he allowed himself to think back to how he had lost it, the memory dominated by the ten euro the useless taxi-ride had cost him. Sure enough, there it was. A transaction in absent-mindedness coming to a close.

It was only back out on the quiet street, rushing to the métro to get home that he opened up the bag to check its contents. It was a black shoulder bag, bought at some Chinese importer in the 3rd, lined with foam to protect a laptop. There was the book he had been reading by a Norwegian, Karl O. Knausgård, a present from his friend William in Oslo. The jiffy that had contained the book along with William's long letter that had allowed the Prefecture to contact him. His mobile, an ancient Nokia 3390 with a Harry Potter cover barely protecting it. A notebook, his teaching folder: he had given an hour's private tuition earlier in the day before meeting Jean-Baptiste, one of the many small jobs he did to pay the rent. A yellow piece of paper he picked out. Folded twice, he saw it was a menu. It was from The Old Navy. He stopped at the top of the entrance to the métro when he noticed there was writing, a message in a careless hand, a scrawl he had trouble deciphering:

JE
VAIS
MOU
RIR
BIEN
TÔT
ET
LE
MONDE
ME
SUIV
RA
AIDE
MOI
SI TU
PEUX

The yellow-toothed smile came back to him, the huge bulk of a man unhappy in the world. George. *I'm going to die soon. And the world along with me. Help me if you can.* John read the message, mouthing the words to himself, dumbfounded at their absurdity. Their pretentiousness. It must have been him: John knew instinctively. But why?

He looked up from the piece of paper in his hand. People had to avoid him as they turned to hurry down the steps. On the other side of the crossroads was a little carousel, ugly and old and too compact to be impressive in any way, wrapped up in dirty plastic covering. And laugh is what he did because right then he felt the whole city and everybody in it deserved nothing more than to be laughed at.

The metro carriage was almost empty: just John and a few others, mostly older, the time of afternoon not seeing many people on the move. A man, tall and heavy in dated denim jeans and jacket, a faded yellow shirt, stood to attention at the far end. The man stood rigid, his face diverted toward the ceiling, mumbling his words whatever which way. John looked down to the bag on his lap, faded freckles of ash still visible. Any feeling of satisfaction he had at regaining it was muted due to the oddness of the note. He was well-used to eccentricities, especially in Paris where his efforts to get to know people had often been frustrated by mock-ironic pleasantries, as passing and ephemeral as the attention of a friends' dog or cat. Shows of amusement, of folly. But this message, so much effort for so little immediate gain, he couldn't help but feel something was different. Not exactly serious but not folly either.

The man of no fixed abode ended his spiel and walked down the aisle, nodding his head, his hand at the ready.

– Merci mesdames, messieurs. S'il vous plaît. Mesdames, messieurs, floated shakily from his mouth.

John surprised himself by giving him a coin, the price of a coffee at a *bar counter*. One less for the day, and what harm?

With each stop some new passengers entered the carriage. It was slowly filling up on its way to Montparnasse, John's changeover. And with each stop John found himself looking over his shoulder, a need to eye everybody entering making him watchful. Watchful of what, he did not know exactly. Montparnasse-Bienvenüe was a busy station. Bag on his shoulder he grabbed hold of the comma-shaped metal door handle, blindly staring out the window, his mind idle as only it could be when waiting to be released from a train pulling into a station.

In the crowd alighting he was in the rear, the change for line 4 was at the far end of the slightly curving platform. Looking up something caught his eye. Somebody caught his eye. A wide fan of fur, swaying above the diminutive crowd. John frowned, focused, quickened his step, dodging people, bags, as he went. It couldn't be, he thought to himself, what would he be doing here? Following him? The idea was ridiculous and he pushed it out of his mind in the same instant it had come to him. If it was the Serb he wanted to talk to him, clear up this strange meeting, ask him if he knew anything about this note. But his fellow métro-travellers resisted his efforts. He was almost running but it was no good. By the time he reached the first set of steps he had lost sight of the coat. At the elevator further down the tunnel he couldn't get ahead of the people barring his way. At the top there was a juncture, a busy T-shaped meeting and this made it impossible to decide which way to take. He cursed, confused. He went on his way, it being all he could do, and moved to line 4, direction Porte de Clingnancourt. Try as he did, he recalled no mention of where this George guy lived; he had turned right outside The Old Navy, he remembered that, but this told him nothing. He could live anywhere.

Uneasiness settled over him. The ranks of waiting Parisians grew on either side of the tracks. He no longer thought of laughing at them, rather he just felt the long recognised need to fold himself amongst them, into their perfume-tight dream of sophisticated otherness.

On the number 4 line it came back to him from the early morning encounter with the man: LGB. He got off at Châtelet and moved through its labyrinth, emerging at the side of Les Halles. He walked to the internet café he used the most often and logged on. The system allowed the user to buy an hour's credit and to log on and off whenever they wish and for this reason he was never online for long. He typed in the three letters and pressed search. He spent time looking at websites about trains and other dead ends and kept refining his search until what came up were mostly pages in Serbian, a language he guessed to be Hungarian, maybe Slovenian, German, some in French and clicking carefully, English. And there: Djordje Bojić. That must be his man. Bojić: he felt the word rest in his head a moment, before continuing with his clicks. The French and English material he read quickly, hunting for information about this man and his group of friends. Press releases for exhibitions in different European cities gave potted summaries of artwork that seemed as disparate as they were impressive. There was an interview with a woman that gave details of what kind of an artist Bojić was: he came across as being interested in language and politics, a conceptual artist whose medium was text and whose interest was the relationship between word and image. John eyed it and stored it all away. Some names he recognised and some he didn't, some others he could appreciate thanks to his last publishing enterprise: Lucy Lippard, Lawrence Weiner, Elaine Sturtevant, important figures in conceptual art over the last number of decades. He also found a review by a guy called Beardsley that was an elliptical overview of The LGB Group. Suddenly the screen flickered and he was presented with a log-in box: his session had expired. All he had read confirmed one thing: he wanted to get his hands on the Serb's manuscript, that he definitely had potential to be someone John could publish.

When he got home the first thing he did was carefully unfold the note and place it on his desk. Then moving with a sense of urgency as if forgetting something important, he pulled at the blind, jerking the jalousie and throwing open the old casement window. He leaned out, searching the street. He was expecting to see the Serb's huge bulk lurking somewhere, looking up for a sign. But there was nobody looking for a sign, nobody interested.

There was just rue au Maire, the same as it always was, routine along the narrow space. A busy little street disconnected from the rest of the city, the old line of buildings on either side slumping amusedly over the little, narrow cobblestone street running between them. The street itself a battered market place, thoroughfare, storage space or open-air drainpipe depending on the time of day. The light was dull, out of focus, the growing cloud and wet wind dampening down any hope for a last burst of autumn sunshine. It was the kind of unapologetic afternoon that announces the warm times are over, that they're secreted away and the only trace to be found of brighter days are the golden, yellow leaves so without life which play happy in the air.

He faced the room, one elbow still on the railing that gave him his perch, considering the paranoia that had been following him since the métro and which was making him on edge. There's no reason for it, he told himself, none at all. He picked up the piece of paper and tacked it onto the wall in amongst all the other papers and notes he had arranged there. Along the opposite wall lay his mattress, single, worn down, only an old pillow and sleeping bag to comfort it. Emptying the retrieved shoulder bag he threw the Knausgård book onto the mattress; the jiffy containing William's letter and his teacher's folder he placed on the desk. He moved to the kitchenette and put a new filter, along with coffee and water, into the machine. Soon it was wheezing like it was in the throes of some ancient machination. He poured himself a bowl of the watery coffee the machine produced and he thought again of how he came to get the note. He remembered how when he had said he was a publisher he surprised the man; could he say that it had 'delighted' him? Yes, he seemed to remember the sad man momentarily light up and engage with a world for which he had otherwise no time.

Publisher. He always felt it was a strange self-designation to make. The Serb had listed all those things John had played with being when he first left college: a writer, an artist, even an eternal student, a return back inside the sanctuary of academe. But his interests had always been far too eclectic. His engagement with what he felt was a lugubrious resuscitation of the past only lasted so long, and when he turned away from it he found his own creative originality, his own discipline say, to be wholly lacking. Publisher, this is what he had settled on, a kind of facilitator. A publisher he started to state, in the clearest sense of the term. It was just that sometimes he had little to publish. Or very little means. But this had not stopped him during the four years since he graduated: there had been four poetry collections by two different poets, one Irish, one Scottish. The early books had been more chapbooks but they all bore ISBN numbers and had garnered small reviews, had served the poets well and still sat on library shelves as testament to something or other. Then a book of ekphrasis, poetry and image, a hasty idea which ultimately ended in despair. It was a regrettable collaboration between a mediocre French poet and a mediocre Irish painter, who, it became quite clear early on, could not stand each other. But the book, printed on heavy-set cream paper and bound beautifully by an artisan printer in Reims, made up for the trouble. He retained two out of the 100 copies they had been able to afford and held them dearly. Then there was another friend, Christophe, whose art he found slightly more stimulating than the Irish painter's, and who had a large, collaborative and sprawling show in Belleville back in May and who had chosen John to compile the catalogue. This, the best funded project Broken Dimanche Press had got to work with, proved a success: they ended up producing a hardback, multi-authored artists' catalogue that had a 26 page full-colour inset. It sold very well and gave John his first profit and during the process he met and worked with a lot of people, including Jean-Baptiste, giving him his entry point most recently to the two girls, a world whose exacerbated sexuality and attraction to art seemed to cling to every aspect of life.

He rolled a cigarette, slurped from the bowl and thought what little hope there was in the strange note – it was almost like a suicide note. From what he had seen on the Internet it was clear that texts such as this one were part of Bojić's trade, this was the form his art often took, cascading narrow bands of text. The press releases he had skimmed were full of a cryptic foreboding, the work of Bojić and The LGB Group having seemed to be bred out of violence and turbulence and suffused not with bland theoretical emptiness that wafted from much of the contemporary art John came across, or indeed any optimism at all, but the very opposite, like the tone of the note now tacked onto his wall.

John sat facing it, then turned and looked out the window, the view truncated by the angle but not the sounds. Chinese traders shouting to each other, water being sloshed over pavement stones. The uneasiness lifted. He felt a heaviness fall through his body: he would have a nap, clear the head, go out later and find the girls, try to meet this George guy again. The heaviness made a grab at the edges of his wide-awake self and managed to pull him down with it. He dreamed of a world that was dying all around him, whole cities flooding with seawater and millions of people on the move, following the world's migrants to Elysian fields already ruined and made barren by the blighted blossoming of man.

De: Lubardamx@wanadoo.fr
Envoyé: lun. 12/10/08 20:44
Répondre à: lubardamx@wanadoo.fr
À: Djordje (djorboj@googlemail.com)

Djordje,
so sorry brother for not calling. how you been?
It was a bit of a long bender you could say! ended badly with gojković losing it over the idea of this thing youre writing. I think we need to talk. you need to tell us exactly what youre writing about us.
Ill call around tomorrow and see how you are. The girls went crazy about this new show on in Espace Paul Ricard curated by your nemesis Nicolas Bourriaud! La consistance du visible, or some crap.
We must go.
Even if they are out to get us!!!
A demain mon grand,
L.

III — 'DON'T YOU KNOW ANYTHING?'

John awoke and felt like he had aged and the entire world along with him, his room full of a pervasive sense of loss. He'd had a dream and in the dream a dirty child came to him down from the streets of Belleville with something written on a carte du jour whose code he could not decipher. Through the filth he knew that the child was himself sixteen years heretofore and the message was mute and would stay mute. He looked at the Serb's note from where he lay in his bed. He still didn't understand his finding it. The four-minute conversation he had with the man came back to him and John knew then that he would have to talk to him again and ask him if he wrote the note.

Leaving home and going out into the city unease followed him. The café was on the corner of the boulevard de la Villette and rue Rébeval. It wasn't until he entered it and ordered a drink that he calmed down. Bourgeois-bohemia had a Belleville palace in the café, its clientele going up and down depending on the esoteric, infrared dictates of city fashion. An unfinished chic left the floors and walls untreated and the furniture was basic: sturdy wooden tables and chairs that rattled about, a red light suffusing the place. It was quite empty: two guys and a woman, speaking English, sat languidly by the window, another man beside John stood at the *zinc*, engrossed in rolling a cigarette and a group loudly laughing, self-absorbed, filled out a table by the door of the toilets.

– You know Camilla, don't you? She worked with Jean-Luc for a while. They got on very well but then he bought a dog and...

John stopped trying to follow the conversation, and drinking down half of his beer in one go, turned the other way. Looking out the front window onto the boulevard he thought of the US, how sometimes he thought he could see Europe collapsing into its ways, somnambulantly like the way society drops one set of mores and picks up a new set, ways of living that had at one stage seemed reprehensible, disgusting even. It was like falling for a bad advertisement, a decadent capitalism, an opposing way of life, without fully thinking it through. It wasn't that he disliked the States, on the contrary. The US was a rare bird in the world of nations, moving from a state of barbarity to decadence without first paying its dues at the court of civilisation: and John admired it for this very reason.

He had been to the US on one occasion only, if you could really term it the United States: New York. The more acceptable side of the beast, he was sure: just as he had imagined it, like something out of the movies, a composite picture assembled from a life time in front of the box. It had been at the end of the line for him, he'd been broken by boredom, aimless: he had come to the end of university and no calling had claimed him, no possible future seemed worth his time. And then in the autumn, his mother gave her son's distress as an excuse to take the two of them to New York. Standing then at the bar in Belleville almost exactly two years later, the memory of the trip overtakes him and he looks blindly out the window. At the time he had known it was one of those bizarre shopping trips that had marked the closing years of the Irish Celtic Tiger when middle income families felt it their duty to go to New York on their credit cards, spend money they barely had, marvel at the Americaness of it all, come home, shout about it, do the tax man out of his duty charges, tweak the accent a little bit more. So, yah, like, y'know.

Thinking about it, he may well have been clinically depressed at the time. All his friends had entered jobs, fixed, irreproachable. He had known he wasn't an artist, of any description, and this realisation, such charity to a world over-flowing with them, had left him at a dead end.

The same nameless – he knew the proper word was ruthless – drive that first overtook him in New York had appeared again and had grown in weight in his mind since awakening from his afternoon sleep. The desire to publish a certain book formed itself in ways he did not recognise, this desire was always a nameless nebulous thing created from his own wide-ranging interests and curiosity. He recalled now where he first came across this nameless drive to make things happen in the world, to facilitate.

John had been a good tourist in New York, even if he hated the sight of them in Paris and he had followed the designated course upon reaching the city, and he had duly visited the Metropolitan Museum. And it was there, in New York, in the decadent States, and not in Paris or Europe, that he had stumbled into an exhibition that would give him his necessary inspiration, kick start his drive to make books.

Cézanne to Picasso: Ambroise Vollard, Patron of the Avant Garde. What had struck him first was the inventiveness of the curation: here was a dealer, Ambroise Vollard, of all the great Fauvists, Van Gogh, Picasso, of that whole generation who were a cornerstone to modern painting, hang his name up and you had a wonderful historical cluster of painters that could be rustled up to congregate below it. The man had been an eccentric, rarely offering his customers what they wanted, a giant of a man, oafish, he nevertheless ended up having enough portraits done of himself that he could fill up a room at the Met. An achievement of sorts, John had thought. The exhibition was the story of a man who had the personality of the collector and the dealer – buy low, sell high had been his mantra – and the exhibition laid out the stories of his dealings with them all. And what had stayed clear in John's mind was the part of the show displaying Vollard's side career as a publisher. It was a history of fine art books, prints, livres d'artistes as well as biographies he wrote himself of Cézanne, Degas, Renoir – later on also, his own multi-volume autobiography.

It was this display of books and publications that had caught John: the paintings were forgettable somehow, as if too self-important they only obscured themselves with their largesse, but the books were so beautiful in their compactness, so bound up in their form and their content. This was an expression of intent, of a time:

John saw for himself that the movement of artists around this man Vollard and his gallery shone more brightly due to their involvement with his career as a publisher. Ambroise Vollard, a name that now echoed with all the great names of modern French painting. The man died, John could still recall, in a car crash.

During that week John saw a lot of art: the grand museums of course, but he had also toured Chelsea.

Who pays for this? He had asked a cute gallery attendant in one of the spaces on 24th Street, inspecting a very expensive artist's book.

– We do.

– Why? Do people buy them?

– Most of the artists we represent get a book every so often. If they have a solo museum show for example, we publish a book to accompany it.

– But why is it full of poetry and philosophy?

– Haven't you seen many artists' catalogues? She said it as a joke.

– To be honest, no. But tell me: do you make money with these books?

– Look at the selection. She had waved an arm across the shelf, all of those are as different as the next, and yes, people buy them. This one here is one of my favourites. It's really well finished, with a dustcover which folds out into a poster.

It had been a beautifully made book. The girl, not any older than John and who seemed to be acting a role more than actually believing in what she was talking about, was one inspiration for Broken Dimanche Press. He could admit that: John could appreciate the work of other people, but what drove him was the possibility of making objects so beautiful that an extra fiction surrounded this work and people would pick a book off a shelf in an art gallery, handle it with care and act out a role of deep, heart-felt appreciation. Like that girl had done. He had bought the book.

He was brought out of his thoughts as the two girls appeared outside the café windows, two streaks of blond hair, and he watched them enter. They appeared limpid to him, their clothes an effervescence, a mere suggestion of something more.

– Bonsoir John, Seita grinned. Comment ça va? He liked their accents, more pointed, the air catching more of the inside of their tiny mouths, giving their hysterical talk a saliva-tinged vibrato. It is possible to say that he liked them more when they spoke their own language.

– Ça va, ça va.

– Ça va, ça va, Seita said in a bass monotone, mock-imitating the deep voice that came out whenever he spoke French.

– C'est bien de vous revoir, he looked at Saffa who girlishly smiled back at him, as if eager to impart a superficial innocence deserved of defilement. When he glanced at Seita and saw the same smile, perfectly mirrored, along with her finger twirling a lock of her blond hair, he saw the mockery.

– Ay, ay, ay, girls, you need to go easier on a guy so early in the evening, I might get upset and go home.

– No, Seita implored, baritone, grabbing his arm. Don't go, John!

The two broke down in hysterical laughter, as if speaking English was a joke in itself. He asked if it was still happy hour – it wasn't – so he ordered a pastis in lieu of beer.

– Santé, they all joined glasses, met eyes slowly, carefully. The girls calmed down; all three drank.

– Where is Jean-Baptiste tonight? asked Saffa as if suspicious of something.

– I don't know, John replied simply, it hadn't occurred to him to contact Jean-Baptiste. I haven't seen him since last week when we were all together in Saint-Germain.

– That's not very nice of you, Seita reproached. Tut-tut.

– Jean-Baptiste has my number, just like I have his, John smiled.

The two only ever met when they were both at loose ends. It was better this way, less obligation or expectation. Jean-Baptiste had been to architecture school with the two girls but, unlike them, did not practice it upon graduation. He worked as an artist's assistant for Christophe, the artist John had made a catalogue for that May.

That had been how the two had met. Ever since their paths had crossed often at vernissages or in the bars of Belleville: Aux Follies, Café Zobra, Café Chérie, le KD.

– Where's George tonight?
– George?
– Djordje. We met him the other night.
– Oh yeah, George. Who knows where he is.
– At home, crying over his life. Or out with Lubarda and Gojković.
– Lubarda and Gojković?
– Don't you know of Lubarda and Gojković?
– No.
– Ah, they both said in unison.
– Then you don't know about The LGB Group? Did you guys talk about it the other night?
– Just a little, John said hoping they would continue.

They jumped over themselves to inform him:
– Well, these three guys, Lubarda, Gojković and Bojić, started it –
– An art movement –
– They were really quite successful, everyone knew them around town –
– It ended up badly though, there was trouble in the group. Gojković got into selling art instead of making it.
– At times it felt like a criminal network more than an art movement thanks to Gojković and his wheeling and dealing.
– And does it still exist?
– Well, it hasn't been going so good, shall we say. We really like George, but the art and those other two guys…
– … young girls can never be too careful, Seita finished and the two of them burst out in laughter as if such an idea could only be said in jest.
– They reminded us of the Nouveaux Réalistes, Saffa said mock wistfully, they were an exciting avant-garde group.
– Who were they?
– Don't you know anything?
– Raymond Hains was one of them! We love Raymond Hains.

– And he loved us! We met him once in Galerie W.

– But relax: all his books have been published. Laughter again. Their childish giddiness was beginning to grate on him but he suppressed his annoyance.

– I think I'd like to meet George again. He said he was writing a book and -

– Yes, yes: your little publishing enterprise, Seita interrupted, you want something special. You should ask him to read it. I know he doesn't get any support from his friends.

– They don't like anything these days. God, they're so depressing.

– Yeah, I think it could be something for me.

– Well if you're nice to us, maybe we can do you a favour, and the two girls clung to each other, their laughter forcing them to seek support from the other.

– Always looking for things, aren't you, our little Irish boy.

He just smiled and shook his head as if to say she was wrong in what she said.

– George is full of sadness and crazy ideas these days, Seita said, I don't know if we can put up with him tonight.

– It could be nice, John said flatly in response.

– You really do want to meet up with him! Saffa shouted out.

– You think he's handsome, ha? Is that it?

He drank again from his pastis.

– I think you're handsome.

– What? Seita asked, not hearing properly.

– Ha, Saffa clung onto her friend's arm. Il vient de dire que t'es beau!

They both collapsed again into their familiar show of laughter, a fixed unit of daftness.

–Non, non, non: je suis *belle*! She stood up off her stool, shifted over to John and squared her shoulders, macho-style. Je te jure mec, je suis une vrai meuf. She licked her lips slowly, a smile breaking through, the teasing and burlesque putting an end – not for the last time that night – to his enquiries.

IV — SHINING ONE

– the mystery of all this is found in the man's weaknesses and the girls' strengths – there on the bed one of the two girls like an advertisement for something worth remembering though which has no name – not like a mannequin, they are not like mannequins in a shop window these two girls they are the opposite, they are twenty-seven year old women in full control of what makes them so bored, turned on, titillated – there is the wear and tear of their supple bodies, their blood rate, their body mass index, the clothes being agitated and shifted, the bands of sweat building up along their perinea – the other girl is in the bathroom and leaves only when the man of this adventure swears loudly – fuck he says, fuck – all night he has been frustrated, frustration coming to those who want but do not get and he tries to bring up the Serb again – but they just continue to have their fun and ignore him, ask him for some wine – in his hands two bottles of wine bought along rue Faubourg de Temple in a shop, a little greengrocer, une alimentation générale, and he is saying how he cannot find a corkscrew to open them – what's the matter, you silly boy, she says as she goes to turn on some music – the other on the bed removes her shoes, and with thumb and forefinger catches the top of her tights and pulls them down from sights invisible in a show the man fails to register, down her thighs and around the turn of her ankles and throws them wherever they may fall – his hands shake from want of finding the corkscrew, of asking these girls once again for what it is he wants to know – and you never know what will come to pass in such a situation, who will stay who will go who will kiss and who will fuck – the bottles go 'phop' and then 'phop' again – he drinks she drinks and the one below lights a cigarette and says: I'm bored of drinking – the one standing now moves to him and kisses the side of his face, his cheek and he moves his free hand around and feels the curve of her ass – a slow moving, lightsome hug – from the laptop on the unsteady table a delighted sounding Japanese woman sings in English – the one on the bed puts out her cigarette, closes her eyes – the two standing are kissing, more and more contact the length of their tired bodies, each as skinny as the next – undressing they begin with the zip of his Adidas sports top, that's the starting point – the shirt, his shirt, the man naked to the waist – the girl's buttons undone as she drinks once again from the bottle, drinking more than the world can hold – small breasts in a bra, black and white lace giving a border, an endline that welcomes beautiful pale skin – she reaches for his trouser buttons, undoes them and she slides her hands down between the trouser legs and hirsute skin – he stands on the accumulated fabric and marches once, twice so that he is free of them and is left in his boxers only and white socks – and they are kissing all the while – and she then puts the bottle down on the ground and goes back to his mouth for more – the girl below in her near sleep lets a leg loose and it kicks the bottle so it falls over and spreads a red lake under clothes, books, unnoticed and uncared for – and again: what about the Serb, he says, when are you going to give me his number – but she just slides her hands around and down under the boxershort elastic and his dick in its excitement feels her fingers before they touch it – so one process ends and another begins – the haunting of the end of day coming to those two still awake with whispers, calmings, susurrus – they move apart and one changes the music and the other turns out the light – and meeting again they greet with hands all over skin – sensation overtaking the man thinks how, as a way of holding back, such an ass would look better in a wide-bottomed pair of panties rather than a thong or g-string – she thinks of pleasure and the welcome size of his dick – and underneath her trousers he finds her ass covered as he thought fit – the last garments are removed and fall down amongst the fag-ash, the dull clutter of the man's den, a crumpled letter sent from Oslo, Norway, the blood-red wine so cheap and tannin-clad the white of the underwear is slowly died a putrid red – she whispers in his ear: rue Danielle Casanova, 15, that's where he lives, now shut up and fuck me – and with nowhere else to go she takes hold of him before pushing him down, a long way down onto the mattress-bed – the sleeping one turns and in her sleep smiles – first he touches her then she touches him, takes a hold of his dick – her fingers slide down between his ass cheeks – in his mind he sees a lake that shines green, in her mind the escalator ride at the Beaubourg and the sleeper dreams of animated glossy magazines – and the one awake touches herself before welcoming herself to his dick, her arms then stretched behind on his legs to carry her weight – he forgets his pleasure of getting information and feels only the pleasure of getting fucked – you never know who will stay and who will go –

V — WINTER

It had grown cold, the air masses shifting, as if the sky had lifted aloft its protective cover, allowing chill winds to rush down off the continental shelf, catching the dead leaves tiredly playing and blowing out the dust motes the low-lying sunbeams had been catching every evening. Though these rays too had grown old and with the change into wintertime, lost their routine power: the sun now set by five o'clock, its weak rays disappearing behind the townhouses in the afternoon. All was grey, the colour draining away day by day. It had become a suicidal season, slashing itself of its characteristics, toting the life-force of trees from leaf to bole to root and sap until one day it quickly transpired into another season: winter.

Rue Danielle Casanova stood bracing itself like every other street in the moribund city. A narrow side street running off from the avenue de l'Opéra, leading a way to Place Vendôme, it carried its share of passengers, a conduit lined with parked cars as it had to be and full of its own secret ways. From the avenue to the first corner there was a telephone shop (SFR), some shoe shops, a pipe shop, cafés, a sushi restaurant, a bookshop (Brentano's, rear entry), a brothel (Bar Casanova), a Moroccan restaurant, a sandwich bar (Bioboa). Above all these were countless other spaces filled with endless other uses, all the uses space is put through, the tired ordeals of human life. People were moving hurriedly along the street, cold, their breath making itself visible before them, a light, low fog covering the sky above, reaching down and taking in the city-dwellers' contributions.

John thought he would have no trouble finding the address. He overstepped the mark and had to do an about-turn. Turning onto the short street he quickly saw across from him the large entranceway, the little blue square with number 15 to its side. The arch was very large and above it the worn words Hotel De Coigny were just about legible. There was space for three of his lengths, standing on shoulders within its expanse. Two solid-looking, roughened wooden doors sealed the span of the entrance.

He noticed the little hatchback police car immediately, of course he did. He felt apprehensive suddenly and the appearance of a police car only heightened the reservations he had calmed since finding the note in his bag. Just then as he made to cross the street the inset, heavy door slowly, silently moved inward and a policeman stepped out like a surprise foil to a doomed project. John cursed and surprised himself by stopping right where he was – in the middle of the road, a car approaching from the avenue – and the policeman, naturally, looked at him. A suspicious act of hesitation. He was a low, rounded man in his thirties, his hair cut so short that it must have only been a couple of days' growth. He put on his stiff cap as John moved out of the approaching car's way and stepped onto the narrow pavement. The two were linked in a silent communiqué, one of expectation but both men stayed silent and John continued on his way through the door, stepping carefully into the vaulted dimness of the hallway. A stroke of luck: in Paris usually you need the code to a building, and directions: second stairwell, third floor, left hand side for example. He didn't have the code, so he could tell himself that the policeman had been of help. But it was only when giving his nod to the policeman that he realised he had no idea where it was Djordje Bojić lived: what floor, what part of the building, which stairwell. He would have to simply call on the concierge and ask them for the missing information and go knock on the door, explain himself and, he hoped and half-expected, be welcomed by this man as a bringer of good tidings, a bright point of hope in this worn out, ever-darkening city. A divine facilitator sent from who knows where.

On the left was the door to what he guessed (correctly) to be the concierge's home. On the right was a wide series of steps leading to an elevator, a stairway, people's apartments. Straight ahead was a wooden and glass panel with a door leading out into the courtyard. He pressed the concierge's doorbell and heard the shrill sound of it come out from a little rectangular window. Nothing happened. Just then the voice of a woman, loud and authoritative, came from the courtyard. The glass-panelled door swung open and a stocky woman, a shock of dyed red hair on her head, moved through it. Followed by another, much larger, policeman, and a skinny, shabby looking man in a white suit with steel-rimmed glasses. More surprised than anything by these three figures moving together, John briefly didn't know what to do.

– Bonjour madame. Êtes-vous la concierge? He could barely speak his French sensibly, realising that all three had arrived as a party and that he was interrupting their business.

– Oui, oui. Yes I am. You want to speak English?

– Yes English is fine. He looked at the two men. The man in white, a foreigner too, he couldn't help but prejudge – resembled the young Trotsky, that is he looked strangely like he was from another age – seemed to be aggrieved or impatient, harried; the policeman, taller even than John, blinked his eyes disbelievingly, the language out of his grasping need for control.

– What is it you want? She had a bundle of keys in her hand, and was concentrating on those as well as John.

– I am looking for Djordje Bojić. The name made all three stiffen ever so slightly. The woman stopped moving her keys around the circular key ring and looked straight at John, who went on feebly: I believe he lives here…

The policeman looked from John to the woman who was at her keys, shaking her head.

– Il a dit quoi madame? The policeman was growing more uneasy. John was now wishing he was away somewhere else, far away, wishing that he had stopped and thought about going through that door as a policeman had come out of it.

–Il lui demande.

–Et vous êtes qui? The policeman was trained on him now; who are you, an existential question he did not know how to answer.

–Je suis un ami de deux filles qui connaissent Monsieur Bojić...

–Hélène et Julia? This came from little Trotsky who, shook loose from his aggravation, was now involved.

–Oui, John was unsure even of this; perhaps the girls he knew weren't called Hélène and Julia but really Seita and Saffa. Or maybe the girls hadn't been joking when they said LGB was more of a criminal network: maybe this guy George had become just a common everyday criminal and this was the arrest team?

– Mais vous ne connaissez pas Djordje? Vous êtes qui alors?

– John, he blurted out. Je suis John.

– John? John? The cop was excited now. Pff, moi aussi je suis 'John'. Et alors? Monsieur Bojić est mort. On a trouvé son corps dans la Seine ce matin. Donc si vous avez des informations sur cet accident, vous pouvez nous accompagner. Sinon nous vous prions de nous excuser, nous sommes pressés.

Meanwhile the concierge had found her key, stepped around John and opened her little door, the lattice rattling, sounding ready to fall off at any moment. The policeman followed the woman inside her little den.

– Vous êtes qui alors? Un ami de Trifke? The man was rolling back and forth on the balls of his feet, psyched-up from the situation John imagined, the oddness of the police, the concierge, a drowned friend in the Seine.

– Trifke? No, no, John said, in his confusion switching without noticing into English. Just a friend of the girls. I just wanted to talk to Djordje about a conversation we had in a bar last week.

Little Trotsky grew more furrows over his steel rimmed lunettes.

– About what?

– What? John said, confused. Oh, about art, well I don't know. But what happened in any case? I mean: I'm sorry–

– Yeah, so he's dead, he said cutting John off, impatient with grief, we don't know the details exactly, but at Charenton fishermen found his body.

The other two returned and the concierge handed a pile of post, one package and some letters to the policeman, who in turn passed them to the man in white. Both men, an odd couple thrown together by circumstance, began their goodbyes, their words of gratitude, to the concierge and turned in the gloomy hall to be on their way. Business like. John was left to regain a steady heartbeat, nod to the concierge.

– C'est la vie, she said without any apparent sense of irony, making John smile, despite himself. I like to speak English, she said pensively to herself, before adding: au revoir monsieur. And with that, the little door closed with a bang, the grille rattling about in protest.

VI — WHAT TOURISTS SEE

At first not at all surprised by what had just passed, John walked across the avenue de l'Opéra, noticing two tourists walking ahead of him, a man and a woman, both wearing matching tartan raincoats and who seemed perfectly happy with all that they saw, oblivious well-heeled Parisians walking briskly passed them. But as he watched them slow down and stop, standing still to better look up at the Haussmanian facades of the long street, the meaning of this fact, this information which he had just received at 15 rue Danielle Casanova, slowly sank in and created a hole in his knowledge of the world: joining up with his anxiety of the previous days and his curiosity to talk again with Djordje Bojić it somehow changed the tale being told. He had to remind himself to keep walking, not to stop like the two tourists just in front of him, that he had to keep walking and figure out where to go next, what to do.

John thought how any story must have its vanishing point, the invisible dark matter that weighs heavy, doing its best to let the listener know it exists, that what is being recounted actually happened. He looked up at the Palais Royal as he approached the end of the avenue, then he looked over to the Louvre and imagined it when it was somebody's home, trying then to imagine it in the future when it would be nothing more than a grandiose ruin. He thought of how history rolled crestful over the same days of different weeks until it crashed down on the go ahead present day, out of sight. How the nature of the apocalypse is that it, of all things, remains off stage, hypothetical, mythico-biblico in helical expanded times that aren't his times. Id est: unseeable.

What had become invisible for Djordje Bojić, John wondered as he entered the fray of rue de Rivoli? What, he wondered, was he failing to see himself?

In the grey brightness of the morning, the city laying dead all around him with the first tourists stepping out of their hotels to photograph its mummifying corpse, what could have been said of this disbeliever of progress? He himself had been saying for many years by then, his audience always wrong footed by his displacement in a world united around peace and harmony and continuity, a world of fallen walls and collapsing ideologies, that the earth quaked nightly with the broken face of man speaking in place of the gods, speaking his own gibberish and destroying that part of himself which is counterfeit, fabricated, a handed-on illusion of nearly-attained perfection. It could have been said also that the night the gods tried to return to the living world, when this Serb's broken self was captured by his friends and by strangers in mourning, the branded strangers acquainted from all the city's abandoned and licentious stairwells, that they had attempted to drown the world with infinite orgasms and ejaculations, that they had lived out their ends by forcing those ends, the termini of many secret paths, the dreams of many others, to be more marvellous and better than any found in workaday life, of everyday life. An apocalypse of abandon.

But that was merely the dream, the morning saw them all awake as the markets closed up, splashing water on their faces, brewing rough-edged coffee, back once more as dissatisfied émigrés in the city that did not want them, the city that held its mummified body upright and proud, as intimidating and benevolent as any old whore running any old bordello, crying out down the street the truth of her virtuous innocence.

All of them awakening save one: the Hungarian, Warmann.

INVISIBLE DARK MATTER, WEIGHING HEAVY

John recognised Lubarda by the same tattered white suit he had been wearing on their brief encounter a few days before, complemented this time with faded tennis shoes, broken with a red band. When the two girls told him where he could find the dead man's friend he first thought them to be joking once more. He spotted Lubarda immediately upon walking into the PMU tabac. They had said that was where he spends each and every afternoon, betting on whatever is being played out on the TV. He sat smoking, his legs apart bracing his chair back on its two hind legs, his face at a severe angle so that his chin disappeared into his collar and his eyes fixed on the screen suspended from the corner of the room. A hand lay on the table over a closed notepad with a pen beside it. He looked like a stick insect John thought, a white praying mantis.

– Miloš Lubarda?

The man simply nodded his head, his eyes turning from the screen for a brief moment only to take John in before turning quickly back to the football.

– I think we met briefly last week? My name's John –

– What is it I can do for you?

He was sombre, somewhat phlegmatic and his hand made a slight wave as if following the flight of some invisible fly.

– I'm really sorry about your friend, John said, trying to keep himself calm and evenly paced, I met him only once but I think he asked me for help. He said he wanted me to read a manuscript he was writing, and then he wrote me a note and I was going to ask him myself but then I met you and the policeman and his concierge, and I, I …

– And I still don't know what I can do for you. You want to know something about Djordje? He continued staring straight at the screen. Just then a waiter came around from the counter and John ordered a coffee, which gave him a welcome reason to sit down.

– I want to find out more about what he had written, yes.

– You don't know anything much about Djordje, do you?

– Other than he's dead, that he was friends with Hélène and Julia –

– Friends! Lubarda snorted. So you don't know much then. Or at least you say you don't know much.

The waiter placed his coffee down in front of John.

– Tell me, why do you want to find out more about Djordje's writing?

– He offered for me to read it, I'm a publisher.

– You're a publisher?

– Yeah.

– You're young to be a publisher. How old are you?

– Twenty-five.

– I would say that's young.

– Perhaps.

– What's the name of your press?

– Broken Dimanche Press.

– And what is it you publish?

– Poetry, art books. Last book was a catalogue for Christophe Bachalard, the French artist. Did very well.

– Here in Paris?

– Yeah.

– In May?

– Uh-huh, yeah.

– We went to see that show, I remember. But can't remember the catalogue.

– You went with Djordje?

– We saw a lot of art together. Even this week we were supposed to go to the Espace Paul Ricard for the Bourriaud show. Have you seen it?

– Espace Paul Ricard? No, no I haven't.

– You should. The fucker is doing what Djordje should be doing, if the world was more just.

Lubarda brought the two front legs of his chair back in contact with the floor, saying nothing more.

– But Djordje, he wasn't an artist, but a curator?

– Yes, I'd say Djordje was very much an artist. But listen, if you don't mind, what do you want exactly?

– Well I think I'd like to read more about you all. He asked me to read what he had written. Maybe we could collaborate in publishing his history of The LGB Group-

– Look my friend, you don't know what you're talking about. Let me try to be as nice as I can be: there is no history of The LGB Group to publish. Djordje was writing nonsense nobody in the world would want to read. I don't know what he told you, but I'm telling you to forget about Djordje and LGB. Okay? If you'll excuse me this match has a lot riding on it.

– But the manuscript, could I read it all the same?

– Why are you asking me? It's not as if I wrote the thing.

– Do you know where it is?

– How would I know where it is? In his apartment I guess. Gojković and I have to go through his stuff later in the week. I'll tell you what: give me your email and I'll let you know if we come across it. How does that sound?

– Okay.

They were in silent agreement that they were both lying.

– God knows if it's there. I've been to the apartment briefly with a policeman – yes, you know – to look for a suicide note but the place is a mess. Djordje was a collector and never threw anything away. It's like a fucking shrine to Warmann.

– Warmann?

Lubarda measured silently a pause and looked at John coldly, his eyes looking catatonic, from grief or otherwise it was impossible to know and these eyes were unable to hide a tired fight with the seen world.

– Imre Warmann was the big love of Djordje's life. His fucking Lebensmensch, as he said. They spoke German to each other like secret code. If you ask me it's thanks to this fucker that Djordje's dead. You can't picture big Djordje with another guy? Takes a while for most people.

He let a cackle of laughter out for the first time, a reverberation full of caught mucus that was incongruous with his thin body.

– Well here's my email address, John said and handed him a

used betting stub with his email scrawled on it. Let me know if you come across it, I'd really like to take a look at it.

– Sure. Will do.

Nothing more came from the Serb. John paid the waiter, turned and shouted a little too loudly goodbye to the man he had been talking with and who just stayed braced regarding the TV, winning or losing it could have been either.

John walked from the 10th to rue Danielle Casanova and his feet were tired and sore. He stood smoking a cigarette and tried to imagine the lives of those filling the footpaths around the busy little crossroads – mostly tourists, but they didn't interest him – rather he was thinking about the business people coming and going from the large BNP banking office across the street, their ordinariness, their apparent precision about all things. Only of course the whole world of banking wasn't precise: it was dirty, rotten, bloated with bullshit and its own hype, John knew that, events of the autumn had shown the world as much.

He heard a click from the door and someone pulled on it from the inside; he continued to stare across the street, concertedly nonchalant as he had planned. He watched the old lady step out of the dark archway and into the bustling day. As she tottered off John reached out his left hand and in one swift movement kept the door where it was as he turned from the wall and hopped through the big, slow door into the dark space. He walked quickly without as much as a glance at the concierge's door.

The courtyard was narrow as he had expected it to be, and full of rubbish bins and the smell of rotting food and kitchen waste. To his left was a door into the neighbouring sushi restaurant, a bucket on wheels and two mops lay abandoned at its lintel. At the back of the space straight ahead was an open door, showing the service area of the Fuxia restaurant that lay on the corner of Marché Saint-Honoré. He could see some tables, filled with late lunch diners, rue Gombust out the window, some service staff. The kitchen seemed to be somewhere to the right, the loud noises of the kitchen chefs ricocheting out into the courtyard and against the four walls. The big green bins were overflowing. There was a low extension coming out of the first floor that must have belonged to the sushi restaurant. He took it all in rapidly: the strange life courtyards in the city have. He walked carefully toward the open restaurant door and a very narrow passage appeared between the extension that housed the sushi kitchen and the back wall. This led to the door of the second house, what would have been the building's servants quarters in the long ago.

Looking into the restaurant as he passed the open door he reminded himself that there was always the concierge if things didn't work out here first, whatever 'working out' entailed. He looked at the panel with the number code, the letters along the bottom: A B C. Pressing one randomly he realised it was dead and there was no electricity running to it and he raised his arm from where he stood, tried the door and, hanging dead on its hinges, it opened. The darkness of the stairwell surprised him: the walls were host to raw craquelure, the gloom total: it was like stepping back in time to when people couldn't afford the luxury of caring for veneers, when the wall's existence was more important than the wall's appearance. Straight ahead was another door belonging to the sushi restaurant. To the right the stairwell – narrow. There was a door at each turn, but the first two seemed boarded up, long out of use. The steps were wooden, smooth with worn-out curves from years and years of boots and shoes. The handrail was iron, black, topped by a wooden rail. John went up slowly, inspecting each door for a sign of a nameplate. Finally, there was a blue piece of paper tacked to the wooden, dull green doorjamb: Bojić. John reached out and tried the handle. Locked. He moved in and put his weight against the door: it was light, a split fold was on the left-hand side, allowing for extra room to manoeuvre furniture through the narrow turn in the stair. John placed his palm on it, just above where he thought the bolt ran into the join from the door, and leaned against both sections. It moved inward in the middle, almost enough to release the bolt, open the door, but at the top it didn't budge at all, an extra bolt holding the side panel in place. He stood back, swore. It was getting on to four in the afternoon, the building quiet, with an air of being deserted. The only noise came from the restaurant kitchen, sous-chefs busy preparing the evening food, and suddenly he was flushed with adrenalin and barraged the door with his shoulder just below the extra bolt and it gave way with a loud splintering.

He entered quickly and closed the door behind him, breathing heavy.

– Hello? He hazarded. Bonjour?

The apartment was dark. Even though he stood facing a window, it looked straight onto a wall and was covered in birdshit, grimy and may as well have been curtained so little daylight did it transmit. There was a large space to his left with two doors in its corner, to the right two doors facing each other. He looked in both quickly: a kitchen, small, poky, normal, through the other was a single toilet bowl, some ancient cleaning products, faded art reproductions, a film poster in Cyrillic. John didn't recognise any of the images. He moved into the large space. Lubarda's words came back to him: the space was an explosion of complete disorder. The walls, the dining table that served as a study desk, the two bookshelves – the only furniture in the space – became but the borderlines ready to burst under an infinitude of books and pages, rubbish, odds and ends. There were stacks of books, sheaves of papers, folders. On the walls were a couple of canvasses, one had food cartons stuck to it, another a series of words, obscured and obscure, a tactile palimpsest, a roughly executed metaphor for the chaos of the room. There were candelabras on the floor, overflowing ashtrays, an army of empty wine bottles. By the window lay paint: large tins of industrial matte to small tubes of acrylic. There were paintbrushes, a roller. No other signs of painting though, no easel or anything, just a roll of paper, eight-foot long or thereabouts, lay propped in the corner. John stood still a moment, trying to detect all the sounds that reached him, in that loud collection of a dead man's objects. Nothing. Just the muted kitchen noises from the courtyard, the fridge in the kitchen humming to itself. He finished the inspection. One of the two doors opened to reveal the rest of the bathroom: a narrow shower, a sink, peeling wallpaper. The other led into a living room. The curtain was drawn, but he could make out the sofa, the TV, the coffee table. Stacks and stacks of DVDs and video cassettes, strewn across the floor, the coffee table, some magazines and books between them, empty wine bottles, ashtrays overflowing. It smelled like a nightclub before smoking was outlawed. This thought made the place seem suffused with melancholy to John. A throwback, a nostalgic bare living space somehow disconnected and completely out of sync with the world outside. The final room led off from the living room and was the bedroom. Nothing but a mattress, a duvet sans bed sheets, a mirror on the wall, clothes all over the place. John walked into the centre of the gloomy space, sniffed the air, felt a shiver go through his body. He could make out a bowl of coffee, yellow and chipped badly on the lip, laying abandoned by the mattress, white scum growing an outpost atop its slowly evaporating surface.

It was empty: the flat had nobody in it that is. Abandoned. It was like the home of the last man to leave town before the bombs dropped. It was horribly lonely, and John couldn't help marvelling at how removed it was from the city outside, the busy little cross-roads, the mandarins of financial exchange, stockbrokers, bustle, other people – happiness – all just a couple of metres away. He had half hoped to find someone in there, a living human being: if not Djordje himself, back from the drowned dead, then someone else, anyone who would tell John how the man had died, what he had been thinking the last time he moved through these three connecting rooms so full of his person, where the dead man had thought he was going when he opened the door and walked out, down the narrow stairwell John had just moments ago walked up and if the note he found had anything to do with him never returning. But there was nobody, just the traces of someone now no longer of the world, an inaudible murmur of a disappointed prayer.

A sense of urgency came over him once this feeling of abandonment made itself felt: he moved quickly into the first space where

Djordje seemed to have spent most of his time. The arrangement of the clutter seemed anguished in itself, as if the carelessness of this hoarder spoke of all the pain, the difficulties and injustices he had felt with the world. On the wall facing the desk was something John hadn't seen when he came through: the letters DadaDaDada-DaDadaDadaDada, in a large arc, scrawled in black paint. On the rest of the wall were large texts, spray painted and sharp from the use of stencils. John stood a moment looking at the wall. A well executed, orderly scream at the world. He looked back at the desk, shaking off the idea that he had no right to be where he stood, that it was too private somehow for him to now start shifting through all the things assembled there. But he knew what he was looking for. He was worried at first because there was no computer, no sign of a laptop or even a printer. He pawed around in all the dross on the desktop. There, with a box of stamps sitting on it, was a large, Manila envelope. He picked it up and immediately felt the floppy heft of a manuscript. Turning it around in his hands he saw that it had on its back:

Envoyé par:
D. Bojić,
15 rue Danielle Casanova,
75001, Paris

But there was no address on its front. He looked again at where he had picked it up, the stamps, the envelope itself. If it wasn't for the fact that the owner was dead he would have said this package was due to be posted at any moment. Had Lubarda seen the readied package when they had come looking for a suicide note? With all the loose pieces of paper, the pens, the books, notebooks and such, perhaps he would have had to have been looking for a manuscript to have noticed it.

John peeled open the seal and took out the wad of paper. It was certainly a manuscript, and over 100 pages. A number of sheets at the back were held by a paper clip. He thumbed through these, they were in French and English, a press release for the exhibition Lubarda had talked about when they had met in the café the day before, other texts he recognised as art manifestos, some Internet print outs. There was no cover letter, or even title page, that he could make out. The main body of it was in Cyrillic and John was surprised by this for some reason forgetting to expect it. He smiled realising he was disappointed: he was after breaking and entering into this dead man's apartment, getting his hands on the sought after reward, only to be unable to read it. On the first page he could make out *Warmann*, in what seemed to be a dedication. Looking up then he saw what Lubarda had been talking about: the place was full of Warmann. Or at least, what he guessed to be him. Pictures mostly, some line drawings, printouts of emails signed off by him, notes – in German – bearing his name. He was a dark-eyed middle aged-man, a bushy moustache that looked like it was glued onto his face made him look out of step with the times, a face already resigned to the past, that of a foot soldier in the Cold War, his sport jackets, the faded happiness in the photographs that showed the two men together – a story over and done with, a memory. One photo was of a birthday party in a cramped kitchen, another showed them getting into a Škoda, Djordje and Warmann both halfway in the open doors, their arms mechanically held up in a posed wave. In the gloom of the indifferent present it was still possible to see that this had become a command station in sadness, a bureau to control melancholy and regulate fading memories.

John hurriedly put the manuscript back in the envelope and took one last look around before going back out the door he had come through, happy to see that the doors came to a neat close despite his forced entry. Having never done anything like it, he didn't want to stop now to think of what he was doing. Taking the stairs two at a time and moving back through the courtyard he met no one, only heard the shouting voices of the invisible sous-chefs, busy and under pressure. Adrenalin was pumping through his body, as was relief. What he had just done slowly dawned on him as he walked back toward the avenue. His sweaty hands were leaving damp impressions all over the envelope as he moved it around, taking a grip on all sides. Photocopy it: that's what he would do. Then he would get someone to translate it for him, at least a sample of it so he could find out what it was about and whether or not Broken Dimanche Press wanted to publish it. Questions crowded his mind as he ran to jump on a number 29 bus. Standing up, holding a handrail, he wondered whose permission would be needed to ask if he *did* decide to go ahead and publish it? Perhaps he could say Djordje had given it to him? And where would he find a translator of Serbian? Now that he actually had the manuscript he was more impatient than ever.

He looked up at the bus route and saw that it went up Boulevard Saint-Michel: that would do, the Latin Quarter was full of busy photocopy shops, he could get off there and have a copy made quickly. Leaning against the sharp turn of the bus going through the archway of the Louvre John thought back to Djordje's flat, trying to think how abandoned it actually was. There were little things that made him wonder: the coffee bowl by the bed. Even if you plan to throw yourself in the Seine would you still need your morning coffee? Probably more than ever, John thought. Would you clean up after yourself? He peered out from the bus as it rumbled around the Carousel du Louvre. Tourists. The Tuileries. Far off the Champs-Élysées, the Arc de Triomphe. But then there was the envelope, sealed, with the sender's address so carefully marked on the back of it, the box of stamps sitting atop. An errand waiting to be done, the day's task that needed to be fitted in. Strange thing to leave behind. But then, what did John know about 'leaving things behind'? He admitted to himself that he hadn't a clue about the mentality of suicidal people. After spending so many countless hours writing the thing, for all John knew the all powerful depression that had in all likelihood consumed Djordje obliterated them, like so many countless minutes wasted in trying to remember something by rote only to go and forget it in the next instant.

Being back on Boulevard Saint-Michel calmed John somewhat: if any part of the city was familiar to him, it was the area of the

Grandes Écoles. He crossed the windy, ascending streets, taking in the young faces, the fresh students – their channelled attentions soothing his anxious distractions. Place de la Sorbonne was the same as ever, though the bookshop on the corner was burned out from the student protests the year before. It gave an air of tiredness to the place. John could remember warmer days, his last days in the city as a student, waiting in late afternoon for a date, the anticipation and then the sighting through the milling crowds, her braided hair.

He got the manuscript photocopied and bought a second envelope for it. Later the same day he put ads online, in search for the distinct intellect that could help him get the text translated.

> Serbian–English Translator Needed (Paris)
> Reply to: com-9311800@craigslist.org
> Date: 2008-11-06, 3:09 AM CET
>
> I'm looking for someone fluent in Serbo-Croat to translate 130 pages of text. Good English style favoured. This is a personal project so email me a bit about yourself and what you're doing in Paris etc. Translated text will possibly be published in book form. Knowledge of 20th century art history a plus.
> For more information please email me.
>
> Location: Paris
> it's NOT ok to contact this poster with services or other commercial interests
> PostingID: 93103640

APPENDIX 1

Dada is a new tendency in art. One can tell this from the fact that until now nobody knew anything about it, and tomorrow everyone in Zurich will be talking about it. Dada comes from the dictionary. It is terribly simple. In French it means "hobby horse". In German it means "good-bye", "Get off my back", "Be seeing you sometime". In Romanian: "Yes, indeed, you are right, that's it. But of course, yes, definitely, right". And so forth.

An international word. Just a word, and the word a movement. Very easy to understand. Quite terribly simple. To make of it an artistic tendency must mean that one is anticipating complications. Dada psychology, dada Germany cum indigestion and fog paroxysm, dada literature, dada bourgeoisie, and yourselves, honoured poets, who are always writing with words but never writing the word itself, who are always writing around the actual point. Dada world war without end, dada revolution without beginning, dada, you friends and also-poets, esteemed sirs, manufacturers, and evangelists. Dada Tzara, dada Huelsenbeck, dada m'dada, dada m'dada dada mhm, dada dera dada, dada Hue, dada Tza.

How does one achieve eternal bliss? By saying dada. How does one become famous? By saying dada. With a noble gesture and delicate propriety. Till one goes crazy. Till one loses consciousness. How can one get rid of everything that smacks of journalism, worms, everything nice and right, blinkered, moralistic, Europeanised, enervated? By saying dada. Dada is the world soul, dada is the pawnshop. Dada is the world's best lily-milk soap. Dada Mr Rubiner, dada Mr Korrodi. Dada Mr

Anastasius Lilienstein. In plain language: the hospitality of the Swiss is something to be profoundly appreciated. And in questions of aesthetics the key is quality.

I shall be reading poems that are meant to dispense with conventional language, no less, and to have done with it. Dada Johann Fuchsgang Goethe. Dada Stendhal. Dada Dalai Lama, Buddha, Bible, and Nietzsche. Dada m'dada. Dada mhm dada da. It's a question of connections, and of loosening them up a bit to start with. I don't want words that other people have invented. All the words are other people's inventions. I want my own stuff, my own rhythm, and vowels and consonants too, matching the rhythm and all my own. If this pulsation is seven yards long, I want words for it that are seven yards long. Mr Schulz's words are only two and a half centimetres long.

It will serve to show how articulated language comes into being. I let the vowels fool around. I let the vowels quite simply occur, as a cat miaows ... Words emerge, shoulders of words, legs, arms, hands of words. Au, oi, uh. One shouldn't let too many words out. A line of poetry is a chance to get rid of all the filth that clings to this accursed language, as if put there by stockbrokers' hands, hands worn smooth by coins. I want the word where it ends and begins. Dada is the heart of words.

Each thing has its word, but the word has become a thing by itself. Why shouldn't I find it? Why can't a tree be called Pluplusch, and Pluplubasch when it has been raining? The word, the word, the word outside your domain, your stuffiness, this laughable impotence, your stupendous smugness, outside all the parrotry of your self-evident limitedness. The word, gentlemen, is a public concern of the first importance.[30]

---

30 Hugo Ball, Manifesto, delivered on the occasion of the first Dada soirée, July 14, 1916. (Editor)

Today would be something other. A wayward leering stance that would attempt to take him away from himself, but really it was going to just bring him back to his work. These thoughts stayed a moment as Tom put on his socks, his belt through his corduroy trousers' loops, looked at himself in the mirror. A thin man growing old, alone. This thought then, seeing itself, was no longer a thought but a seen thing and so an action: he moved toward the mirror and felt out an in-growing accumulation of pus and matter and with his thumb and forefinger slowly pushed it out into the world, murmuring to himself:

– But not too old. Not too old at all.

The man, not old by many estimations, turned from his reflection and moved to the hallway and into the toilet running water cool and brittle over his thumb, the ochre snotpus washed away to join infinite bodies of kindred foulness. Back to work, a return to the same day in a different week.

He moved out into the living room where he also slept and would now also work, avoiding a last look at his visage. At desk he poured a cup full with a strong coffeebrew from his dirty, limestone-stained cafetière à piston, rustled in the crisp paper for the croissant he had bought a little over an hour ago on Montorgueil and sighed, pathetically, probing the freshly shaven cheeks now that little less filled with the body's badness and thought of his French lesson, later on that same day.

Essayer encore. Rater encore. Rater mieux. To read our own in their language. To move toward the other only to find yourself moving back toward oneself. He thought of the poetry he wrote in Serbian, so ornate and impenetrable in its Cyrillic flourishing, left behind in a notebook lost somewhere.

Thomas O'Neill had two projects underway that autumn in Paris: the first was of a monetary nature, to finish the translation of a report from the Serbian National Security Council to the International Criminal Tribunal for the Former Yugoslavia, a burden of length and aridity. The second was to master a third language, French. In Cambridge he had always proved more confident at

French than at Serbo-Croat but he could see now, some years free of the milieu of the university, that this was largely due to his determination to impress those at university who heard him speak the language. In his Serbian tutorials there had been merely himself, old Zoran and two others, a girl from Hull and a guy from Manchester, people he never really got to know despite the size of the class.

After four years in Belgrade, language, Tom had decided, was inherently social and mastering a language was a social undertaking.

A belief that echoed back to him everyday he had to return to board and commence anew the solitary workings of his mind and computer, the lonely task of translation, in a city where he knew almost nobody and nobody knew him. Today would be no different, he told himself: a return to work that subsumes itself and nobody to see until tea time.

> – *If I could see*
> *the land until*
> *tea was served*
> *how happy I'd be:*
> *fait-accompli!*

Silence then rose up broken by the odd crinkle of paper as he damped his thumb and retrieved croissant crumbs.

As he worked his mind kept returning to the ad he had read on Craigslist the night before. He could see no reason for not responding to it. Today was a cool morning of increasing stillness, the orderliness of November long established, the warmth promised each morning in the confectionary at his boulagerie on rue Montorgueil carried itself into his routine and numerous coffee breaks. Ice christened the window-panes each night. Grey accentuated itself everywhere. The arc of the morning started later and the days shortened their breaths making them seem busy and hurried. Tom was tired of the translation he was doing for the Tribunal. December gave only the cross examinations of the Srebrenica trial and his resolve was gone, the remove he had given himself shortened itself, like the winter-day's busyness facing the dark of five o'clock evenings, and he came closer and closer to the horrors of war and genocide. Stirring sugar into his coffee and examining the streaked dirt on the window, sliding down from the force of invisible forces to form rings, becoming like the depressions around knots in a tree-trunk, he couldn't help wondering if there was a syndrome akin to Stockholm's in which a translator or writer, worrying over words and clauses, building up a portrait piecemeal, failed to notice any increase in compassion. Biographers, he knew, often fell out with their subjects but what if the subject was disliked from the outset: was there only room then for emphatic understanding, exoneration?

Away from the words circled in red ink, accompanied by a question mark, he fell into a moment in the company of images of Radovan Karadžić as guru: the seemingly grainy, as he recalled them now, shots of the man and his white beard as he spoke amused yet tired, behind red oak-panelled walls. Or the scene of him in the snow, dancing. Tom reached across the table and with his thumb extended, ran through the arrowheads of dirt, leaving a clean furrow behind. On his thumbface the stain boredom leaves behind. Tom O'Neill liked dirt on windows, a small reward for city life, it was a small pleasure to gather filth on his skin and leave it there: it gave him a feeling he wouldn't be able to describe if he had to. He would reply to the ad, if only to leave his desk for an hour or two someday, get the chance to go out and meet someone in a café.

APPENDIX 2

Dada is a farce, a legend, a state of mind, a myth. An ill-bred myth whose underground survival and capricious demonstrations upset everyone. André Breton had thought at first to dispose of Dada by attaching it to Surrealism. But the anti-art explosive was short lived. The myth of the entire no lived clandestinely between the wars in order to become, as of 1945, with Michel Tapié, the guarantee of an 'art autre'. Thanks to the change of absolute aesthetic negativity into a methodological doubt, it was finally possible to incarnate new signs. A necessary and sufficient blank slate, the dada zero constituted the phenomenological reference of abstract lyricism: it was the big break with tradition, whereby broke the muddy wave of formulas and styles, from the 'informal' to 'nuagisme'. Contrary to general expectations, the dada myth survived Tachism's excesses very well; easel painting marked the occasion, causing the last remaining illusions regarding the monopoly of traditional means of expression to disappear, in painting as in sculpture…

We are witnessing today a general phenomenon of depletion and sclerosis of all established vocabularies: uselessly repeated stylistics and redhibitory [i.e., latent academisms (Fr. Redhibitories)] with increasingly rare exceptions. Certain individual approaches confront – fortunately – this vital deficiency of classical methods and tend, regardless of their scope, to define the normative bases of new expressivity…

The Nouveaux Réalistes consider the world a painting, the large, fundamental work from which they appropriate fragments of universal significance. They allow us to see the real in diverse aspects of its expressive totality. And through these specific images the entire sociological reality, the common good of human activity, the large republic of our social exchanges, of our commerce in society is summoned to appear.

In the current context, Marcel Duchamp's readymade (and also Camille Bryen's functioning objects) take on new meaning. They translate the right of direct expression belonging to an entire organic sector of modern activity: that of the city, the street, the factory, mass production. This artistic baptism of the ordinary object nevertheless constitutes par excellence the 'dada act'. After the no and the zero, here is a third position of the myth: Marcel Duchamp's anti-art gesture assumes positivity. The dada mind identifies with a mode of appropriation of the modern world's exterior reality. The readymade is no longer the climax of negativity or of polemics, but the basic element of a new expressive repertory.

Such is Nouveau Réalisme: a rather direct fashion of getting our feet back on the ground, but at forty degrees above the dada zero, and on the very level where man, if he succeeds in reintegrating himself with the real, identifies the real with his own transcendence which is emotion, sentiment, and finally, poetry.[31]

---

31   Pierre Restany, 40 Degrees Above the Dada Zero, first appeared in French as À 40° au-dessus de DADA as the preface to the catalogue of the exhibition at Galerie J, 8 rue Montfaucon, Paris 75006, 17 May - 10 June, 1961. (Editor)

The streets seemed quieter than usual, the pavements more orderly and the ten or so centimetres they rose above road level reassured John: this simple fact of urban life, the raised border of the simple footpath, spoke to him this bright winter day of safety and reassurance. Cement sealed the pavements, cars were parked obediently, shop vitrines gleamed, reflected, offered forth goods and services and at the end of the street sat mutely the edifice of La Madeleine. John had sat with the manuscript for two days, dumbly looking at the opaque language it was written in, waiting for a reply to his advertisement. When, after the second day there was still nothing he went to the trouble of putting an ad in FUSAC, the expatriate classifieds and decided to go to the exhibition Lubarda was to visit with his friend soon-to-die.

The gallery was off the assuring rue Royal, through a plush arcade and up an adorned flight of stairs, the thick red carpet absorbing his weight and his noise and through a small anteroom to the right on the first floor. He did not know what to expect as he picked up the press release and strode into the middle of the space, a long room filled with artworks, the light at once artificially bright and dark in places, a bar, or what seemed like the model of a bar, a fake imitation of a bar, broke this first room into two. He walked past the bar into the next space, glibly took in the artwork and went around the corner into the last impasse of the gallery. He was aware, as one is when you visit such a space during the weekday's working hours, of people in offices through the small doors that led off from the exhibit. He heard the compressed whine of a coffee machine. Now that he knew the layout of the gallery he relaxed and looked around him: the artwork appeared to him as disparate, slight, some projections, some things in glass cases, small spades on a wall. In the first room, out on its own, defiant, was a piece that drew his attention: a matchbox, a softback matchbox, the sort you get free on your way out of a middle-of-the-road restaurant. It had been reproduced to, at a guess, 500 times its normal size. He stood looking at the matchbox, the need for a cigarette coming up through his body. Someone walked briskly behind him in the last space (he pictured a tall, elegant lady with a coffee cup in her hand), the parquet flooring rang out in alarm but when he turned to look the person and the noise of their shoes had disappeared. He went to look at the wall label and for reasons he vaguely understood, and which he put down to his extra perception from his recent anxiety, he was not surprised to see that the name of the work was *Seita* (1970) by an artist called Raymond Hains. Confusion at this apparent clairvoyance was soon replaced by a revulsion: looking at the bright, mute presence of the box he thought of one of the girls who called herself, for whatever perverse or inane reasons, after it, and it struck him that it did the artwork more harm than the girl. And that perhaps was the point: the girls often seemed to want to imitate in some small way the reality of such an object: functional, to hand, the friction of surface leading to the release of bright energy.

He looked around, too distracted to take in all the artworks, his default mode of perception when it came to group shows such as this one. Suddenly the raise of a nicotine craving grew into something he recognised as a sense of overarching fear, anxiety borne out of being lost in this orderly, warm gallery. He stared at the sheet of paper in his hand, the press release, holding it with both hands, but he couldn't focus on it. He asked himself why he had come, what had he expected to see – to see what Djordje Bojić had seen? He would have known, John guessed, of Raymond Hains and that these two blonde women were nothing more than possibly the strangest acolytes an artist has ever known. But did this mean anything? Who were these two girls who called themselves after old artworks? Their ease at shuffling their personalities right down to the tone of their voice became an unsettling capability: objects in a total present, ubiquitous everyday objects (and he found himself thinking of those two girls at the same time, carrying out, that is, the perfect male chauvinist act of female objectification) came to him then in the middle of the empty gallery in a flood of utter mundanity, startling in their inanimate presence in the world, menacing. Tables, chairs, mugs, computers, pens, pencils, park benches, parked cars: all resting, blank and expectant – visible – for someone to come and put their presence in the world to use. Anxiety grew in him in the form of a close, static sweat. He looked again at the large matchbox in front of him. Seita: an inanimate object wanting to be animated by whom? He found himself wondering what would be the price if one did not touch it, did not utilise its dumb, entelechic presence? He turned from the Hains piece and walked briskly back out the way he had come, barely glancing at the work asking him for his interpretation.

– Tom?
– John, pleased to meet you.
– Likewise. How're things?
– Good, you know: Ça va!

The men smiled, as much for friendliness toward the other as at the amusement of their own respective situations: Irish men in France, speaking French, the self-consciousness of home momentarily making itself felt.

– Yeah, ça va is right. Listen thanks for meeting me. What'll you have to drink?
– What are you going to have?
– Wine.
– Sounds good.
– Red?
– Sure.

They got a bottle of Morgon the richest of the Beaujolais family, more expensive than John would have liked but he no longer cared, or tried not to, after his moment in the gallery of seeing the world objectified, stationed with the things he had to put meaning into, he told himself he was enjoying this chance to find out what Djordje Bojić had been writing just before he died, that now he had started, nothing would stop his determination to get the job done.

– Where you from? John asked.
– Northern Ireland.
– Oh really? Whereabouts?

– Newry. You?
– The Republic: Louth. Bordering county. Badlands, he grinned. What's with your accent then? There was a strong British lilt to Tom's words, an echo of the BBC.
– University. Went to Cambridge. Most of my twenties. Changed degrees half way through. Then a Masters.
– And you studied Serbian?
– Serbo-Croat. Yeah, after I finished with French. Whose finer grammatical complexities I now have to relearn.
– And you're a translator? I mean: you translate, Serb to English?
– Translator and interpreter, yeah. It's funny, the whole time I was at Cambridge the wars were going on, you know, throughout the Balkans and I couldn't give a shit, I mean, I barely noticed them, but they've given me so much work since finishing with my Masters. Endless reports on war crimes, on everything else. They follow me around in a way, fill my days.
– Who?
– What do you mean, who?
– Who follows you around everyday?
– Nobody. What do you mean?
– Sorry, what did you mean, your work follows you around?
– Yeah something like that.
– Ah okay, sorry, I know the feeling.
– My days... Tom didn't finish his sentence, tried to get the barman's attention instead.
– Your days?
Tom ignored the question for a moment, ordering an assiette de fromages from the barman.
– My days are getting strange somehow. I spend them in the company of murderers. People who went about committing terrible crimes. You know, the details. I have to work over the details.
A basket full of bread and a wooden board heaped full of blue fourme d'Ambert cheese was placed beside the envelope John had placed between them: it was soft, pungent and ready to be eaten.

– I have this manuscript and I'd like to know if it's well written and so on. It's about LGB, you ever heard of them?

– No.

– They've been pretty successful. I think it could make a great book. What do you think, would you have time to look at it? It's 112 pages. There's an appendix that I can read myself, mostly source texts in French or English, art manifestos and such.

– Yeah, Tom sounded like he was persuading himself he had the time, yeah I could certainly take a look at it.

– I don't have all that much money at the moment, so maybe I could commission you first to translate a couple of pages that I could use to help get some funding.

– Are the artists going to help fund it, what about the author of it?

– The other artists don't seem so keen, and I'm trying to figure out why. As for Bojić, the author, I have a feeling that something in the manuscript might suggest how he ended up dead in the Seine.

– Dead in the Seine?

– Didn't I tell you? They think he jumped in.

– Are you making this up?

– No, no, I'm deadly serious, he said and tapped the envelope with his index finger, somewhat, he was embarrassed to realise, conspiratorially. The one time I met him he seemed to know he was in trouble. And that was just a week before he died. John opened the envelope and took out the sheaf of papers. What does this say? His friend seemed to think that his lover called Warmann could have caused his death.

– It says, 'To Warmann'.

– 'To Warmann'?

– Yeah, it's more like a dedication. This isn't the proper title. You must be missing the title page. Both men looked again at the sheaf of papers, John flicking through the paperclipped appendix.

– Strange to dedicate a book to the person who'd cause your death.

– Well I can read it and tell you what's in it.

– Great, I'd really appreciate your help, John said and looked at his phone. The girls are coming, you should like them. They're quite odd. I don't think you'll have met people quite like them before. They introduced me to Djordje.

When the girls arrived all four of them sat at a table by the window. They weren't at all interested in Tom at first, barely acknowledging him when John introduced him and the latter was surprised by this, but told himself he shouldn't be. He thought they would have found Tom's well-coiffed, starched-shirt collar manliness attractive. It struck him that he knew nothing, when it really came down to it, about the two girls, their tastes defined always in the negative. The tiredness of the world was reflected readily in the thinness of their personalities: they seemed to have long ago given up maintaining their individual opinions, their view on the world a shared set of viewing glasses handed back and forth when the time came to express an opinion, say something scintillating.

– What are you little Irish boys doing this evening?

– Well, said Tom, we're getting drunk it would seem.

The two girls laughed at this and put hands through blonde hair, a level of attraction slowly being reached with the soft tones of Tom's accent, suffused as they were of money and a healthy, upper class childhood.

– And what do you do? asked Seita.

– I'm a translator, from Serbo-Croatian into English.

– And how do you know John?

– I was looking to find someone to have sex with on Craigslist when I came across John's ad, said Tom, doing his best to get a laugh out of the girls. He succeeded, both girls laughing dryly, and they both recrossed their legs, drank from their drinks.

– You had an ad for sex on the Internet John? asked Saffa.

– Very funny.

John shifted in his chair and then, knowing it was going to cause a shift in their conversation and curious to know what the shift would be, John added: But Tom here is going to help me translate Djordje's manuscript. Have you heard anything more about Djordje?

– No, they both said together.
– Oh.
– We still can't believe it. But I guess that's how these things end, said Saffa.
– What things?
– Tragedies. A man like George, all he's been through: it's a tragedy.
– I don't know why, John said, but I can't get rid of the idea that he knew he was going to die.
– Knew?
– The night in The Old Navy, when he turned up just before we left: what was he doing there?
– The Old Navy?
– Ah yes, I remember. The night I went home with you. He just stopped by, wanted to say hello. George lives, lived, by night.
– It's just I think he left me a note, saying he was going to die. I mean: I think it was his note. And then he goes and dies.
– So?
– So it's all very strange, no? I wonder how he died. Do you think he killed himself?
– Killed himself? Tom said.
– Yeah: killed himself.
– Maybe he was pushed, said Saffa with a smile.
– Or thrown in, Seita continued the joke, already dead.

They all stopped a moment as if to think over these possibilities.

– George had a lot to be sad about. It's impossible to know. But let's not get all sad and ruin our night.
– And if you got the manuscript you should publish it.
– Yes and we're probably in it, so you have to publish it! He told us all the time he was writing about us.
– Lubarda didn't seem to think it would be so interesting.
– Don't mind Miloš. Such a sad old man. He always knew that George made better art.
– At first he thought I was a friend of Trifke.
– Ha, how did he manage that!

– Who's Trifke?

– Trifunović. Trifke's his nickname.

– Trifke is the real gangster of the gang. The three Serbs owed him. He got them here without visas, when visas still weren't so easy for Serbs to get. They did some work for him, even when they were recognised names they could still make more money with Trifke.

– Doing what?

– God knows. Couriers, messengers, debt collectors – we have no idea, they never speak about it.

– Take some advice, Seita said quietly, just be careful of Miloš and Aleks, they want some things to be forgotten about LGB, about their youth. They want to move on. And people like Trifke can be dangerous if you cross them.

– I'm sure it's possible to convince them. I'm going to let them know my plans once I've got some more people on board. There are one or two institutions that would be interested. The LGB Group were big.

– Yes they were, you could make a really successful book. Just–

– Just make sure we're in it!

And the two girls broke out in their mirrored laughter, their fatuous giddiness no longer a surprise to John. Tom shrugged his shoulders and turned to get the waiter's attention and ordered another bottle.

APPENDIX 3

For this, the 10th anniversary of the Prix Ricard, it seemed important to me to complete the normal function of this exhibition (a thematic presentation of emerging artists from France's artworld) by having a critical preamble which would include 'historical' or confirmed artists. This inclusion poses a very simple question: what marks the boundary of an artwork? By what gesture is its terrain brought about, puts in place its limits, outlines the perimeter of its exploration?

In thinking of the concept of 'bricolage' with which Lévi-Strauss defined mythological thinking, I thought to present this subjective story in the form of a reunion of fetishes: that is to say, objects which, despite their appearance of detail, represent a complex thought which is found suffused throughout them. Such as with a hologram.

This question, regarding the 'plan of composition' of an artwork, is not innocent or free, nor without repercussions from the choice of 'young artists' that continue it on.

In one way it underlines the importance of initial gestures and of the necessity, when making a work of laying out a terrain and defining a specific manner of surveying this terrain. As so many artists today content themselves with the production of objects under a vague 'theme', more often than not borrowed from the contemporary ideological notebook, it is better not to forget that an artwork resembles a journey more than a mere tour of the local gallery quarter.

Elsewhere this question shares a surprising point in common, without doubt not the only one, between two key actors in French art to whom this exposition would like to pay homage: Pierre Restany and Bernard Lamarche-Vadel. They were, for the young art critic I aspired to be at the turn of the 1990s, two unique role models. Between 'the technological humanism' of one, directed toward social production and the totalisation of the visible, and the subtle aristocraticism of the other, through the singular and the inexpressible, we find ourselves in the presence of two dissimilar trajectories belonging to two different generations, but united by the same independent spirit and a similar engagement in the French artworld.

Restany celebrated in 1960 'the autonomous expression of the real' in launching the Nouveau Réaliste movement, which insisted in the radical gesture of 'direct appropriation,' founder of all artistic practice – 'automatic manifestation of the sensible' – explored in a new 'urban nature.' Twenty-six years later, Lamarche-Vadel was to regroup twelve artists for his exposition What is French Art, by the pertinence of their 'posture' or their 'process,' that is the invention of 'ways to put in process (their) existence in the course of creating their artwork.' At first glance dissimilar, these two propositions constitute in my eyes two levels of the same conceptual discourse.

The nine artists that I have chosen for this 10th edition of the Prix Ricard respond to this double promulgation: supporting their work on the one hand with a collective sensibility and on the other with a personal composition, riding the waves emitted by the social but dissociating themselves from it by a singular point de départ. They can subscribe to the formula of Lamarche-Vadel which gives this exhibition its title: 'Therefore what we consider in the visible, the artwork, must above all have the texture of an extreme doubt about the consistence of the visible.'[32]

---

32 La Consistance du visible, exhibition curated by Nicolas Bourriaud, with Gérald Decroux, Julien Discrit, Cyprien Gaillard, Camille Henrot, Emmanuelle Lainé, Gyan Panchal, Abraham Poincheval and Laurent Tixador, Lili Reynaud-Dewar and Raphaël Zarka. This exhibition also had a 'Preamble' that featured work by Martin Barré, Daniel Buren, Erik Dietman, Alain Jacquet, Pierre Joseph, Raymond Hains, Bertrand Lavier, Édouard Levé, Roman Opalka and Agnès Varda. Ricard Foundation, 9 rue Royale, 75008, Paris, October 10 to November 22, 2008. (Editor)

John enjoyed it when there were openings across the Marais, the closely packed streets of the 3rd arrondissement became busy with art-goers, from the young to the gracefully old: on one night he could see expensive 19th century work or up-to-the-minute multiples or videos made by artists younger than he was. Faces would appear, recognisable and repeated, a critic or curator, or it could happen that he would admire the shows at Thaddaeus Ropac, Yvon Lambert, Chantal Crousel or the Marian Goodman Gallery with the same strangers, brokered for some time with a pace that was similar, following the same route. He would always end such evenings at La Perle, the bar on rue des Archives that was always so full he had never once sat down in the place, had always stood, heaving with all the other young *bo-bos*, drinks in their hands and cigarettes lit with difficulty due to the lack of space.

This evening there were a number of openings he planned to attend at some of the more established galleries, names he knew and work he admired, and he planned to meet up later with Jean-Baptiste in La Perle for a drink and to see what either felt like doing for the rest of the night. It had only been a few days since Tom O'Neill took the manuscript home with him and he felt himself restless with anticipation and had to work hard at not calling him up to ask questions, harass him for details. He knew he would have to wait. In the meantime however he had Galerie Gojković to visit and once he had called in to galleries along rue du Temple he made his way along the hushed, dark streets to rue de Turrene where he had located the gallery of Bojić's friend, if he could be so called, and in which their winter show was opening, an exhibition by a German artist John had never heard of, not that that said much about anything. Walking along in the dark, hands in his pockets and his shoes landing lightly on the footpaths, he hopped between cars, bisecting streets, his collar turned up. John wondered if this guy Gojković may have had something to do with the death of Bojić. When he reached the street where the gallery was he decided the best thing to do would be to just spot Gojković, if he was present, and go back again during a quiet moment in the week. The gallery itself was much like any other of the commercial storefront galleries in the neighbourhood and he stood outside and took it in, rolling a cigarette in order, he was surprised to realise, to check the place out and see the situation – he might after all know some people attending. Gojković was written neatly on the front of the gallery, tasteful in very small, assured letters. Through the window he couldn't see anything but the outlines of figures, people moving around absently talking to each other or protecting themselves behind the shield of a warm glass of wine. It was well attended and people continued to move past him on the street where he smoked and bustle their way inside. He tried to guess if any among them were Serbian, and many could have been, but mostly the crowd seemed, in that distinct, well-attired handsome way, Parisian. They may have come from all over, but they all lived here and the city branded them all in its unique way.

He finished his cigarette and throwing it into the gutter moved to go into the gallery and as he did so he spotted Miloš Lubarda ahead of him, with a man and a woman, and for some reason he wasn't surprised to see a look of extreme fatigue on the man's face before he moved out of the darkened streetlight into the brighter light of the gallery space, a look that seemed to speak of an anguish so debilitating it left no energy left, like a fire guts an entire building before burning itself out. When he was inside, nervously and with distraction taking in the artwork (line drawings on assorted material, rough notepaper, menus, newspapers) John wondered if they had gone to rue Danielle Casanova to clear Bojić's belongings. Furtively he looked around at the people: the usual crowd of small-talkers and loud-laughers, people at ease with being social. He spotted who he guessed was Gojković due to his manner, a mix of business and social facilitator. John was surprised because the man looked mean, huge and mean and menacing, dressed in a brown suit that made him look, only just for a moment, like a parody of a Russian mobster, his blonde hair on his rounded head cut short like an army conscript, the man exuded power as he solemnly introduced two people, both quiet young ladies, before making a joke which made them both laugh as they shook each other's hands. He just stood back with his hands slightly encompassing them both, as they started to make small talk with each other.

Then as he stood dumbly taking in this little scene he saw Lubarda step up behind Gojković and talk to him in a distracted way only people who are well used to each other's modes of reception can manage, and slowly, for John saw it happen slowly, both men looked up and stared directly at him, not twenty metres away, as if intensely disappointed by his presence. Taking his hands out of his pockets, hands he noticed that were slick with sweat, John turned around, agitated. Suddenly the unease he had been feeling since first reading the note collected itself in the pit of his stomach and screamed at him to get away from the gallery. He moved to get out, tried to take in the work in a final nonchalant sweep, saw then the two girls, blond streaks in the far corner and he raised his hand automatically and smiled in greeting but one just shook her head, as if also gravely disappointed and the other just looked away. Lubarda was gone from view and John's last sighting of Gojković was of the burly man talking to what seemed to be his twin brother: a heavyset man with a big nose stood nodding as Gojković spoke into his ear, one hand on his shoulder. John was out on the footpath in the cold night walking away as fast as he could, his relief like the soothing calm of the claustrophobe upon release.

He hadn't gone far when he realised that someone was following his steps very closely, and full of nervous energy and self-reproach at what he kept telling himself were his own made-up paranoid delusions, he turned around to see the very same man with whom Gojković had just been confiding. Quickening his pace he laughed at himself, he tried to laugh at himself, for being the central character of a bad thriller, the thought passing through his mind that the Serbs and the two girls were making fun of him, entertaining themselves at his expense and he tried to transform his growing fear into anger but to no avail. He had taken a wrong turn and was walking along quiet streets, rue Béranger, rue Dupois, crossing with a little jog the rue de la Corderie and looking briefly over his shoulder saw the man still following, close enough to make out the shallowness of his little eyes behind his great nose. What could they do to him? Nothing at all, they're just scaring me, he told himself over and over. Seita and Saffa flashed in his mind and he felt terribly stupid because really he didn't know any of these people; they had histories together he knew nothing about. His self-reproach was acute in the face of the current situation. Lubarda and Gojković must know that I have the manuscript but they won't do anything, he told himself a bit frantically, they are just letting me know that they know. It's quiet here but there are people behind each of those windows – and there's rue des Archives. Bright lights; almost there.

Then, quite suddenly, these thoughts were broken by the unmistakable sound of brakes, a loud, long drawn out screech of brakes, a quick klaxon not fast enough and a horrible, definitive thud, metal on metal, breaking glass. Putain de merde! rang out and all the quiet streets and all the countless invisible people behind the warmly-lit windows were sucked toward the point where the two cars had collided into each other on the corner of rue de Bretagne and rue des Archives. Pedestrians stopped and stared at the two machines that now looked like tired-out mechanical slugs, the damage not so severe, though one driver seemed to be hurt, the ambulance already called.

John had jumped with fright, the collision happening just to his right as he crossed the street and his heart was racing and he was covered in sweat, not breaking his stride for a moment, jolted into motion he ran then, ran from the source of attraction which the crash had become for everyone around it and jogged onto rue des Archives, all the way to La Perle, into its packed humidity, wall-to-wall with hipster bodies and he felt relief and didn't care about his fear and his running away from whatever the man threatened for he couldn't do much to him in here, there was barely enough room to order a drink, but order a drink John would.

APPENDIX 4

LGB![33]

1. We would like to declare the Republic of Red Doorknobs. The subject of our work is everyday life, uttered for some in the language of a politics of the here and now, for others in an attempt to overdraw the power of little red doorknobs.
2. We dismiss any need for war, starting as we must with war. We proceed with rigour and belief but without chauvinism.
3. The belief in the good life and how to live it exists for each man and needs not an order or regime to dictate the terms of it. That is not to say that it is unknowable or relative but that each person is free to choose the terms drawn up under the rubric: The Good Life. Art works by scribbling down each term, then erasing them, then scribbling them down, then erasing them...
4. As artists we have experienced war and know its consequences. The fall of man is in his very self-belief – art then, as an age-old hope in the enlightenment of man, cannot delude itself with questions of progress. A question: How many generations does it take for a society to be orderly, for buses to come on time, for democracy to function, for our leaders to be honest, for clean water to come out of the tap? Who knows, we're not interested in finding out because there are so many other questions to ask, for instance: How many

---

33 First Manifesto of LGB Art. Distributed on the occasion of the exhibition LGB, Akademija Lepih Umetnosti, Belgrade (10-14 May, 1995) and Pančevo Biennal of Young Artists, 1995. (Editor)

generations does it take for a society to build train networks that end in Auschwitz, Dachau, Buchenwald etc? How civilised are we that our civilisation merits the rape and pillage of other civilisations, conducted in our name, by soldiers and young men whose life should be spent not in uniform but in a creative everyday civilian world of red doorknobs?

5. We would like to declare a circadian revolution! Twenty-four hour insurrections! One day only, everything is ours!
6. Yes to the products of bourgeois degeneracy: Grundig TVs, Coca Cola, Sony Walkmen, Levi Jeans. The frames of the new art are to be built over the entrance ways to shopping centres. These alien tools inherited by us with the fall of communism allow us to conquer not only ourselves but the entire world.
7. We recognise the fall of Utopia, its agents, the Utopian project in general. We agree with the terms: 'Eastern Modernism' and 'Retrogardism'. In these words we find connection to our distinct past but also connection to our future which will be distinct from the future of others BUT AT THE SAME TIME WILL BE SHARED BY ALL.
8. The Form is never one but many. The more the better for this Republic is multifaceted, pluralistic, non-exclusive.
9. We are for inclusion, our art is inclusive, a forward-moving progression of humility.
10. 'We have to get going. Lord, but how quickly it gets dark here.'[34]

---

34 „Сада морамо да кренемо... Господе, како се овде брзо смркава." Last line of Garden, Ashes by Danilo Kiš, trans. William J. Hannaher. Edition Dalkey Archive Press. (Editor)

The sound of feet running away in retreat: he heard people pass through the streets, reverberating louder as they passed behind him then shuffling slowly out of earshot as they continued on down the adjoining street. Tom would often go for a walk at this time of night in order to get out of his small apartment where he sat and worked all day. By nightfall, which came earlier and earlier everyday, he was restless and bored of the walls that grew closer and closer to his desk. He would turn on and then off different lights around the room in which he did all his living, sleeping and working and eating; he would turn the heating up and then down, telling himself it was cold, then on doing some work that it was warm; he would decide to play some music and then decide against it until finally he would put down the sheets of photocopied paper and close his MacBook and stand up from the desk and realise that it was late and that he had yet to be outside at all that day. Of course he was satisfied putting on his coat and wrapping up: he tried to work intensively like this as many days of the week as he could, getting through the reports quickly and sending them to The Hague long before they were due. Especially now that he had this peculiar project to do for John, the translation of a document he did not know how to describe, having only read it through extremely quickly, he had felt like a lost man in the open country, only a small torch in his hand to illuminate piecemeal the vast territory around him, a territory he could as easily call home as he could call it the moon.

He closed the door behind him and heard the sound of feet echoing away behind him, down toward Montorgueil. When he went out for a walk like this he tried to avoid the bigger, busier streets, navigating between the market street and the Boulevards to his left: it was not easy to stay only on small, quiet streets, but it was possible. He had a lot on his mind from the translations, things he didn't want to think of, pointless technical things he hated but knew would not go away until he settled on them. Questions of idiom, of his register in the English he transformed the irascible Serbian into, matters he did not care about before, but since the arrest of Karadžić and especially since reading the manuscript John had given to him he had become, what? Self-conscious? Paranoid? Suddenly, as if he was blind before, he saw himself clearly in his translations, his voice all over the work like a thief's prints all over a forced window and he knew it wasn't guilt he felt but rather a self-conscious awareness of accenting it all with his own voice.

The feet came back, slowly, and of course he paid no heed: you were never alone in this city, no matter how much it tried to convince you otherwise at times. But suddenly he realised that they were fast steps, and two sets of them. Just as he turned around to take a quick look a fist came down on his face and his body gave out under it. He didn't register that it was a fist in particular, just like he didn't make out what language his assailant spoke when he called him a motherfucker – perhaps it was even in English? – and perhaps he had used a dull piece of wood, or some disused end of some long out of use mechanical machine or other, he couldn't know because he was now on the ground and whatever it was, fist or object, it was continuing to fall down on him. Get up, get up, Tom shouted at himself, but he stayed down. His hands went up to cover his head and he felt the surprise and adrenalin that he should be getting the shit kicked out of him like this, on some quiet street behind Boulevard de Sébastopol more than he felt the weight of his assailants' blows. Thoughts came to surface: they were just common thugs looking for some cash, he had nothing on him other than his house keys, they would leave off any second once they found this out; protect your head and you'll be fine; don't antagonise them; pain; my kidneys; they're speaking Serbian. They are speaking Serbian. The blows continued on and the street was too quiet, nothing speaking save for the clothes of the assailants, a soft whispering between conspirators. He had been beaten up before closer to home, in West Belfast, many years ago, at least what felt like many years ago. A different lifetime, a different part of history, a different corner of the continent. They didn't want anything that time either, just the fight, and when he didn't fight, just the physical release of hate which had been built up so much inside them that when his accent let the lid fall off it, their hate had poured out, hot and punishing and without end. Facts came back to him: he was last in Belfast in 2002. The city's population is almost 300,000. The population of Belgrade: almost two million. Two million. The *Jugoslovenska Narodna Armija* split officially on May 19, 1992 to become *Vojska Jugoslavije* and *Vojska Republike Srpske*. His date of birth: 1972. He was from Northern Ireland: he knew what violence was. He knew what violence was! He was of military service age when the war in Bosnia started. He had pictured himself many times visiting Keraterm, Omarska, Luka. In his nightmares full of white noise and the static of screams which nobody knows how to translate, he drives in a military jeep through broken streets and he knows each time where it is he is going, just like this time: to the Partizan Sports Hall in the town of Foča. He is standing in the dock and there is a judge and a prosecuting lawyer and he is being asked about exhibit number 99 and asked to explain just how it is he kept his prisoners in a state of total fear and submission. Or how his Muslim guards beat him and abused him. He was Serb one minute, Bosnian the next. Irish to one murderer, English to the next. He knew what violence was. Each time he turned the corner he knew exactly where he was going, it was July 1992 and he was going to the Partizan Sports Hall in Foča, Bosnia. Every time. Until this time when he told himself he was no longer asleep and that he could open his eyes. And open his eyes he did.

– I had a dream last night.

– A dream?

Tom spoke without enthusiasm. Confined as he was to his hospital bed he had no choice but to listen to John, who was somewhat manic or nervous, it was hard to say which.

– Yeah a dream, and I never dream, at least I never remember my dreams. And it really scared the fuck out of me. All this paranoia I've suffered since Djordje Bojić dropped a note for me in my bag, it all came out in this dream. It's hard to explain. And somehow *his* paranoia was in the dream too! At least, I mean, that his paranoia created the dream somehow, the atmosphere. The language of the dream was a mix of German and English, like Frisian or old Norse, the kind of words you almost feel, like you can see it being inscribed as runes on some old northern granite. Cries, screams, the sort of crazed dementia you would never wish on any language you spoke because you'd be worried that one day you would end up in the same state as that person, making the same sounds, those cries. And in the dream I was in a car, don't know what type of car, though a real *car*, you know, as in some sort of American car I've never even been in but know from Hollywood. A 1950s car. And it was a pitch black night and the car was in the countryside and something happened, some adventure or other had just come to an end, I can't remember that part of the dream, and me and the driver, there was this man driving, turned the car in a three point turn on this country road in the middle of the night, grass and fields opening up ahead of us in the car's lights. And then there was a chase, a very scary chase. And then boom! Out in front of us across this huge dark plain everything was suddenly illuminated. A hydrogen bomb exploded and there it was, this beautiful, I'd even say majestic, mushroom cloud rising up and it was all silent at first and then there was this thunderous dull boooom. And the cloud just got bigger and bigger and we could see the grey of smoke after the yellow flash subsided. And we were now exposed, you see, and we knew there would be more bombs and we had to get the hell out of there and the Russian driving the car, he was Russian yeah, he backed us up and we sped off down another road but it just brought us to an embankment, a raised up dead end with a wooden gate at the end and from here we saw another bomb burst out of the night, and then the dream sped up and there was nothing we could do and it was all over. Then the dream changed slightly and I looked at the driver, imploring him to get us out of this, to save us somehow, and I realised that I knew him, at least I had seen this man before. Once I was at Bar de la Luxure, you know, by Gare de Lyon with Jean Baptiste and Christophe Bachalard and there was this dude next to us, a Russian guy, from where exactly I don't know, but he was well out of it, he was a ghost, I mean he was *dead* man, and his friends all rushed around screaming and they rang the cops and he was dead. Well, it was this guy that was in my dream. And this was when the screaming started and the dream changed. There is a Norse story about the end of the world, you know, and I think, and I mean I don't know that story, the myth, the Norse myth at all, but I think that is what I dreamed, or like a version of it, in a time that was not my own, in a time that reminds me of the last century, now that I come to think of it, and Russia and shit, a kind of materialisation of time where it stands still because objects and products don't change, haven't changed, so the car became a Lada, another type of car I've never been in, and everything in this car, the smell and the cigarettes and the fabric and dust even, all that was from my childhood, you know, timeless for me, and the driver backed it up and we sped through the night in reverse until behind us loomed tower blocks, the type from centralised planning, the type built after the war and which now seem strangely out of date, the end point of functionalism with nowhere to go, grey taking over and consuming them, like the same grey of the mushroom cloud …

APPENDIX 5

At dusk, in mid-April of 1992, soldiers came to our village. I do not remember the exact date but it was probably around April 10th or 11th. I cannot remember for sure. We knew of course there was a war. We saw via the media that there was war going on, there was shelling, and we could hear the shelling also. Well, for example, we couldn't go into town anymore. We weren't able to buy food, cigarettes, anything like that, any toiletries, anything, anything you wanted – you needed, whether you needed to go to a doctor or anything else, you couldn't go. I saw soldiers chase people out of their homes, they killed three old people. We saw more of the army and our neighbours wore uniforms. They had weapons. And we were afraid that we might be burnt in our homes, which had started to happen in the surrounding villages. We saw the flames at nightfall and the smoke in the morning. And for these reasons, and other reasons, we withdrew – we went into the woods. I don't understand. Oh well we went further into them, to a place, a spot and built a type of tent there. We would go from there during the day back to our house and cook food. Eventually we had to go to town, for food and cigarettes. It was on the third day we went together, my sister and my mother. Yes that is correct, this is when we met the soldiers in person. We came onto the road that went to the town, we needed food and four soldiers dressed in uniform were out before us, and one of my neighbours was among them. I knew him. Yes, his name was ——— but I don't remember right now his second name. I heard my neighbour was captured and died in ———. The other three were young men and I didn't recognise them, they weren't old at all. Just boys. They had Belgrade accents. I've known my neighbour ever since I was a child. Yes I can. One was tall and skinny and wore glasses. I don't remember his name. Another was very big with square shoulders and yellow teeth from cigarettes. I can remember his first name was ——— —. The third one was smaller with a round head. I asked for his name because I hoped one day I could do something like this. Yes, that's how you spell it. We didn't expect anyone to be on that road, it was never busy. I do not know what they were doing there. That is something that I remember most vividly, whereas what happened before is all a haze to me. I remember it faintly. Well, nothing. That neighbour came up to us and he said that there was no reason to be afraid, that as we were good neighbours, we would be taken to ———, to free territory, that we're not to blame for anything, and we weren't to blame, because we were just women and children. He said that they would just help us to be transferred to ——— and that everything would be all right. First we walked with them by foot until a truck came, an army truck, and they brought us to ———. How do I know? Anyway they took my freedom then. We did not know it but that was what they did then. No, I never saw any of these three since the war. The other three were young men like I said, not any older than I was, I remember this fact and that was why I thought we were being sent to free territory. I don't understand. No, they didn't use force that afternoon, not until later that day. Yes in the motel, we were all brought in there, women and children and there were two very old men who couldn't walk and they told us they would leave us here to wait for transportation. The arrow points to the motel. The buildings around it, these buildings further up here [indicates], when I was talking a moment ago, I thought these were the barracks. This with the black roof is the motel and restaurant itself. Yes. These are the barracks [indicates], over here was well, all this. All these are barracks. The room we were in was a reception room, narrow and it was crowded. Soldiers came and went from upstairs, there was a room upstairs, and bedrooms at the back. Then our neighbour came in and asked me to follow him. He took me to another room, approximately in this last prefabricated building, on the bank of the River ———. I think that this room was at the end of the hallway, because its window faced the ——— River. He closed the door to the room, it was a bedroom. It had a bed and a dresser, a normal room. And then he told me to take my clothes off. No, he pushed me onto the bed. But I didn't. He was saying things like: What am I afraid of? Don't I know what sex is? Haven't I done it before? That kind of thing. Let's enjoy it. That kind of thing. Yes. I did not understand your question. Can you rephrase it? Yes. Someone came and said it was time to go. But one of the younger men we had met on the road came back. The smaller one, with a round head, ———. I can't remember. Yes. He did the same thing. But with more force. Then they put us onto a bus. And they also said that they were taking us away from there, that we would be reunited with the other women and children who were also waiting to be transferred to free territory, and straight from there they took us to the high school centre in ———. We were all put into the sports hall. No, all we had were foam mats from sports practice and some army blankets, that is all. There was one toilet at the bottom of the wall down some steps in the ground. It wasn't very good at all. Perhaps about 80. I don't know exactly. Then we stayed in a classroom. For those days, yes. Yes. On the second day, in the evening, a group of soldiers came. They entered the classroom that we were in. They stood in the middle of the classroom, and they were pointing their fingers at girls and women who were supposed to get up and go with them to the other room. Five, I think it was five. Into another room, also a classroom, the one next door, I think. There were a few mattresses there too, and they said that every one of us should stand by one of these mattresses or sit on it. That's what one of them did. And the other one said that they had free choice, that they could choose the one they wanted. I went and sat down. Yes. In army uniforms. They all had weapons.

He sat down beside me but then said we should get out of there. We went to another room, another classroom. He ordered me to sit down. Yes. To take off my trousers. Then he raped me. This time he raped me vaginally. Yes. I don't recall what he said to me. I never described what happened to me in detail to anyone. If I wanted to say what happened, I said the worst had happened, referring to rape, and from then onwards, throughout my stay in this camp, I never talked to anyone about anything from that event onwards: I kept silent. Awful. There are no words in this world that could describe my feelings. It is the worst thing that was happening to me. Yes afterwards, they were sent back to the classroom. It is hard to say. It's hard to tell. They would take them out when they wanted to, when they felt this urge to take this out on them. But at any rate, every night some girl would end up someplace with the same soldier or with a different soldier. They looked dreadful. They were all crying. They would all be crying when they came back. Some of them would be bleeding from the nose. They would be screaming, tearing out their hair. Different things. I was taken out many times, I lost count. Sometimes for a day for some hours, other times for up to three days. In flats of people I did not know and never saw again. Yes, that day I know where I was, it was an abandoned house. We were made to clean it up and then kept there for two more days when they raped us. Yes. Every other time it was the same thing, every time after that it was always the same thing. Well, the day before we left, people from the ——— came and asked for a list of names. They told us that we would have to leave, that they would organise buses to take us away, and they printed some permits for us, exit permits, with our names on them and our dates of birth. I heard that the reason was that it was thought that the International Red Cross Committee might be coming to ———, and that is why I assumed we had to disappear from there. I didn't quite get your question. What do you mean? I think there were other times, yes. I wasn't taken off to other places, but at the places that I was taken to, I was raped a number of times. And when I gave my statement, on the day I gave my statement, it was actually the first time that I had ever told anybody that, and it was very difficult for me, and I'm sure I didn't say everything that had happened to me. I don't know the exact date, of course. It was after I had left ——— I went to see a doctor, because the whole time I was in ———, I never had my periods. Of course, I was afraid of what might have happened, and when I went, it turned out that I had an inflammation of the ovaries and my uterus, and I didn't get my periods. And the doctor explained to me that that was out of fear. And then later on, two or three months later, my periods came back and became regular again. Of course. There were moments when I felt so bad. All my fears came back to me. I felt psychologically unwell. I would get very excited and very upset, and this fear would keep coming back to me. The doctor I went to see, the psychiatrist or psychologist, I didn't tell him any details. I didn't talk to him about the details that I'm talking about here today. We just had a conversation; that was all. I don't really know.

Yes, of course: my name is ——— and I am ——— years old. I was born in 19—, and I lived in the village of ——— near ———. My mother is ——— years old. My father is ——— years old. I have a ——— year old sister.[35]

---

35 Witness 56 testified on 29 and 30 April 2000 at the International Criminal Tribunal for the Former Yugoslavia. The author had retyped it from the Tribunal's webpage and in the folio it was the last of the appendixes. (Editor)

– Can you please shut the fuck up about your dream?
– Yeah, sorry. Of course.
– What has it got to do with anything?
– I think they're after us.
– No shit Sherlock. You're fucking right they're after us. I can barely move.
– I know, I know. Is it very painful?
– Yes it is. Tell me: did you know this would happen?
– What do you mean?
– Did you know people were this against the manuscript being translated?
– No, not really. I felt followed myself. I *was* followed even, just the other night in the Marais.
– What happened?
– I got away, went into a bar. But then I had that dream-
– Shut the fuck up about the dream, John.
– Yeah right, sorry.
– I went out, like I do every night, almost every night, for a walk and every night I take a different route, almost always a different route. I had walked a little bit, not very far, a few turns, and that was when they attacked me. Now, what I would like to know is if they know where I live or what? Because if they do I want to get the fuck out of this little translation enterprise you have got going on here. You know that these guys, whoever did this to me, have probably killed people in cold blood? I mean: do you know anything about the wars of the 1990s? Really bad shit went down, every day I have to read about it and process details you couldn't get a demented lunatic to make up. So right now, I want to know if they know where it is I live and how the fuck I persuade the people who put me here I'm having nothing more to do with this job.
– It's not a job-
– It is for me John, that's what you need to realise.
– But you've read it?
– I don't know what those girls were so excited about. I could make a guess as to who it is who beat the shit out of me.

– Who?

– Do you think the girls told the other LGB artists who I am?

– Who do you think beat the shit into you?

– Djordje Bojić's fucking ghost! I don't know, any one of his friends, he writes about them all and every one of them could have a reason not to see it published. Including the girls.

– Could it be this guy Warmann? Lubarda thought he caused Bojić's death.

– Warmann is dead.

– Dead?

– Yeah, it's all part of the story.

– I guess that makes sense now that I think of it.

– But this beating is obviously a nice little postscript to this fucking story you got in your hands. And what a fucking beating it was! The only people who know I have anything to do with you are those two girls.

– Yeah, that's right.

– So what, am I going to have to go and ask them if I should thank them for my little holiday in the fucking hospital?

– Well, you've read the manuscript. Lubarda laughed at me when I said they were friends of Bojić. You heard them say I should publish it. What does he say about them?

– He wasn't really all that into them. More like a father figure. But when I read it I flew through it. I wasn't thinking who he was libelling or implicating, was I? From my reading, he comes across as the centre of a large group of people. The LGB Group. I mean, you know that he was gay?

– Yes.

– At least he had sex with both guys and girls. With everyone. Yet he wasn't, at least he doesn't come across in any way from reading his words, as camp or anything. You know, you wouldn't guess he was gay. He loved Warmann and his death really fucked him up. They were certainly quite a group of people and he comes across as the most likeable of them really. But that's no surprise seeing as he wrote the thing. And there seem to have been mates of his that were opposed to him writing about them.

– But in your opinion are they justified?

– Sure, well, I don't know. Maybe, maybe not. He was slowly working up to telling a story. He tells a story that isn't such a rosy tale. It's in the way he tells it.

– How does he tell it?

– Well, he starts off with the art, The LGB Group and slowly twists and turns and goes all over the place. You can see that the manuscript is made up of sections that he wrote from start to finish, even if they tell stories from different times, and other sections, like notes and stuff, that start on new pages and are quite separate. But he had them all together, ordered in a way, at least if what you sent me was how he intended it to be read. And it is hard to say where it begins and ends, at least if it ends. If he killed himself or whatever, the manuscript doesn't tell us anything about what he thought of it. It just ends, like he couldn't write anymore. Did he say if it was finished or not?

– No, just that he was looking for a publisher. So you mean it's not finished?

– Finished enough, I'd say.

– And what's it like, how does it read?

– I don't know. It is funny in parts, depressing in others. I know nothing about art really so…

– But is it a good read?

– Well, there's a word for what it feels like to read it.

– And what's the word?

– Ah.

– Well?

– You're just going to have to read it for yourself.

TO WARMANN

Written by Djordje Bojić
Translated from the Serbian by Thomas O'Neill
Edited and proofread by John Holten
Broken Dimanche Press 2009

'FLY TO YOUR OWN HEIGHTS': BEGINNINGS AND FOREFATHERS

Our relationship with history, in Belgrade like everywhere else, became ever more complicated in the last twenty-five years. The art of The LGB Group was only in the first instance interested in the present, the everyday, using the parameters of neo-Dada practices as a way of circumnavigating the increasing politicisation of society, and indeed war, once it arrived. What needs to be examined in any overview, any contemporary archaeological investigation of The LGB Group, is its tenuous place alongside the other current trends of the former Yugoslavia and the Balkan region, placing it concurrently alongside such movements as *Neue Slowenische Kunst* and separating it theoretically as well as practically from those very dissimilar art movements and trends. Indeed NSK works well as a critical tool enabling a very clear set of aesthetics and political alignment with the world that are in contrast to those of The LGB Group.

Like Tzara and company before us, LGB began with a rallying cry in the face of those collective vociferations that a society can produce in times of war. In an environment of shifting borders and changing everyday reality, the spectre of war quickly engulfing most facets of society, we choose a heritage that we felt was out of fashion, out of kilter with the time, our choice in itself a protest and a means of beginning anew, free of any insidious political body threatening to overrun our work as young artists. With the war of 1914–1918 the consequences reached far and wide: three great empires died out and there was the formation of a new Yugoslavia, while to the east a great revolution brought about the first socialist regime in history. From the rubble then arose a new world, and new ways of seeing it. Yugoslavian avant-gardes of the time originated as leftwing ideologies opposed to any domination by bourgeois values. They did not have much in common with the large avant-gardes preceding them, those of German or Russian origin, but had more to do with the smaller movements in Hungary and Czechoslovakia.

We placed our foundation stone at the feet of Dragan Aleksić, a personality that shines like a scintillation in the dark of night, when toward morning the cold grows and, ever so slowly, the western sky lightens. Zagreb, Vinkovci, Osijek, Novi Sad, Subotica, Belgrade. Dragan Aleksić moved across this constellation in the early 1920s trailblazing the anti-art of Dada, joining a social negativity to a personal freedom and so subsequently creating an art that was at once subversive but full of potential. His group grew and became for a short time the first avant-garde network of Yugoslavia under the distinct slogan *Yugo-Dada*. We choose this bout of activity, across this geographical constellation during a mere three years, as an imaginative starting point, or indeed imaginative blank slate (nearly all of the material from Dragan Aleksić's activities ended up as rubbish, disposed of in a Belgrade dump in 1958) because in so doing we could resuscitate the spirit and continue it onwards, unburdened by influence or an insistent visual vocabulary. In fact, we were completely *un*influenced by almost anything the early avant-gardes created. I remember meeting the critic Ivan Stilinović in the toilet during the opening of our first Belgrade exhibition and very quickly he had got it out of me that I had no idea what the word 'Zenitism' referred to, nor that a large part of the show, Miloš Lubarda's work in particular, was Zenitist derivative! Not that it mattered: in fact I think this only served to impress Stilinović, who once persuaded of my genuine ignorance only seemed to grow more receptive to our efforts. I can still remember the uneasy feeling I had as I finished up at the urinal as he leaned casually just behind me as if together we were waiting for a bus we both knew to be delayed indefinitely, trying not to make a big deal of shaking myself dry and acting suave. He was smiling a very charming smile when I turned to face him. Of course he died later, Ivan Stilinović, a stupid death in stupid times.

But I digress: Zenitism certainly had things to offer us once we turned to it after the first exhibition in 1995, but its power always lay in the magazine, the publication, and we were all, even Miloš Lubarda, not so inclined. The idea of a Balkanisation of Europe, Ljubomir Micić's ill-concieved 'The Second Barbarian Raid on Europe' (his *Zweiter Barbarendurchbruch*) always seemed far fetched especially, as they say, with the benefit of hindsight.

We put on the LBG show with little or no experience of exhibitions. I had never curated anything before, but this fact gave the show its boldness and eager spirit. We simply wanted to do something outside the norms we saw as controlling and infecting our city, our society. There was no doubt that after just three years at the Akademija Lepih Umetnost[1] Aleksandar Gojković was an extremely gifted painter: his combines, stark canvasses with objects attached which were associated obliquely with the curse of war, together with the text art of Miloš Lubarda, made for an exhibition the likes of which hadn't been seen for a long time in Belgrade. I think we were fortuitous with the timing – cultural editors of newspapers, those who still had a job, wanted something that would distract from the Dayton agreement and Bosnia and our show seemed the perfect mix of culture, indifference to the war after nearly three years of it (if not outright pacifism) and youth. Life would go on, their reviews said, these men show that our young men fresh from the front will continue on with life, full of the truth and the past and will continue to uphold Serbian culture. Et cetera, et cetera.

Most, if not all, of the press and the establishment's response surprised us and I didn't really want a dwell on it, as so much of it continued to uphold a defence of Greater Serbia – as if that could be found in our work! But what it did allow for was a group from Vojvodina to read about us and our little show. They became interested and hunted out the manifesto that we had hurriedly

---

1 The Academy of Fine Art (Trans.)

written for it. They were a small group of Hungarians, and the one amongst them who showed the most interest was the curator Imre Warmann, a man who would become a key collaborator and friend. He sent me a letter that was full of enthusiasm and excitement for what he had read about our show, and he wondered what we had planned next. Of course, we had very little planned. The three of us were still students so to speak, we were still learning. I was at least a year away from earning a degree in philosophy and had spent far too much of my time reviewing contemporary art and reading about art that I was in danger of failing my final exams. And in fact I slowly dropped out over time: the lectures and tutorials couldn't hold my attention. I had written our manifesto with Miloš Lubarda, and that had been a lot of fun. We had studied the old manifestos from the century before and at once parodied them and exalted them. Then his letter arrived at my parents' house and changed the route, if not the map of our journey itself. Warmann and myself exchanged letters for a year, all the while expanding our acquaintances in Belgrade, Novi Sad, Budapest, telling people about the ideas we were formulating through our correspondence and searching out the art being produced that conformed to them. By the time we met in person we had already agreed to hold a group exhibition that would travel between both cities, from which it would also take its name: Budapest and Belgrade. At the time we weren't interested in conducting raids into Western Europe, but we were interested in breaking out of the Balkans, and this show was conceived, I see now, as a bridge out of the difficult times in which Serbia found itself, with its reputation slowly sinking and isolation growing like a yawn of a tired old man faced with a delinquent youth. One big coup with regard to the construction of this bridge was the calibre of artists that we managed to include in the show: the internationally known and very well respected Elaine Pettifer, Jan Offe and photographer Ivan Veselin, to name but three, ensured that there was international interest.

But if *Yugo-Dada* was not the archetypal antecedent what was? The truth is that The LGB Group fell in between too many cracks for me to offer a clear lineage to Ivan Stilinović in 1995. By the time we held this first open LGB exhibition *Budapest/Belgrade* in 1997 we could certainly empathise with Ljubomir Micić in his *Manifest Zenitizma* of 1921, indeed we could almost tell ourselves he wrote it for us personally!

> We are naked and pure.
> Forget hatred – sink into the naked depths of Yourself!
> Dive and fly to your own heights!
>
> ZENITH
>
> Fly above the criminal, fratricidal Present![2]

But we were not strict Dadaists – as if you could be in any case – no, we were climbing over the century that was coming to a close in order to manage somehow to get clear of the barbaric, war-torn fin de siècle that confronted us as young men and women. We applied an equal measure of Situationism and Conceptualism to the Yugoslavian legacy of Dada to come up with the unique practice that defined LGB art: a non-aligned engagement with everyday life, in line perhaps more with European conceptualists such as Buren, Broodthaers and, not least, the most influential figure for us: Braco Dimitrijević. But then, our group also had the mythologising reconnaissance of Elaine Pettifer, as well as Maarten Varekamp, broaching out into the legacy of Beuys, Darboven or Erhard Walther. What you could term Eastern European art of the high tide of Conceptualism – the late 1960s and 1970s – was by necessity political due to its adherence to a decentralised framework in a bureaucratic monolith controlled by the Party, but with the dissolution of the real-socialist state at the end of the 1980s and the beginning of the 1990s these concerns were not our concerns. Indeed having had direct experience of the wars we were opposed to any overt political gestures, relying instead on the comfort of the anti-gesture of non-aligned artwork. It is crucial to remember that the starting impulse of all

---

2   Ljubomir Micić, first published in *Zenit* number 1 in Zagreb, 1921. (Editor)

LGB art and activity was to disavow ethnocentric/chauvinistic/patriarchal nationalism of any description. We would leave that to the politicians, the army, the rest of our respective societies in general.

With the advent of postmodernism's last virulent blossoming and a strengthening in favour of the neo-expressionism coming out of Germany (as well as the US), we started with a pluralistic platform where painting, concrete interventions of text art and a revision of arte povera techniques all fell under a theoretical umbrella of left-wing engagement with the everyday. It was the challenge after all: to somehow make an art that would lead to the unremarkable, not to peace or any such political abstract, but just to a normal everyday. The impossibility of such a term (for what is 'normal' and to what standard will anything you term 'normal' be measured by?) meant that we strove for a new, international set of signs with a history as eclectic as postmodernism would allow us. The Wall had fallen, war had arrived – we wanted out but we also wanted in: LGB became an ark where the signs of the century would be used to create anew, together, as a group.

This collection of people would, at its apogee, number up to thirty or so different artists of a dozen different nationalities working in the fields of literature, visual art, theatre, video, sound art and performance. A total of sixteen artists were included in the *Budapest/Belgrade* exhibition, and they could roughly be broken down as follows:

Painters defined by a neoexpressionist and bricolage vocabulary: Maarten Varekamp; Branko Savić; Zoran Živković; Željko Radić and Peter Tomc.

Text artists and writers: Miloš Lubarda and the present author.

Sculptors including combine painters: Aleksandar Gojković; Elaine Pettifer; Jan Offe.

Two photographers from Hungary: Matthias Nagry and Ivan Veselin.

The performance artists Biljana Pusić and Vesna Jović.

Video artist Marko Krivokuća.

The curator of the show was Imre Warmann.

Other successes include being invited by the Hungarian government to organise a series of events in Dublin in May 2004 when Ireland held the rotating presidency of the EU and ten new countries from the east all joined on the same day. They wanted to organise a show of Hungarian contemporary culture to mark the country's entry into the European Union. The invitation put us in direct competition with Laibach and Neue Slowenishe Kunst who had also been invited as part of the celebrations: it was to be a great invasion of the east and their arts. We were unsure as to what we should programme: our group had grown so wide and each member had such full careers that we could have held week-long programmes of theatre, contemporary music, film or video art or large solo exhibitions. What we decided to do was something of a compromise between the range of our repertoire and resources (the Hungarian Ministry of Culture didn't have an endless amount of money naturally, and in truth expected us to foot a lot of the bill, which we refused to do. And if it had been Paris or London maybe we would have made more of an effort, it is true). We held a rather modest retrospective exhibition of the work of Elaine Pettifer, Jan Offe, Aleksandar Gojković and Matthias Nagry. Of course, the Hungarians who invited us weren't very pleased by this exhibition, containing as it did only one Hungarian, but they couldn't really complain: The LGB Group was a well-known name in the international artworld by then and that's why they invited us there in the first place. We had a film screening in the city's film institute where we showed the work of Marko Krivokuća. And on the weekend of the actual accession we had Biljana Pusić and Vesna Jović perform with their relatively new theatre group, Trupa Blokovi[3]. Personally I think Krivokuća's evening was the most successful. The theatre piece was a dance performance so there was no problem of the audience not understanding the language. The problem that did occur was its refusal to take dance seriously as a form of expression inherent in a contemporary theatre of the body. Biljana and Vesna

---

3   The Blokovi Troupe (Trans.)

left Dublin confused and upset by the attitudes they came across but thankfully they have since gone on to enjoy great success across Europe and the United States.

From this we got invited to partake in no fewer than three conferences held in the United Kingdom in the coming years: their art academies and universities became fascinated with East European art. A generation came of age across art history departments that had grown up with the wars on the television as they tried to remain focused on their schoolbooks studying Van Gogh and Munch earnestly at the kitchen table. We met a slew of scholars and curators who were enthralled with the idea that we were a group founded by soldiers fresh from the front line. Thankfully Gojković never joined Miloš and myself in attending any of these conferences as I can only imagine how he would have reacted to some pimply undergraduate asking him about his time in Bosnia. And how did we react? We evaded, ducked and dived, and we most certainly lied through our teeth – we bandied around ideas of blame and never apologised. We acted hard and indifferent only because we knew they wanted us to be hard and indifferent. For instance: nobody ever, not once, seemed to think that we would think the war crime tribunals were fair and just, they just presumed we hated them and thought them unlawful, unnecessary and grossly biased. We should have been up there in front of the TV cameras posing for the evening news. The whole damned region should have been up there with us. It has been strange in the last few years because we felt like we became historicised overnight, people weren't always interested in our art, our current practise: they wanted our opinion on Dayton, on the NATO attacks, on the latest news from The Hague. That's what Laibach got so right, or at least what they got right at the right time: people just presumed that underneath all LGB's talk of the everyday and the artistic intervention there really existed a bedrock of latent fascism just waiting for the right interpretation to draw it out. Why? Because we were Serbs, ex-soldiers who had fought in Mladić's army, we were the old enemy. I remember well during the coffee and biscuit break of a conference on relational aesthetic practices over the last decade in Goldsmiths how an artist and tutor at the school had come over to me and introduced himself. I pretended to him that I knew his work, persuading him and myself while I was at it that I had seen his last show in Paris (maybe I had, who knows). Fuelled by the lengthy talk about the English language in the artworld and its growing dominance we had just come out of, this little English shit cocked his head and asked:

I was just wondering George, why is it you speak German amongst yourselves?[4]

Amongst ourselves? Who?

You know, your group: LGB.

Well, I speak it with Warmann because he's Hungarian. We both studied it as a second language. And Elaine Pettifer and Jan Offe both speak it. Why are you asking?

No I was just curious. Probably envious. We don't speak languages so well, us Brits. It's so precise, isn't it, German?

Depends who's speaking it.

At this he let out a big camp laugh and swung his coffee around in the air, eyeing me mischievously.

So there's nothing reactionary about it?

Reactionary?

Oh you know, harking back to the old days.

The old days?

I think it gives you guys a layer of mystery and power, y'know.

Mystery and power?

English is so... transparent. Goodie-two-shoes. There's no threat with English, if you know what I mean?

I hadn't the slightest idea what this guy had been talking about until it dawned on me at Heathrow airport, queuing up for all the hysterical security procedures they put one through because one is so obviously hell-bent on destruction and murder. We have the Bomb, but you have a bottle opener. Beep beep. We'll have to confiscate that. It hit me and I laughed out loud, people looking at

---

4   This conversation was in English in the original. (Trans.)

me in the queue: the little faggot was suggesting we were some sort of Nazis. The Laibach diagnosis we've since termed it. I have since gone about promulgating the rumour in the artworld on both sides of the Channel that this guy is a member of the British National Party and once propositioned me for ritualistic, fascistic group sex. I make no secret of my sexual deviancy – or my anti-fascist political makeup – so I think I have been believed.

But back to The LGB Group and the artists that comprised it. For after all, and however misguided it may be, the current study is an attempt to give an overview of LGB art and the artists connected to it.

LGB. Three letters. In Cyrillic they are ЛГБ.[5] Three shapes. A moniker, nothing more; I am going to take the opportunity to clarify that yes, these three glyphs have their origin in three surnames – Lubarda, Gojković, Bojić – dating from a frenzied number of days and nights running up to our first exhibition in the weird and faraway world of Belgrade, 1995. We had no time to come up with another name so just scribbled this down and Lubarda and I wrote a manifesto hurriedly beneath it. (My work was all about rubrics at the time: canvasses headed by single words or phrases, the space below filled out with the rapid thought associations of a desperately ambitious young man.) We agreed on nothing. Gojković never recognised our manifestos, the idea was out of date for him, and insisted on calling them press releases. We in turn never agreed with his commercial aspirations, told him we weren't a commercial gallery or public institution. But, there were other people involved and this is the point to be made: the three of us happened to know each other but it, the phenomenon of The LGB Group, never would have happened if it wasn't for the inclusion of countless others. Right at the beginning there was Marko Krivokuća, who was in Gojković's class at art school. Biljana Pusić was also there from the start, telling us how to go about putting on a 'production', i.e. an

---

5   In the original these opening sentences were reversed: the Latin being the shapes, the Cyrillic the letters. (Trans.)

exhibition where everyone involved would properly be included, their talents utilised and their affect maximised. Biljana was successful before we came along with our big ideas and indeed she has continued to be, with Trupa Blokovi, the most internationally well-known and established member of The LGB Group. Biljana was someone Aleksandar, Miloš and I knew from our youth in Belgrade. She was a bit older than us, more like an elderly sister. She has had her own difficulties, her work being considered extremely unpatriotic back home, but nevertheless she continues to work relentlessly on new projects from her base in Zurich.

Our apolitical stance was strong and we made no effort to hide it when it became troublesome for some of our fellow erstwhile Yugoslavian brethren. We saw through the new borders erecting themselves and this was not easy in 1995. A good example of our disavowal of all ethnocentric/chauvinistic/patriarchal nationalism, saw the alignment of Željko Radić, a Serb who grew up in Niš, and Peter Tomc, a Slovenian who grew up in Ljubljana. If you listened to our leaders on TV you would think we only wanted to kill each other, that a Serb could never agree with a Slovene, a Croat, or Muslim.

Peter Tomc came up to me during the vernissage of that first show and shook my hand and, in a matter of moments, informed me politely that he would like to be involved in whatever it was we were in the process of establishing. Peter grew up the only son to parents that should never have had a child and his shyness and timidity with the world knew no bounds. His art has always been a universe he inhabits in order to avoid the far more prosaic world of reality; it is another universe and his quiet fervour has led him to the recognition he deserves. Željko Radić was brought on board through the long bond he had enjoyed with his cousin Zoran Živković. Niš and Ljubljana couldn't really be more different, especially in the formative years of Tomc and Radić and yet since their first meeting in 1996 the two have become life-long friends, enjoying a relationship that is so deep-seated that it defies outside categorisation or understanding. The two would not see each other for months, even years in some cases, and yet to be in their presence one would think that they could read each other's minds. It was only around Radić that one could hear the beautiful and sad laughter of Peter Tomc. It was Vladimir Pištalo that wrote that Freud was wrong: the psychological need to dominate the other is stronger than any sexual need [6]. And I would say Pištalo wasn't too far off the mark (this is something I will look at more in the next chapter [7]; I don't know the details of this remarkable friendship, all I can offer as elucidation are the world famous collaborative works that have resulted from it as proof that some of us subverted this deep need so ingrained in the Yugoslavian mind of the 1990s, and how the Serb and Slovene turned it into a domination that was symbiotic, democratic and which gave equal returns to both. Peter Tomc is the one person on this worrisome planet in whom I can trust completely. This also is the only compliment I can offer one who has no shortage of compliments.

---

[6] Vladimir Pištalo, *Milenijum u Beogradu*, 2000.
[7] Suggests that Bojić had a chapter scheme planned for his monograph on LGB that he never got around to following. (Editor)

Peter Tomc, *Tisch* (2002)
Video, 03'00. Courtesy the artist.

Željko Radić, *Autechre* (2002)
Video No. 7 from the series Taste of Life.
Courtesy the Museum of Modern Art, Belgrade.

NOTES TOWARDS A POLITICAL CONTEXT OF OUR ART[8]

Imre Warmann, one of the key figures in establishing a curatorial framework for LGB art and facilitating its theoretical reception in the artworld, was from Hungary. This is something to remember when considering the origin of what Haeg, via Slavoj Žižek, called the 'LGB screen of the reversed Other'.[9] He was also responsible for consistently including Hungarian artists in LGB exhibitions, dating back to the earliest projects. This collaboration between countries became a key feature of our work and was acknowledged in May 2004 when LGB were invited to participate in the official celebrations of Hungary's entry into the EU. Yet the respective countries of LGB members and their cultural contexts, as well as national discourses, have marked differences that when placed together in practical terms have resulted in the uniqueness of the aesthetic that was made up of this metaphorical screen.

While Tito's Yugoslavia, into which Gojković, Lubarda et al were born, had been tied through the years to an Ottoman Empire and part of trade routes diverted toward the Middle East, the country that Warmann, Matthias Nagry, Ivan Veselin and the other

---

8   This section title is handwritten above the typed title: 'The Readymades Are Coming' which has a line going through it. (Editor)

9   This reference to Haeg has not been traced, the author perhaps misremembering or misspelling the name, but the Žižek may refer to the following: 'Far from being the Other of Europe, ex-Yugoslavia was rather Europe itself in its Otherness, the screen on to which Europe projected its own repressed reverse'; Slavoj Žižek, 'Taking Sides – A Self-Interview' in *The Metastasis of Enjoyment* (London and New York: Verso, 1994), pg 212. (Editor)

Hungarians in the group were born into had been part of countless grand Germanic empires, not least the Austro-Hungarian Empire that reigned strong before the catastrophe of the first World War. It lay on traditional trade routes, irrevocably linking it up to the rest of Mitteleuropa. If dissent was missing in Tito's federal dream, Ceauşescu's megalomaniac theatre set or Todor Zhivhov's Bulgaria, it was present in Communist Hungary. We know that. But the Hungarian Revolution of 1956 put a wet blanket on any smouldering hope that communism, after the death of Uncle Joe, could exist side-by-side with the smallest, free-willed drop of freedom or independence. The hyperrationalist, the scientific and minutely executed project of the Soviets knew the infinitesimal nature of *all things*: there was no need for discussion, and none for dissent. But Hungary never played by the rules emanating from across the Elbe. It seems in retrospect that even among the most doctrinaire padres of party policies there always existed a lofty belief that this little country, erstwhile home to empires, and kept alive in their unique, Finno-Ugric tongue, should go its own way. Shortly after Imre Nagy and his ill-fated anti-Soviet revolutionaries were crushed by Soviet tanks, the passive resistance of Hungarians on the streets fed itself up (toted by the shared disgust at the humiliating events that had come to pass in May and June 1956) to the Central Committee. A study group headed by a member of this team called Rezsǒ Neyers assessed comprehensively the state of the economy, and less than a decade after the humiliation of Moscow's put-down, his conclusion was the need to re-enter the world market in order to improve mechanised labour which was so badly needed in order to fill the void left from a lack of manual workers. This resulted in one of the most intriguing, long lasting and, if it can be said, beneficial economic policies of any Eastern Bloc country: the New Economic Mechanism. In 1982 Hungary had become a member of the IMF and the World Bank. This most rebellious of Eastern Bloc countries had in place the wherewithal to weather the storm coming in 1989: a 'second economy' was allowed to flourish; towering intellectuals such as János Kis advocated loudly for a separation of powers in the social sphere, driven on by the events of Solidarity in Poland; 'The Danube Circle', a group of harmless, apolitical environmentalists mobilised 30,000 people, the most gathered since May 1956, in protest against the construction of a dam on the river Danube. This nonconformist attitude I think is important because Imre Warmann brought it into the mechanics of LGB from his very first involvement in the group: nobody was going to tell him what he could and could not exhibit.

For good and bad, nation states have proven to be the heaviest of baggage for many LGB artists: existing only by their (so often brutal, barbaric, atavistic) pull on things and peoples, an influence on the world's tangible front. Invisible lines that nevertheless make the visible perceptible, international boundaries show up the supposed differences among people, culture, land, making white an apparent opposite of black (one immediately thinks of the work of Zoran Živković, whose oneiric paintings represent the texture of these heavy lines). This is what has to be talked about if one wants to point out with full honesty the contexts from which LGB artists have emerged. These rumbustious environments and expanding worlds that had been demarcated with concrete, barbed-wire-topped walls, became during the last decade, thanks to some of Gorbachev's bright ideas and the onward march of History, for many LGB artists (though not for the Serbs among us), once more invisible, though very heavy, lines drawn around people.

If internal dissent was less flagrant in Tito's Yugoslavia than in post-'68 Hungary, the erstwhile country still had its rebellious image abroad. Tito broke with the tiresome, overly patriarchal Uncle Joe in 1948 and never looked back. Borders were open, the International Monetary Fund gave money and set regulatory reforms, the General Agreement on Tariffs and Trade was in a manner of speaking agreed upon: Tito's was a socialist project open to liberalisation and political decentralisation, making deals and doing the rounds with the European Community and the European Free Trade Association. The world that I was born into in 1973 was one around which my own parents could move freely, enjoying the diversity of a multicultural pluralism and prosperity, at least for the first seven or so years of my time in the world, an environment free of paralysing uncertainty, violent disharmony, or any overt repression from a monster as ugly and determined as the USSR. It was a world that Warmann and his family could have only dreamed of, and it was precisely such dreams that made what was to come in 1989 so momentous.

What must be remembered is that it was this 'foreign' position of the erstwhile country that in part precipitated the crisis that befell the Balkans once the Berlin Wall came down. For a while the power vacuum in the Yugoslav Federation led to disastrous infighting and political meltdown brought about by severe economic deterioration. The international order that had brought importance and even prestige to Tito's Yugoslavia shifted its whole dynamic, leaving its trade, economic and military standing on uneven, you could even say, disappearing land. By the end of the 1980s the need for economic reforms was being loudly voiced by foreign creditors: the market economy had won after all, the tide had turned and socialism was to be quietly dismantled and buried with its tattered dreams. So, in a time when civil order was needed in the country most of all, less government was called for, and the government's influence on state affairs was brashly reduced. The civil and legal world was falling all around us when we entered university: there was widespread unemployment; rife black market conditions and petty crime all over the place; out of work soldiers and secret police who turned gingerly to alternative sources of employment; guns were being trafficked out of the emptying barracks; drug trafficking from the eager east; human trafficking resulting from too many dreams and fears.

The state of grace, in retrospection, at times seems to be predicated on invisible misfortune, the disaster that awaits just around the corner, the flip side of love, hate, brewing its indignations, waiting for the dams to burst, its moment to come. The wars that would finally break up Yugoslavia started in 1991, first of all with Slovenia after it declared independence from the Federation, then in Croatia and then from 8 April, 1992 onwards in Bosnia and Herzegovina with the recognition by the United States and many Western countries of the new country.

> [Bojić wrote: 'Off point + boring!
> Come back later' but failed to do so]

[10]...yet Jörg Haider had, like the rest of us I am tempted to write, many milestones in his life: an exceptional career as a law student; notorious, reprehensible comments about German National Socialism in 1991 and 1995; the 27% of the vote he received in 1999 as leader of Austria's Freedom Party. All of these are recorded historical facts, we have the words, the texts, the balloted votes, the images and moving pictures and the European Union's sanctions dating from when his anti-Semitic party was included in the Austrian government. There exists the man: populist, charming, his words and thoughts so controversial to the world, so endearing to his supporters. I don't mean to distract by bringing up Haider but, as with so many other tangibles, he came into direct contact with The LGB Group and hardened what were already strong apolitical and anti-nationalist strands within the group. Because the extraordinary thing (although within the world of contemporary visual art perhaps it is not that surprising) is that almost all the artists attached to The LGB Group have at one time or another been immigrants in various European countries and a certain amount of LGB art has always had the weight and fallout of xenophobia as its theme.

Of all the milestones in his life, the recent car crash that killed Haider will surely be the most portentous: the Ballardian fusion of man and machine that somehow sates the latent, subliminal desire

---

10 This section begins in mid sentence and appears at a later stage of the folio. Bojić was somewhat obsessed with Haider throughout his career, perhaps for reasons that will become apparent below. We have placed it here due to the political context it gives. (Editor)

of our technological, speed-freak make-ups.[11] Driving fast near the city of Klagenfurt over twice the speed limit, Haider, I like to imagine, was fuelled by his sedan's power for celerity, or perhaps he was late to bed or to making plans for his grandmother's 90th birthday celebrations he had been due to celebrate the same weekend of his death. The conversations with those he met the night before might have been on his mind, the drinks he shouldn't have had but didn't refuse for whatever reason; he may have been joyous, elated or maybe downright melancholic. We'll never know what this public man was feeling, not with any certainty at least. And then he decided to overtake another car that shared his route. Maybe he was thinking about the more than successful election results of just two weeks previous and those figures and what they signified. Then his car veered onto the side of the road. And the acceleration of the machine, its parts, its tremendous power of traction – none of it allowed him to wrestle back control. His life, as the cliché goes, perhaps he saw his life in a rapid succession of frosted film frames as his car smashed into a concrete pillar. And as the car rolled over several times, the world fading from view, perhaps this man thought of those he loved, or of the disappointment people would feel if he were to die, or indeed find out he had been over the alcohol limit. Way over the alcohol limit.

The intensity of the life brings the extent of the fallout from the death you could say: revelations of drink-driving, of a gay life and relationship with his party's spokesperson, Steffen Petzner, in opposition to a background of having voted against any lowering of the age of consent for homosexuals. The secret lives of politicians are not commensurate with the people we get to know in the first place, and this is their amusement with us.

But Jörg Haider spoke publically as an embodiment of a strand of European historical and everyday reality: an anti-immigrant

---

11 Haider died from a car crash on October 11, 2008, just four days before the author's own death suggesting that these may have been some of the last pages revised by the author. (Editor)

and prejudicial conservative, tying his colours to the flag of bigoted traditions and xenophobia. This was his politics. But perhaps there existed a double life, like the one Steffen Petzner maintains that they lived out together behind a veneer of conservative homophobia, of a man who felt keenly the results and consequences of his anti-immigrant, anti-Semitic, homophobic stance, behind the lone personality he himself so eloquently created, all too happy to keep the divisive and all too exclusive populism that belonged to the darkest parts of 20th century politics alive and well amongst the good peoples of Mitteleuropa? It is something to think about. Because this is the very opposite, it must be stressed, of an LGB artist.

Miloš Lubarda, *Карађорђе* (1999)
Paper, found documents, unlimited edition 40.6 × 34.3 cm.
Courtesy of the artist and Galerie Gojković.

Miloš Lubarda, *Другови и другарице I, II, III, IV* (2001)
Black and white photograph, tape and ink on paper, 20.4 × 13.6 cm.
Private Collection, Novi Sad.

ПОПУШИШ МИ КУРАЦ!

ЦРКО ДАБОГДА!

Miloš Lubarda, *Биће боље* (2003)
Installation view of exhibition Around is Back Again, Today, 2002
in Gallery Michael Jetzer.

POST SEXUAL ART: LGB AND HOMOSEXUALITY

I believe that the homosexual public has shown more interest or curiosity for modern art [than] the heterosexual.[12]

— Marcel Duchamp

One thing I would like to be able to do here is talk about sexuality and art. The connection between sexuality and death is a science in itself, and we have lots of death in our group and I can see that clearly: but who wants to talk about death drives and dead loves? One of the most unique selling points of so much LGB art is its campness, its homosexual origins. Most of us came from extremely patriarchal, chauvinist societies where to be gay is tantamount to being a criminal, and a weak criminal at that. Therefore, like many other commentators, I myself never fully understood this strand of our art but would like to stop a moment to consider it. Chauvinism is never the goal in a work of art, it just sometimes makes itself the means like a traitor becomes part of a team only to undermine its victory. So much of our success has been Pyrrhic, but that's the cost of making art you can stand over and defend. It is the price of exposing yourself when nobody else is willing to expose themselves, when all around you are cowards and prudes. LGB art is rent open by the honesty of the lives of the artists who make it: pure commentary on the honesty of those brave enough to say the words: this is me and this is my art.

---

12 Bojić notes simply 'Western Round Table on Modern Art contra Frank Lloyd Wright's homophobia' as the reference for this quote. (Editor)

It has been an interest of mine for a long time: the gay man and his circle within the world of contemporary art. Whether it be Paris, London, Berlin or New York, you can be sure that you will come across them, gay men, with loud, rigorous opinions on the art of the day, a beautiful lady friend or two, and sex lives that leave most straight people running for the wings. For a while people thought that The LGB Group was nothing more than such a grouping of gay guys who happened to make art but really preferred sex and camp jokes, but this prejudice didn't last long. The continuing success of shows in Budapest, Zurich and Paris, to name just a few, allowed the work to speak for itself. A certain campness may have been a selling point at one time or another, but it was certainly never the only one.

Art theorists have come up with the idea of the homosocial and our grandfathers in Dada and Surrealism were most certainly homosocial, big gangs of boys running around joking and playing like a litter of puppies and this much has also been true at times of The LGB Group. In the early days we travelled, lived and created together: there was no boundary between the private and the creative. As individuals some of us may have been homosexual and may even have made art that could be termed homosexual in content but I feel that the two levels aren't dependent on one another, and shouldn't influence any judgement levelled at either the artist as a moral agent or their artistic work.

But this raises the obvious, less tenacious question: is there a link between an aesthetic sensibility and emasculation? I argue that there is absolutely none and much of my life to date has been proof of this, hence my inclusion of these ridiculous ideas here, early on in my...

> [This section ends in mid sentence. The author never fully returns to his chapter scheme]

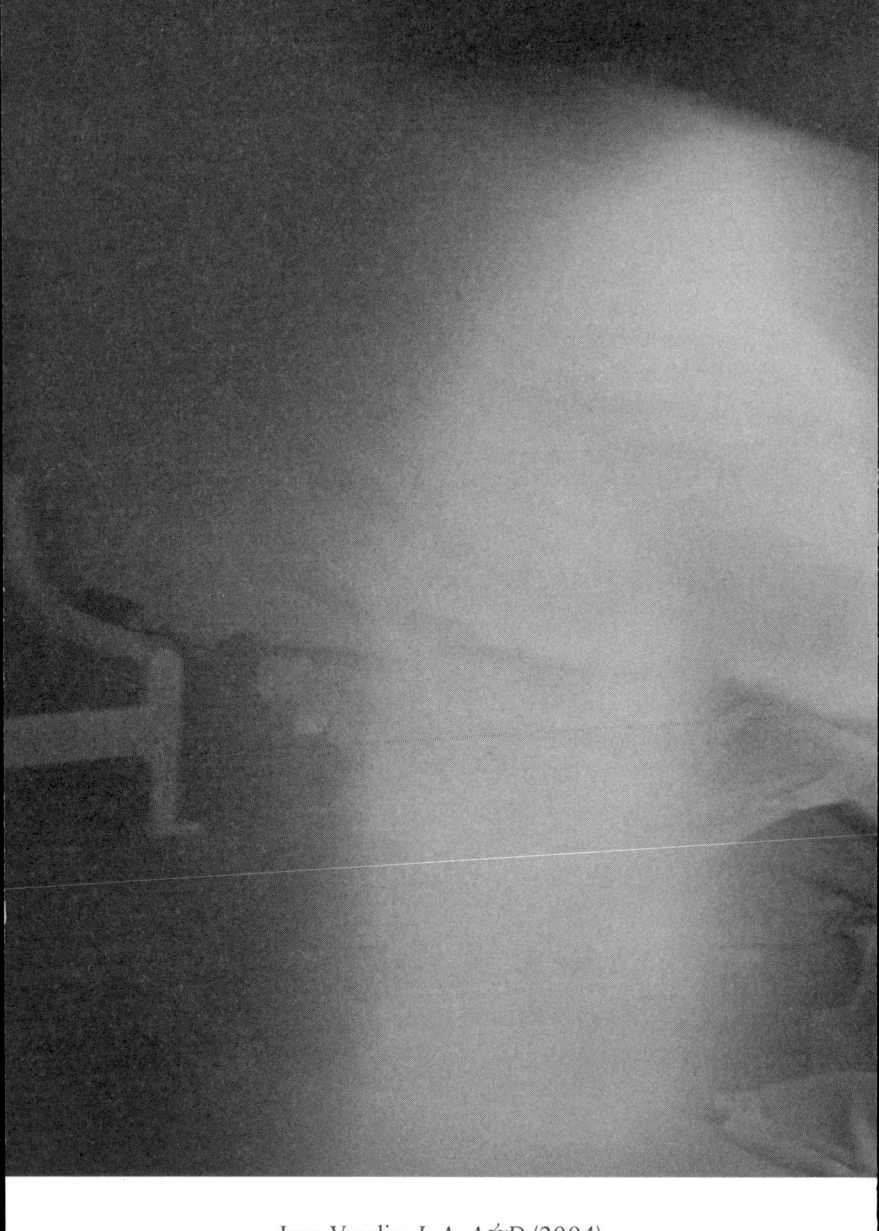

Ivan Veselin, *L.A. A&D* (2004)
Black and white photograph.
Collection Fricke-Waldhausen, New York.

Ivan Veselin, *L.A. III* (2004)
Black and white photograph.
Collection Fricke-Waldhausen, New York.

Elaine Pettifer was born to an American father and a Swiss mother and grew up not in one place but many: her childhood was a series of destinations across Europe and the United States, her father dragging his young family with him during his diplomatic career. As a sculptor there is an abiding sense of displacement in Elaine's work, yet there was nothing of the 'ephemeral' or the 'fleeting' with her, these are words that have nothing to do with Elaine. Rather one finds a vocabulary of weighted signs and forms not readily recognisable as belonging to any one tradition, geographic region or indeed temporal span. I guess what I'm saying is that Elaine's work was original to the point of defying any attempt at labelling it.

But that, somehow, sounds like a load of clichéd bullshit.

Let me try and write about her without cliché or artspeak. Rather diminutive she had nevertheless an aura of strength that reminded one of the physicality of sculpture itself, with a face as kind as they come. I first met Elaine in her studio in Budapest and the gregarious expression on her face as she welcomed me warmly, at the time nothing more than a shadowy stranger to her, has always stayed with me. That first day I remember being struck by her vitality – Warmann and myself were visiting Budapest in anticipation of the group show *Budapest/Belgrade* and I knew nothing about the artists working feverishly in the city, but soon after just a few hours in her studio I knew that this was an artist concerned with life and the art of living life, and that this concern was so strong it would instinctually, like a reflex, unconscious and unwilled, inevitably find its way into her artwork. She told stories that day that had no discernible direct link with her artwork but which betrayed her love of the randomness of life, and her having lived her life as she did, speckling the world with her presence, the random soon seemed paradoxically connected. With Elaine you felt that everything mattered, not that it had a 'reason' but that in simply occurring, by one man telling you a strange story or a car accident happening as you walked along the street, it had an importance you could not ignore. Elaine was the antonym of apathy.

Elaine's parents met in Geneva when her father was doing work for the UN. Coming from a family of diplomats her parent's connections would enable her to travel all over Europe and the Middle East for much of her life as she travelled back and forth to visit her relations and meet her friends and of course to see the art being made in each respective city, from Tel Aviv to Budapest, Ankara to Berlin. After school in Switzerland it was clear that art was what she had to do with her life, that it alone could help to channel the buzzing diversity of the splintered world into forms she could find understandable, manageable. Having been accepted into the École des Beaux-Arts Elaine moved to Paris where she quickly moved away from her young notions of art toward the world of Conceptualism and Minimalism, the world of Buren or Judd. On finishing her time at the academy she exhibited in Chantilly, her first exhibition, and it was immediately well received, a bold tapestry that was made with a craftsmanship that surpassed itself, erased itself and brought the work into a realm of sculpture not seen often in Paris.

I think what Elaine did next confused the French, because she left and would not return for many years. She got on very well in the École, extremely well, and this was matched in the success and *acceptance* – something many artists can never get in their life, and perhaps we should remember, something they should not want – of her first show in Chantilly. But while Paris had been good to her she moved away from the easiness of it and toward the Other bustling and shouting outside her bedroom window. That was what she needed, a foreignness around her and this is what she meant when she started to call herself a translator and the work she produced translation – she was moving the exotic signs all around her into the realm of the personal, like tourists need to photograph everything they come across, so she captured the difference in her everyday and exalted it into her art.

She moved first to Istanbul where her uncle was initially stationed as part of a NATO mission before he moved to Ankara and where she managed to find a studio with two other artists, both American: Basle Overbeck and Max Evans. Evans was a vain relic of 1960s New York, who felt that because he had been to Warhol's Factory he could look down on and condescend to anyone younger than he. We had the misfortune of meeting him once in Paris and the comment he made about 'you eastern European artists' was almost enough to send me over the edge. He died three years ago at the grand old age of seventy-five. Elaine fell, somewhat uncomfortably, into the role of the young American lady being Europeanised, learning about the Old World while all the time wishing to unleash upon it the laid-back, nonchalant Pop of the States. This was obviously a strange doubling of personality and one that Elaine was all too aware of; it was dangerous almost to revert back to a self she had last experienced at the age of twelve when her family lived in Washington D.C., afterward only ever flirting with Americana through her relations with those schoolmates sent all the way over the Atlantic for finishing school.

Of course things were not that simple. Max Evans took Elaine under his wing and they became friends, close friends, and together they explored Istanbul, the large, sprawling Ottoman city that was full of welcome and also malice, inquisitive market sellers with smiles on their faces behind whom lay in wait invisible pickpockets. The city and all its shapeshifting forced the three artists to stay close together. Evans was a weak man who needed women more than they would ever need him as Elaine quickly discovered, tiring of his insistence on the exotic (and hence for him alien and ultimately unknowable) nature of the city. Indeed, she realised that he was scared of it, the city and its impenetrable dark reaches, and guessed that he must have had a terrible past or secret left behind in the States (which we all now know he did) for him to run so far and scare himself in his evasion. It did not help that Basle Overbeck was in love with Evans, that she had moved from Boston all the way to Turkey in order to be near her art college tutor, after whom she was silently pining. Elaine never took interest in Overbeck's work but believed it when Evans spoke of rich patrons back in the States. Soon the situation became untenable, like a petty mid-century novel Elaine thought, and something she did not want to be part of, something to which she was not even emotionally connected. So off she went.

Hoşça Kalın was the show that came out of her year in Turkey, a loud, almost bombastic exhibition in what was to become her gallery in Cologne: Galerie Baxter. The show didn't sell but had the fortune of being commissioned by the Gasometer in Oberhausen to be enhanced and expanded to fit the huge chasmic space where people like Christo previously had the chance to blow up their work much larger than was standard. While the large scale held no particular interest to Elaine she took the opportunity and relished it, transforming what ended in stress and emotional turmoil – her year in Turkey – into something strong and monumental.

She stayed for the next number of years in that part of the world, making up what the critic Hermann Wölfel later termed her 'Westphalian period', for she worked up and down either side of the Rhine, first in Cologne then in Oberhausen and later near Venlo on the border with Holland and then Düsseldorf. She exhibited in all of these cities and more: Bochum, Krefeld, Bonn. Her output was relentless: an annual show in Galerie Baxter never sufficing, she pushed her work into the Kunsthalles and abroad. The earlier style, founded on craftiness and a light touch, using the European signage of reduction and simplification, was replaced with a heavy use of more Germanic-seeming tools – she took on the vocabulary of Beuys and, replacing the representation of her everyday life with his mythologizing, made the series of sculptures *Die Lebenslügen I – XII*. These works will perhaps, with the strange oxidisation of time, become her most recognisable and iconic work. This was evident in *Lebenslüge IV* where a huge honeycombed structure, made out of a thick, viscous material solidified and pungent, housed mementos fashioned from lead, barely visible as the wall ran out of sight, of all her previous cities of occupation.

Then she left for Berlin where a commission from the state of West Berlin finally ended her remarkable six years along the Rhine. She would experience the fall of the Berlin Wall and the momentous changes that overtook the city during the first years of the 1990s. It was here she met the artist Jan Offe with whom she left Berlin to live in Budapest (due to the need, she would write in the feuilleton of the *Süddeutsche Zeitung*, 'to get away from the history-soaked days of Germany and arrive at those days when one can live, for a time, free of all weight not one's own.'[13])

And it was at this time that I am happy to say my own story crossed paths with Elaine's. This sense of history, of turning one's back to obliging history in favour of your own workaday world, made us get on so well for that was what I was so obviously doing back then, my first day in Budapest. Walking into her studio and into the line of her smile, her compact, passionate warmth as a human being, I remember being scared of bringing in too much 'history' with me, too much war, like a guest worries about bringing in dog shit on their shoes. And I really felt this fear, not out of mere politeness but from the bottom of my makeup as a human person and it is this that makes me so indebted to Elaine Pettifer because I finally purged myself, in her presence, of war, of hate, of terrible, terrible things no man should ever have committed or colluded in but which I had to go on carrying because I was an artist, of the humble kind, concerned with the everyday and the readymades that humdrum life allow artists to imbue, through their creativity, with meaning. This is a power, a blessing in a way, a divine rubbish collector of the blandest most unique order. She had been to Belgrade it was true, and she had seen our work as the little, burgeoning collective LGB and she liked it. Yes she had been down there thanks to one of her uncles, working for the UN, accusing my people (so the Serbian press was saying) but I did not care at all for that and Elaine, I know, saw that in me, this indifference towards, no, rather this desperate need to turn away from, hatred and paranoia and prejudice and she let me in, and we let her in, her and Jan, and she told us stories and gave me the key to my art and it was a very special evening, one that changed, as you know, everything.

---

13 'Denn ich muss loskommen von den geschichtsträchtigen Tagen Deutschlands, und da ankommen, wo man eine Zeit lang frei sein kann von den Bürden, die nicht die eigenen sind.' *Süddeutsche Zeitung*, 23 September, 1994. (Editor)

And then, the next morning we left, with paintings of hers, new paintings – the first paintings the world had ever seen the artist Elaine Pettifer execute – and drove them away in a Škoda much too small for them, and somehow we put on our second exhibition under this term LGB and which, thanks to work such as Elaine's and the intervention of Jan, became a bigger success than you or I could ever have imagined. Her galleries around the world did not like it, this inclusion in a shabby, reactionary East European grouping, it was too defining, limiting her – such things weren't done anymore – but they let her because she wanted us to include her work and repeatedly insisted in her letters to me that she wanted to exhibit with LGB no matter what the case may be with her gallerists, or what fashion wanted to shout so rudely at us. When Elaine and Jan moved to France this relationship became more personal than theoretical – and perhaps that could sum up the whole sorry movement of LGB – and the richness of her self-conviction never waned for a moment. When *Artpress* laconically suggested that her everyday life 'must be as horrendous as the horrors of war', a flippant piece of art journalism they should have known better than to publish but which was, as Elaine knew only too well, a continuation of a threadbare, rather pointless argument started many years before when she had left France for Germany, Elaine wrote a rigorous, honest rebuttal for *Le Monde* that showed just how petty the initial volley was:

The truth remains that war is mundane, it doesn't necessarily have to be, but often it is hard and mundane. Real life, my life of fourteen wide-awake hours pottering around my house, going to the market, shop, café, hairdresser and then to the studio via the RER is not always mundane, it can be mundane, but it does not necessarily have to be so, it can be as rich, shocking, depressing and dangerous as war, and it often is. We are all of us at war; Total War belonged to the last century; daily war on abstract nouns, ongoing, infinite: this is the war for which we are currently fated.'[14]

14 'La vérité est que la guerre est banale, ce n'est pas nécessairement le cas, mais ça

And the strange thing is: Lubarda, Gojković and I, the three founding soldiers of LGB, all agreed with her, though Gojković of course grumbled. And stranger still: I never once talked to her about war, not once. With Ella, my concierge, I talk night on night, over and over again, about war war war, but to Elaine Petiffer, this artist who has always tried to envisage the boredom of the trench, the boredom that drives men to kill babies and rape their mothers, this artist of a belligerent, pernicious peacetime world, I told nothing. We must have had those conversations alright, but in other non-vocal ways I cannot put a name to: felt out silent chit chats.

This spat between critic and artist had its end point, for me at least, when Elaine was nominated for the Marcel Duchamp Prize but of course did not get it. She hated the idea of prizes and barely noticed even being nominated, but it really pissed me off because the establishment just could not let an artist, who was not even French and had gone off to Germany and Eastern Europe for a good part of a decade what is more, speak back to it with the conviction that Elaine had. She never stopped writing to the newspapers, whether it be letters to the editor or articles in the feuilletons, across Europe in French, German, English or even Hungarian on occasion, she was relentless and saw all these journalistic interventions as her duty, as a logical extension of the role she had to play as the artist she had become: it was her obligation to her vocation. Lubarda once had the great idea to edit her collected writing and both Elaine and Jan thought this a fine possibility. I would still love for LGB, what is left of us and our sorry state of affairs, to enable it to happen. Someday perhaps. Although who am I kidding?

l'est bien souvent: dure et banale. La vie réelle, ma vie, veiller 14 heures durant à faire de menus travaux dans de ma maison, aller au marché, dans les magasins, au café, chez le coiffeur et puis à l'atelier en RER - n'est pas toujours banale. Elle peut l'être, mais ça n'est pas nécessairement le cas. Elle peut être riche, choquante, dépressive et dangereuse comme une guerre, et elle l'est souvent. Nous sommes tous en guerre. La guerre totale appartient au siècle dernier, la guerre quotidienne, en cours, infinie contre les noms abstraits: voici la guerre à laquelle nous sommes condamnés actuellement.' Le Monde, 19 November, 2002 (Editor.)

Because of course soon after this diversion of the Marcel Duchamp Prize Elaine became sick and never told anyone, not even Jan at first. And I could hardly bear to see her vitality drain away like that, because it was too upsetting that some invisible, greedy little growth could rob one who was so energetic and strong...

But what is this I am trying to write here? Some sort of obituary? It fails on almost every level just as we ended up failing Elaine. This must be my last half crazy attempt to insult her with my drivel. She got sick and I could barely bring myself to visit – even now I get nauseous, a terrible sickening turning in my stomach rising up in my throat whenever I think of her as sick: such betrayal of the word 'life'! And then you, Warmann, go and die and Elaine hears about it, in the middle of dying herself, and I go and visit her to let her know and her eyes just know how you died, they wash over and she shook her head as if sorry I had spoken, sorry that death had overtaken her and you and that she had to live longer. How terrible life seems when you realise you have to pay for it with death; we all of us will die and I have learned the hard way that there is no such thing as a beautiful death save perhaps from the vantage point of beyond the line of the living. And the last time I saw Elaine that is what she retold me, with the authority of one whose days are marked: she reminded me that our lives are themselves one big lie, not because of a hidden transcendent truth they forsake but because we think of them as being well ordered, civilised, replete with good manners, educated, sophisticated, peaceful, meaningful, materially ordained, the next step in a progression that started way back in some cave in southern France, in short we take on our lives with the rules already governed for us and this leads to a false sense of honesty and freedom. And I told her she was right. Then she died.

Elaine Pettifer, *Down Shall Kill The Bull Up Shall Fly A Kite (After Lawrence Weiner)* (2003)
Installation view of exhibition Around is Back Again, Today, 2002,
in Gallery Michael Jetzer.
Courtesy Gallery Glucksman.

Elaine Pettifer, *Each Moment Depends Upon A Perception A (After Lawrence Weiner)*, 2003
Installation view of exhibition Around is Back Again, Today, 2002,
in Gallery Michael Jetzer.
Courtesy Gallery Glucksman.

Elaine Pettifer, *Each Moment Depends Upon A Perception B (After Lawrence Weiner)*, 2003
Installation view of exhibition Around is Back Again, Today, 2002,
in Gallery Michael Jetzer.
Courtesy Gallery Glucksman.

You always said that history, 'our history together, dear Djordje'[15], was only what we made of it. And that the future was not of us. You would always say that we lived in the here and now only to work on the remainder of the there and then. And not thinking about it but stubbornly going on out of a need to produce, to work myself clean from the past, I never stopped to think about this promulgation until now when I am supposed to somehow formulate where it was we came from and I realise that where we came from was an impoverished recreation of something itself hard to define, something which bled itself into a million different corners like mercury let loose in a darkened laboratory. We came from Dada and like Dada we came from war. Okay. So I try to make something of our history as a group, what I sometimes despair was nothing more than an ineffectual and not very important little group of friends who picked up and dropped off people along the way. I try not to think about the future for what does the future have now? Not much at all. What am I writing then? All there is to look at is this war, this point of departure so hopeless and depressing and in ruins that I feel wholly apathetic toward it. Other beginnings are needed. I tap clean the rubble from the ruins, set it straight upon my dray cart and wait eagerly for the mason to do with it what he may.

This then is my job: rubble cleaner[16].

***

The little red doorknob would not cease in its taunting, telling me that normal life was waiting to be lived. I sat for what felt like hours in the kitchen of my childhood home, staring at the cupboard, the bright little doorknobs. I could barely talk to my parents or anybody at all come to think of it. The days were hard squares I had

---

15 Appears in German in the original. 'Unserer gemeinsamen Geschichte, lieber Djordje' (Trans.)

16 The German term Trümmerfrau is used in the original, referring to the conscription of women in postwar Berlin and other German cities to clear rubble and prepare it for reuse. (Trans.)

to push myself through, rounded with grief and remorse. Sarajevo, Mostar, Foča, these towns I heard echoes of but avoided hearing anything more than just their dull reverberations, knowing too well the sad news that would follow their utterance.

I started to reread a lot of the books I had gathered, mostly volumes stolen from bookshops across the river. I read some Danilo Kiš. In one sitting I forced all the words of *A Tomb for Boris Davidovich* into me, alone in my bedroom hiding from everything except the fates of all the people Kiš kills off. Tales just about bearable in their accuracy of man. What is wrong with us humans? For that is what it comes down to: us people, us humans, and the haphazard things we choose to believe in, through chance or fate I do not know.

It was storing up inside of me, the need to create, to get out of my skin, to escape from myself and the nothingness threatening to engulf everything around me. From one moment to the next I would think: I need to get the fuck out of here, I need to start doing something with my life. Then I would sit back down in a dark world of shame and see out of the gloom a morning form itself into something visible inside my soul, a spring morning like any other somewhere near the village of Brasna with friends and an old man in army fatigues. A deserted road. A forest people called home.

The indecision of how to proceed with my life went on. At the time of this battle with normality I continued, it must be said, to believe in Greater Serbia and the inherent, what? badness? repulsiveness? of Bosniak Muslims. I was sickened with myself but also with the world. I wrote poetry or lines (it was at this time I started to use stencils and make the letters BIG, finding fonts and ripping them off, cutting up text, stealing) in which I battled with the hate of things, of the world, but also that much more intractable, confusing hate – hate of oneself. Regret. Pah! What a disgusting, vile thing. I did not then, nor do I now, want to stop a moment to think of it.

So it was not easy to turn away from Bosnia or the army. Help came when I went at last to the university in search of a way out, a way back into normality. I no longer wanted to study German literature like I had before joining the army. I wanted to read philosophy.

Just a word that seemed the opposite of everything else I could study, an extreme in itself. But at the department of philosophy my nascent drive was shown to me for what it was: delusion.

You want to enrol at the university?

Yes.

Have you got your results?

No.

No?

No. I went to the fucking war. I never got them.

Well did you sit your exams?

Yes. I did very well too. I think.

You'll have to apply for them. My guess is that you'll miss the deadline for the next round of matriculation I'm afraid. There's always next autumn.

Look, I've been off fighting a war. I want to start a new, normal life so please, don't just send me packing like some asshole! God damn it!

Everything seemed wrong, unfair, out of reach. I was about to start hyperventilating in this poor secretary's office when she saw past my rage and anger and offered me something to go away with: a calling card.

My advice to you is to ring Mr. Savić. He's involved in a new group interested in helping people come in contact with philosophy and move away from war. The Belgrade Circle. If you want to prepare for matriculation he is your best opportunity. Here's his number. He's a personal friend. You can tell him Ivka gave you his details.

She handed over the number, smiling. I held the card dumbly for a moment not knowing what to say.

You'd do well to call him. He'll understand your position.

I tried to smile back at her and left then, deflated and unsteady.

Meeting Savić was one of those events that happen only once and only then if you are a lucky bastard. Which I would not consider myself to be, all things added up. So we're talking here about something beyond the realm of luck. Savić was to become what you, Warmann, became later: a teacher, friend and confidant. He lived over in Zemun and had me over to his place that very same evening I rang him.

I am lazy, haphazard. All my life I have been around bustlers, energetic, incessant people, friends determined to carry me along in their zealous carriage. Another slice of luck, or whatever I should call it, you could say. For from the moment I entered his flat Savić talked eagerly, listening actively, I mean piercing me with his cocked ears and picking down countless well-thumbed books from his wearied bookshelves.

I'm so glad you could come Djordje. Ivka told me all about you and I feared you might not contact me out of shyness or something. And what has shyness ever given to the world?

Not much I imagine.

Not much at all. Like me this evening: all I can offer you is a shopska salad and a cold beer.

Oh Mr. Savić I didn't expect food-

Please, sit down and tell me about your family, I'll be right next door in the kitchen. Shout!

I learned quickly that Savić ignores good manners, but does expect them. An old man, short, busy grey hair and moustache, well dressed, slippers that slid him across the wooden, creaking floors. You can imagine. I sat there looking around the walls crowded with reproductions of Miro and bookcases, shouting in to him my family's history, tallying up the names like an exporter signing an invoice. He shuffled back in and handed me my bowl of tomatoes and goat's cheese and set down a beer to the side of me on an overflowing night stand. I ate, he just smoked. Never stopped in fact. He asked me about my schooling and we talked about my teachers in the IX Belgrade Gymnasium (he knew some of them), about what I was reading at the moment (I told him nothing and he nodded), he asked about my hopes for the future. He never mentioned the war or any politics that evening, not an easy achievement at the time. Trust me. You, Warmann, were very good at this too. Savić did well that first evening to keep it all *normal*, sitting in armchairs across from one another, me eating and drinking, him smoking, talking on and on about ourselves.

He had been a maths teacher and had retired the same year I finished school. His wife had died of cancer three years before that and it was obvious this loss stung him still but he did not shy away from it, gave himself forth in the most translucent of ways. Savić was a generous soul, unceasing in his vision of how the world should sit and what he could do personally to make it comfortable. He had been there when The Belgrade Circle was formed in February 1992, an NGO created by intellectuals in the face of Milošević's military ambitions. And it was Savić who brought me along the next Saturday to one of their 'Saturday Sessions'. And nothing would sit the same after that. I adopted his manner, his outlook in life, his social graces, his social faults.

But you don't know for sure what you want to do next?

No.

Philosophy maybe?

Yeah, maybe. I don't know anything about it, but it's either that or religion. I want to figure out...what's right and wrong for myself. It's all been taken over, y'know.

But?

Well philosophy, what could I get out of philosophy? I'm a hands-on kind of guy. My worry is it would be all sitting around reading about things and not doing anything about them.

Or as Marx said: plenty of philosophers have *interpreted* the world, the point is to change it.

Exactly.

But you don't know how you wish to change it?

Except not with a fucking gun or terror, no.

Yes. The guns are unfortunate.

Other than my father, this was the first man I had met who openly dismissed war, this being quite some time before Dayton when people were still enthusiastic about it all. Funny looking back, but he was the first of many who openly displayed a desire for absolute, apolitical peace. My father talked down the war because he was a coward, Savić because he was heroic, or so I thought at the time.

When at last I left he gave me quite haphazardly it seemed, all the more so when I perplexedly examined them in detail at home later, two books from the scores he had taken down and consulted during the course of that first evening. He had talked about education, self-education through reading and the appreciation of art. His humanism stemmed from his generosity toward people and both fed his pacifism. It was a lesson I carried with me for the next number of years. While I could still carry their weight, still believe in them. I left with a feeling of excitement and gratitude, the turmoil of the past few weeks had dispersed for the time I spent in Savić's company.

I walked the whole way back from Zemun to Blok 64, a trip that took me a couple of hours, but hours I needed to think things over. I examined the books whenever I passed under a streetlight. One was an old tattered French book by a critic called Michael Gibson, *Dada-Duchamp*, the other *The Society of the Spectacle* by Guy Debord thankfully translated into Serbian. The sound of nearby gunshots startled me when I reached the Bulevar Arsenija Čarnojevića, breaking the silence of the night and mocking me and my new-found excitement, it seemed.

To take my mind off the sinister night and its threats I started wondering idly whether Savić might be gay. I laughed almost as soon as the thought crossed my mind. At the time it was a common enough thought for me, meeting men and sizing them up. The strange thing being that I never felt ashamed about such thoughts or for what I had done with men, only curiosity if I would ever have the chance to do it all again. The war and the army I was already trying to push out of sight but I have learned over time that I take from them what I want when I want. What scares me is what I don't want to remember and when it will choose to come back to me, unbidden and unaccounted for.

So first there was Duchamp and later there was Nouveau Réalisme. Duchamp was my introduction to modern art. Not Picasso nor Cézanne, the Impressionists nor even the Surrealists to be honest.

Pierre Restany was Nouveau Réalisme's intellectual leader and founder. I have often thought about Restany. He has enjoyed his own champions in Paris recently and needs no accolades from a half-educated European from the continent's murderous, ill-mannered edges. But I have often wondered what he would be like in person, this French intellectual, to talk to at a vernissage or something right now, today, in some gallery or other along the rue Saint Gilles. I would not have very many theoretical questions to ask just perhaps what it felt like to be thirsty and hungry in Paris of all places in the 1950s. The birthplace of modernism in the years of its overturning. Nouveau Réalisme was premised on an engagement with the urban, industrial everyday appropriating or exhuming the facets of Dada, placing the everyday on the easel or rather replacing the easel entirely with a rough quotidian laboriousness that managed not to show overly the hand of the artist.

We knew very little starting as we always did with war and at the same time our starting impulse was a very raw need to be modern.

War does that to you: there is no such thing as pluralism only the right ideology, culture, tradition, only the one true pinnacle that needs to be climbed. Your national heritage. And to scale it you need a narrowly dictated tradition. Pride. Strength. The top-heavy building of an idealised, impossible future.

***

Aleksandar Gojković and Miloš Lubarda would play in the fields together and I would go out and join them, escaping the watch of my mother and slowly over time, a mere hour or two in the terms and conditions of childhood, we grew accustomed to one another. Without the need for any questions or expectations.

Thinking of our faces, our imagined faces of the past, I see the seed of so much distrust and suspicion, the folded flesh so redolent of Serbians. Our ilk grounded in arched eyebrows, furrowed foreheads. But also smiles enveloping and unceasing in peacetime, these too I remember from our sport across the unused field-spaces of New Belgrade. This our first playground, our first kingdom.

Trifke was there too of course: he was part of the gang from the start. Mr Trifunović, as Ella always calls him, which makes me smile. And I'm trying hard to see where the differences started: how is it he has absolutely no taste for art, for culture? For example why can Miloš or I only see the world as a matrix of references to works of art, literature, quotes, homages and criticisms? We are cultural animals. Trifke a drug dealer, a smuggler. Are our lives determined from the outset I'd like to know, laid out like the grids of New Belgrade in hardened, squared fashion that we must follow for the rest of our days? Trifke came from a family that was much like all our families. He'd always be the one to throw the first stone, to try to steal an apple at the market, but Gojković wasn't far behind him.

I remember a party on one of the disco boats from when I was still studying at the university. We were all going mad to the latest Bebi Dol track, it was the sixth time the DJ was playing it, and Trifke appeared out of nowhere and insisted on buying me a drink. He asked me about the army but made it obvious he didn't really want to know. In fact he hardly looked at me, seemed pained to be in my company. I don't know why he offered to buy me a drink. He started making comments about some girls on the dancefloor, he wouldn't shut up with complete smut, the really tiring kind, and I couldn't help but feel he was testing me. He asked what I was doing with myself. I told him I was making art with Aleksandar and Miloš. Shaking his head he turned to look at me with complete disdain. I asked him what he was doing with himself. Making money, was all he said, then some girl came over to him and I went to dance. And that was the last time I saw him on Serbian soil.

***

Those tower blocks and overgrown, litter strewn spaces between them, were not in the business of cultivating artists but somehow that is what we grew up to become. A group of approximations of what a European artist was to…to whom? To my own ignorant prejudice of what a European artist was? I don't know. The first word spoken about Dada or Surrealism I heard was from Aleksandar Gojković on the number 7 tram crossing the old Savski bridge, direction New Belgrade.

I know my artistic antecedents.

What? I laughed, I remember laughing.

No seriously. Like you said when you left, we need something to take us out of it all. Lubarda and I have talked a lot – about art and poetry. I know it sounds like bullshit but you wrote us saying you were studying philosophy and art history and…

And what?

Don't go all hardman dickhead. I'm talking about art and who we're following as artists not as dumbass soldiers or unemployed losers. Or fucking raping murderers…

We let silence speak then for a moment in the half-empty tramcar.

So who the fuck are we following then?

Surrealism and Dada. Surrealism was poetical, non-realist, he said clumsily, Dada was cut-up, non-Eurocentric, anarchic. Both centres of modernism. You know the Surrealist partisans from school, Popović, Ristić, nationalists in a way. But not the Dadists: they'd be anti-everything!

I still had no idea what he was talking about: I could not even remember what I said when I had left Bosnia. I had not really thought that he or Lubarda could have given a moment's thought to art and certainly not that Gojković considered himself an artist. The last time we had seen each other I was almost crying and Lubarda was silent with shock, he physically could not open his little mouth to speak. And Gojković? He had been angry, he was yelling, hollering, shaking his gun like a crazy man as if in its rattle he would find a way out, a permanent return to Belgrade. As if that motel and that river could have meaning for us, as if those buses and those women, all that innocence, could tell us anything. No – how do you go from this to talking about becoming artists, I mean: what did I miss in between? The only thing that the army and art have in common, that I can make out, even after all this time, is one thing and one thing only: a disposition for camouflage.

We were in a tramcar, itself rattling and cold and it was 1993 and we were all three broken men. We were approximations of what people think of as twenty-one year-old men.

Dada? I repeated the word. That sounds funny.

Yeah, well, it can help us grow Djordje, to use what we have but get rid of the rotten shit. The past is over. My past. The here and now will be my art. You said it yourself: we need to forget the war and become whatever it is we want to become.

An artist?

A question he would only answer by the by, but one I had then to ask.

Dada. So affirmative! Even now with its myths decoded and its potential diffused I hear the revolutionary echo of the word. It should not have really been a surprise that Gojković was to become the visual artist, the scissor-and-paste man who would battle his way through the Department of Fine Art and convince us and many others that he was in fact, an artist. A great artist.

***

Relativity was introduced and explained to us early on by Lubarda, though we didn't know the word for it then. In the toilets at school he showed us the meaninglessness of graffiti abuse through disassociation. All three of us were bullied at one time or another. Trifke would sometimes stand up for us, he had respect, but he couldn't protect us everywhere, all the time. It was Mrs. Gojković who came in for some of the worst, ill-dreamed missives marked onto the toilet cubicle's walls. Why that should have been the case I no longer know: it was Lubarda's mother who was the stunner and that even today, I believe she has no fewer than seven suitors chasing her around the markets of Belgrade.

A prostitute, Lubarda spoke the words carefully, is only a prostitute to the sad bastard who looks at her that way. She is after all somebody's daughter, somebody's mother and respected at the very least by god.

I am not sure to what extent this syllogism calmed Gojković's violent rage but it impressed me and, I suspect, even Lubarda himself.

***

In the autumn of 1993 we saw each other wearily, Lubarda, Gojković and I, somewhat embarrassed by what each others' eyes reflected, what they knew and what they had seen. It was hard starting back at the everyday life business, the nationalists, the Church and everybody else making that difficult. We were only getting started in learning how to live normally in a normal everyday: there was no one more surprised than I that we should have made something deemed to be art out of it. But there was still much to come to pass.

***

Who knew what the normal everyday was in the Belgrade of 1993?

***

You never wished to hear about my sex life from before we met, which was unfortunate. Everything had to be so solemn with you which was a relief at first after all that had happened and all those voices and egos spiralling around and getting only louder, and how I yearn for it now, your solemnity and your grave cock growing hard in the morning light slowly, some old dame of Vienna or Paris peeping in through the window trying to get a look as we awoke together, warm, tumescent. With you it was always with a seriousness of face and composure of hands, mouths, tongues, which I have never come across in another.

Not that I have been looking since you and your solemnity.

But my sex life was only full of fun and flippancy. With the exception of Jovana, that was different, but I try to hold no guilt for the confusion that relationship caused. Sometimes I think if I had fallen for Biljana, or anyone else, and didn't sleep-walk into my relationship with Jovana around the time of the army, I may have had less misfortune in love later on.

First there was kissing. No, first there was hugging then kissing. New Belgrade was not a very straight-laced place for us urchins, all being the same as the next in Tito's eyes. Each holy pioneer equal to the next child comrade.[17] Amusement soon came in the bushes and garbage centres. Behind my tower block I enjoyed my first blowjob from a girl of whom all I can recall now is her face, her name gone like so many others.

It was right in that spot that they built one of the first bomb shelters in '97.

I think she gave everyone a consideration: strange that her name escapes me. The sheer joy comes back to me, even now, the disbelief that something that had been up until then only an abstract possibility was becoming a base reality and flooding out from my groin to the rest of my trembling body. Smiling at the collapsing walls and sinister-seeming catalpas this sensual baseness made me laugh, causing her to look up for a moment before I urged her to continue on. Sex was wide-eyed and laughing even when it was still terribly confusing.

***

I always saw my father as a weak man. When the time came for the people of Greater Serbia to rally against the unjust and undemocratic

---

17 Pioneers was an organisation for children and involved an oath-rite and the wearing of a red scarf, it was largely based on the cult of the Partisans of WWII. (Editor)

collapse of the federation he stayed quiet. Never spoke one heated word. So strange come to think of it for a Montenegrin. Growing up he had never strayed far into words hot-tempered or irate and what in a middle-aged man is a peaceful demeanour for peaceful times became in the older man a weak disposition in a time of strong wills. His family had come from Montenegro and he took us to those hills often, once a year if he could manage it. On these trips he would come alive and tell my brother and sisters and me stories of the War and the happy fools that populated his childhood. Every village had its idiot as far as my father was concerned. The heroic age ended for him when no one took enjoyment in the village idiot anymore. This loss occurred, according to my father, in or around the year 1986.

***

Gojković and I would call around to Lubarda's apartment often in the hope that there we would be brought out of the tedium of living at home with parents we inevitably detested. And Gojković could detest: he was already, by the age of fifteen, consummate at passionately disliking people, places, things. This trait many people have come across in Paris and London, a certain shock always discernable in the face of a Balkan put-down the likes of which the sufferer has never quite before experienced.

One Saturday we met up, Gojković and I. He knocked a window through on a boat parked down by the Sava and we got a hell of a chase from the boat owner, a burly fucker in a red and white striped jumper who implored vainly the strollers of the sad promenade to apprehend us. We lost him eventually, knowing as we did the paths of the woods further down the riverbank and decided, under the pretence of caution, to call to Lubarda and hang low for the rest of the afternoon. His flat was in a different complex to our own, Blok 70 and the light seemed different there, though it was just a couple of hundred metres from our own homes.

Lubarda must have been writing poetry or something when we called as he looked flustered and embarrassed all at once when he saw us at the door. He led us in and listened quietly as we excitedly rattled off the story of our delinquency. Lubarda's parents were somewhat bohemian. They were different species to Gojković's or my own parents and their flat showed this clearly. His father worked as a surveyor, becoming the head of his department when Lubarda was still a toddler, the job allowing him to travel as far east as China, researching and learning about various dam projects and land reconstruction schemes. A tall, erudite man who seemed only to charm people, like a snake charmer puts a python under his spell, the shock of his handsomeness a powerful aide. His wife Silva Ereš, the beauty of Novi Sad, was a heavenly creature, a Cleopatra. She had been an actress for almost a decade with the theatre of Novi Sad, having left school early to follow a career in front of the admiring eyes of the people. She stopped upon giving birth to Lubarda and never returned to the stage thereafter, without any need to give a reason. We all knew that she wrote for the theatre and that eventually one day her work would be performed, however this seemed to be eternally put off, a melancholy wait that lasts, I believe, to this day. Gojković and I loved that flat, full of exotica and books and Lubarda writing his secret poems and his mother so beautiful and sex-full that at times it was a torture not to tell our friend our thoughts of his warm-hearted, long-waiting, luscious mother.

We did not always tell each other everything.

I followed our host through into the living room, registering the lovely Silva cleaning up in the small kitchen. Gojković stopped off the telling of our pursuit to flirt with Silva, leaving me to pick up the story. His benign, hyperactive babble reached me as we sat down, looking on as Gojković joined us, followed by Lubarda's mother unhooking her apron and listening keenly as she told us she was going out.

The three of us said goodbye in unison.

Anything to drink Lubarda? I'm fucking thirsty. Gojković proclaimed as soon as the front door closed.

Help yourself.

He came back with a beer and a cheeky grin although that would be an inaccurate description. There is nothing cheeky to Gojković, purveyors of his art know that he possesses just a single-minded assurance that he can do whatever he likes and that it will be deemed – if not immediately acceptable than eventually – for the best. How else could he have ended up running a gallery?

What the hell are you doing with that?

I know your old man is down in Sarajevo with those pithy headed Bosniaks checking their soil or whatever. And besides, I'm parched.

Lubarda had always been contemplative and he would sit quietly through the vagaries of Gojković, like a silent penitent putting up with what has been put on the earth to challenge him. We just sat and watched as he drank the beer in two long gulps that I remember seemed uncomfortable.

You're an asshole Gojković.

Yeah?

Yeah and someday you're going to get me in serious trouble.

Only Gojković was no longer listening. He had his eyes closed and the bottle held in front of him. His other hand rubbing a growing bulge in his trousers. Often I had hard-ons in Lubarda's apartment too and knew I could ascribe them to his mother and her casual sexiness but I did not know what Gojković was doing. He went on to unzip his trousers and feel out his growing dick from underneath his offwhite briefs. I had never seen another man's erect dick before; somehow I had thought maybe I alone enjoyed this phenomenon. Soon all too soon he was wanking himself slowly, giving a method to what were up until then unimaginable physical desires and suddenly he came, good and pure, the white stuff appeared and what had been barely audible moaning broke into a groan and my erection was so hard it hurt and my eyes stung from the need to blink. The whole room was filled with light and the noise of the street as if trying to distract us with the normal way of things. He opened his eyes and smiled and got up and went to the bathroom. I'm not sure Lubarda even realised fully what happened, I did not look at him to see but just stared out the window onto their crowded balcony.

Some time passed in silence. When Gojković returned Lubarda asked us both to leave as he had enough of us for one day.

I did not say much tramping across to our blok. The anticipation like nothing I had had to put up with before. The relief a total revelation. No, we did not always speak to each other. We did not always need to.

***

'The world of perpetual darkness'[18] raised its head and swallowed us whole. Were we ever to truly resurface again? In the old Yugoslavian People's Army you were eligible for military service from the day you turned eighteen. As it happened we were the last batch of young blood that the YPA, as Tito knew it, would ever conscript: we were entering the ranks of a beast about to undergo a most violent transmogrification.

I remember the last day of what I could term my youth clearly. It was banal. Lubarda had finally told me about his poetry and writing, explaining it as some sort of bourgeois affliction he had inherited from his parents. We were sitting on the low wall outside the local grocery shop Kod Sime, smoking cigarettes and talking talking talking. School had come and gone and we were free then, for a month at most, to pass the hot summer days as we liked. Mostly we slept late, annoyed our mothers, talked like we were then outside Kod Sime, went swimming in the Ada.[19]

Lubarda told me he wrote poetry and I said nothing in response. I envied him if anything: behind his glasses and his glazed-over eyes lay a world he kept from Gojković and I and everyone else. I

---

18 *Tamni vilajet* (Trans.)
19 Short for *Ada Ciganlija* which is the nickname for the *Savsko jezero*, a man-made lake on the river Sava, a popular swimming area. (Trans.)

had never enjoyed such a world, my life an ongoing public charade in which everyone chipped in and had their say. Except perhaps my father, something else that made me envious of Lubarda. I didn't reply because I did not know what to say.

Papa says that Milošević is bringing us down a dangerous road.

My friend spoke in order to say something.

No offence, but your papa's an old Titoist.

I spoke in order to hurt. Thankfully I failed:

Yeah, you're right. He thinks we're all one and the same and should stay the way we are.

Pah! Well he would think that, wouldn't he? The old guard looked after him well enough with his trips to China.

A cloud went across the sun and in the dimmed world little Banio, the feral kid we sometimes took turns to look after whenever his single mother went into rehab, ran out and fell over one of the many cracked pavements, skinning his knees and wrists.

Aaooh! he let bawl out of him. We just sat and watched as Sime's old wife, the wench, ran out and picked the little crazy up, shushing him with a mixture of reproach and pity, as is the way of such women.

It's just that I'm not sure I want to go join the army with all that might happen over Slovenia.

Well, you have no choice.

Papa says if there are elections they will change everything, that the government's already changing the constitution to create an unstable state.

Well, damn your papa!

I was fed up with this talk, aware that we knew only what we were told we knew, that since Slovenia declared itself independent the year before everything was changing or liable to change as if it were not enough that our own little lives had to change but the whole country too. If the prospect excited me I think it also tired me.

I want to study too you know. It just looks like it's going to have to wait.

We heard then the low whistle that stayed close to the overgrown grass that we knew to be the call of our friend Gojković. I looked up and, shielding my eyes from the newly revealed sun, kenned his bulk coming out from an alleyway one house down. He eyed the deserted street without turning his head, which was sunk between his broad shoulders like he had learned to do in the movies and he stepped lightly, hesitantly toward us.

This guy already thinks he's in the army, Lubarda said glumly.

And he's probably right, I said trying to sound light-hearted.

Always the soothsayer – that had been my job when we were young. Because I knew it was true, I knew that there was only one thing over sex that Gojković wanted in life right at that moment and it was to get out of Belgrade and seek out adventure. In the summer of 1991 that meant, invariably, a career in the YPA. A ride on the changing animal, the start of a long march at dusk, darkness rising up all around you silently as things fell ever more apart.

Guess what's in my pocket?

Lubarda put his hands deep into his own pockets. I felt for my cigarettes. The sun went back behind another cloud.

My call up card, smiled the self-assured mouth of our friend, the guileful Gojković.

***

I returned from Bosnia much earlier than Lubarda or Gojković. At first I dealt with my time there by throwing myself into the wild and frenzied jingoism that was so pervasive in the city. It lasted about a month, my posturing as a credible chauvinist-nationalist until one day catatonia swept over me – quite suddenly – when my father left me alone in the kitchen. I had been lecturing him on the plight of our Serb brothers in Bosnia, in Croatia, the plight of the Serbs against the Muslims, the Turks, the Jews, the fact that he didn't know shit about anything because he was a weak-minded little man who placed his fate in the hands of bureaucrats and idle federalists. After I expended myself he just rose and got his jacket, slipped out of his slippers, put on his shoes and left, closing the door silently behind him. I was so out of breath from my worked up rant I had no punch left to fire at him, no invective valediction to hurl at his disappearing little body like I would normally have done.

Instead I just sat there and let the silence wrap itself around me where I was, elbows on table and nothing at all to focus on. The banality of the room, the apartment, the sheer functionality of all the implements, the kettle, the sink, the doors of the presses and their little red doorknobs, all this crowded my mind as if they were as exotic as the Chinese tapestries and wares that adorned Lubarda's parents' place. The inhumane, gaping void inside me lurched in the face of what my father had suddenly left me to face: an everyday world the like of which I had just stormed through, gun in hand, thirsty for carnage and guided only by anarchic hate.

Intercepting women on their way to do timeless acts, acts of decency beyond young men like me with guns in their hands. Rushing into people's lives, strangers who had done nothing against me, and ruining their world. Kicking in doors and smashing the contents of homes under the polished butt of my gun. A destroyer of the everyday world for so many people. An everyday world I may never again know or enjoy as I did before. I looked over at his slippers by the door and I heard the roar of war, and saw that it represented ideals that had nothing to do with what I was seeing, with the way I was supposed to then live, *with everything that was normal*. Everything that had constituted life before the call of arms was dispatched and heeded.

The dread that Bosnia would never leave me, that life had without a moment's thought been irretrievably set by the army of the Second Military District and the defence of the hallucinatory Republika Srpska made my stomach turn, a wave of nausea nearly setting me and my chair over.

Gojković and Lubarda and all the acts in the perpetual darkness stood before me and only a little yelp of a cry leapt from my soul for fear that anything more would only see me slide into insanity.

Innocence was lost.
Beauty was lost.
Naïveté, lost.

All handed over for a long list of things that have nothing to do at all with a deflated pair of slippers, a kitchen sink, a cupboard's red doorknob.

***

Every approach to Paris is as different as the next. There is an epic to be written yet and it will comprise the testimonies of every-one wallowing in Paris and their accounts of how they got there. Which would amount not to an unreadable chronicle but an unbearable one. It's some sort of act of resistance to recall accurately your own very first memories of Paris when images of Paris are as iconic as a McDonald's sign lit up, bright and gaudy on some confused junction at the edge of some dirty town. My first sight of Paris in person was from the A2 coming in from the northwest, the whole thing lit up in a grand big parody of itself, scintillating a million lights in a pointillist mix with all I had preconceived in my head. In a Mercedes Benz C200 series with four other men: you, Trifke, Gojković and Lubarda, both of whom were asleep, you just staring out the window blankly and Trifke up front driving like a maniac, fighting exhaustion with too much Red Bull. I was a rat on an ill-fated ship. The snoring I remember. The ramparts and tunnels of the Périphérique I remember, the impressive rise of La Défense, the financial district, high-rises invoking insomnia. I felt the water of the Seine below us, not once but twice, the large arc of the river growing away along below our gangster's car. Then the streets of Neuilly. The first streets of Paris I laid eyes on, deserted all and broken only by street lamplight.

Trifke, lordly and acting the gentleman he was not, helped me out of the car. He felt bad I think about how long the journey from Vienna had taken, what with the diversion we had to take in order for him to drop off a consignment of drugs, but only just then, right then, that evening and thereafter any guilt on his behalf would be gone for good. Men like Trifke do not deal in guilt. I had slept for the first half of the journey, recovering from my attack. During the night drive from Nantes I had sat up front with him while the others slept. I tried to talk as amiably as possible, remembering old friends and stories from childhood and New Belgrade, anything to take my mind off the pain in my shoulder. I had wanted to take in rue Danielle Casanova and get my bearings, enjoy at last the fact of being in Paris. The home of so much of my past learning and future life. But Trifke had no time for such gravity, three other bodies needing to be dropped off at points all over the sleeping city. He had his arm around me and my good arm went likewise over his shoulder, the arrangement being awkward as Trifke is a good measure smaller than me. So when he rang at a street door and we were met by a business-like woman in her forties, I could not shake her hand. She let us through the heavyset portal and silently welcomed us, displaying all at once sympathy and alarm at my banjaxed state as well as warmth and good humour at life in general, all through a series of deft little movements as she admitted me into her concierge's domain.

This was of course Ella, who else. My keeper and first teacher in Paris.

***

Meeting them for the first time after the army I can no longer remember what I was expecting. But I was not expecting two artists. Benoit has told me at length what it is like coming off smack and I think coming off the army and Bosnia was similar. The horror and all that. Only instead of wanting to get your hands on something, coming off the war was all about getting rid of something, the ache of trying to get an indelible mark off your soul's retina. Saying again and again: yet here's a spot more. I have never gotten rid of the stain of course, but after twelve or so months I could function again, look at the next day without fear, go to the market without shame, make tea without crying out silently. So when I met at the bus station my childhood friend, the rough bastard Aleksandar Gojković, I expected to fall into the role of medical orderly and start the difficult process of getting my friend back to where I could recognise him.

We had a short talk about Lubarda (who had been staying with family in Novi Sad for some time) and mutual friends from the army, their levels of hate and madness and all the little hints of the full-scale horror going on down there. His words shut me up until we got on the tram.

Then he started talking about art!

The circumstances of the last time I saw Gojković, crazy reckless Aleksandar, were enough to make this turn in conversation a little surprising.

I found our artistic antecedents.[20]

By the time we reached Blok 70 I was convinced that this was serious, that Gojković had found his methadone, had dealt with things his own way and that art, becoming an artist, was how he was going to look in the eyes of the new day coming without fear or trepidation.

Our art was to be about the day, the unit of each day and how it is constituted. It had to be: it was either that or full blown abstraction, but we were too tainted for that, too caught up in a jaded, proletarian obligation to normality that we went off chasing it, the normal everyday. It is true what they say about people from the Balkans (how inclusive I feel speaking such vagaries!): people disburden themselves of a heavy, hurtful past by living only for the present day.

Only Biljana could have saved Aleksandar from himself. He was a lonely child to a mother who was forced to work too hard

---

20 The discrepancy between this reported speech and the one above indicates Bojić's willingness to work freely with supposed real events and speech and his apparent lack of interest in factual consistency. Such textual and narrative discrepancies are not here amended. (Editor)

just to feed and clothe him, Biljana acted as the older sibling he desperately needed. Biljana was hard, she was always a figure of strength for me and I think it was this power that made Aleksandar respect her, to listen to her, and I increasingly suspect, learn from her. He had plenty of opportunity to listen to her during the hours we hung out with her and her friends by the promenade along the Sava. Aleksandar pretended he didn't really respect women, or at least that he had no time for them but really he had, he just had to keep this fact secret. He would go home on time, the obedient son, and try to get his mother's affection.

Biljana one day came up to us on her own, Miloš, Aleksandar and I, as we sat around on one of the many benches facing the wide, fast flowing river. It must have been autumn because I think I remember leaves falling like snow, the treeline on the far shore on Ada golden and yellow. She bummed a smoke off us and we stared at her as she lit it with her own lighter. We thought she was cool, and she was.

Where's that little creep Trifke?

Don't know, why?

He owes me money, that's why.

How was the show in the Student Centre?

Good. Really good.

Biljana was already performing at the age of seventeen in venues such as the Student Centre.

Just that some men are assholes.

How's that? Aleksandar asked seriously.

They pretend they give a shit, but really they're just a fucking shithead themselves. This country's full of shithead men, trust me.

She stared straight ahead, one elbow held in one hand as the other hand moved in and out to her mouth in a rapid wave as she drew on her cigarette.

Promise me boys never to become macho assholes? You're too clever for that.

Sure, said Aleksandar, then added: is everything okay Biljana? Nobody messing around with you?

And stay away from that kid Trifke, she said ignoring his question, he's going to end up dealing drugs, trust me.

He's already on them, Miloš added with a laugh.

Exactly. Thanks for the smoke.

She walked off then, sullen and moody and we looked at her go. Then went back to looking out at the river. Aleksandar moved off after a few minutes, mumbling about finding out who was messing around with Biljana. After he was out of earshot Miloš spoke up:

Why's he so into Biljana? She'd never look twice at a kid like Aleks.

She wouldn't be the first, I remember adding.

***

I do not know how I went from inarticulacy and ignorance, the last among us to call myself an artist, to becoming the supposed leader or spokesman of the group, the mastermind behind the machinations. Or at best, if I were forced to, if someone, some fucking academic or shitwank critic from California or Harvard with square glasses above a gay scarf and shoulder bag came in here and put a gun to my head, well then, perhaps I could start guessing. I copied Savić: I never asked people to be persuaded, but I did expect them to be – I took it for granted that they would be convinced.

Leaders, fathers, family, institutions.

Peter Tomc once joked in Venice how we were like a big happy family and I tried to disagree with him, joking that we were too different to be a family, but what family has no differences? I didn't believe in what I was saying myself. LGB was the only family of which I was ever proud to be a part.

Benoit reminded me straight away of my father, there was something in his smile, which broke out often, that brought the face of my father, who I haven't seen for so many years, back in front of me, not that my father smiled much. One after the other, I have picked up many substitutes for my father. I can see now, round shouldered and waiting, my heart beating faster than normal, that love means a replacement, an erasure of one to be replaced by another. My real family is just that: faded people I have rubbed out, willing the faces of all these other people, the two guys Aleksandar and Miloš, Savić, Ella and Elaine, to appear in front of this fuzzy empty space.

But then Benoit was different. I met him first in the Connetable, sitting at the counter drinking wine and smoking incessantly, as if both actions could only be carried out in unison, and quickly. Amidst the chaos of that place, late on in the night, I was ordering a round for the table of us people upstairs, and he started talking as I waited to get my order in and immediately he had my attention because of that grin. A sardonic, all-knowing grin, one of a father, that's it: a *fatherly* grin, if you can imagine that. And what he had to say caught me, captured me and brought me into a past – his past and only the past – that for a moment, and late at night getting that terrible champagne they sell in that all night hell-hole in the Marais, allowed me to see myself, briefly, with a smile on my lips, accepting myself. A strange thing to see reflected back at you in the gloom of a two-in-the-morning exchange of words at a bar counter.

He was a waiter by profession, had worked across the city in over twenty restaurants, he never tired of saying, and knew more about the serving of a meal than any mechanic does about the running of a car. His life, for eighteen years, had consisted of the astute and noble art of serving plates of food haloed with invisible Michelin stars, and after his shifts, the quest for perversity and pure inebriation through open-ended white nights. I never figured out the core of Benoit's perversity, nor its motives, nor even its reason for overtaking his life as it did: he was perfectly clouded in it, and like darkness sits over the city for half of its lifetime, so sex and alcohol and drugs hung over Benoit.

I rarely see the light of day, he would joke without laughing. Daylight doesn't allow for any surprises.

We were celebrating that night a big show by Matthias Nagry, a sell out, and it was the last time we all gathered around a table with any sense of unity. I got my order and Lubarda appeared at my shoulder to help me bring up the bottles as I placed a dozen or so flutes between my fingers. I invited this grinning stranger up to join us because I knew he was the answer to the question: what was I, as spokesman, meant to say when my vocabulary had run itself dry of any new words to proclaim?

Do I blame Benoit for giggling, for cementing my primal shameful memory? Yes and no. Having killed people, seeing dead bodies, shaving your head before you put on a uniform – what difference is it to fuck in front of one more dead body? But then not every dead body is the body of the one you love.

***

I awoke to my first day in Paris with a pain shooting itself through the balm of my slumber, ripping sleep away from me with a roar. I tried in vain to sit up. Lying there I heard noises outside, voices, what sounded like kitchen pots and pans. Then I went back under a film of sleep.

Matthias Nagry, *Pillow No. 1 Ann-Marie Johansen* (2003)
Digital print on canvas with emroidery, 104 × 64 cm.
Courtesy of Collection Lindemann, Stockholm.

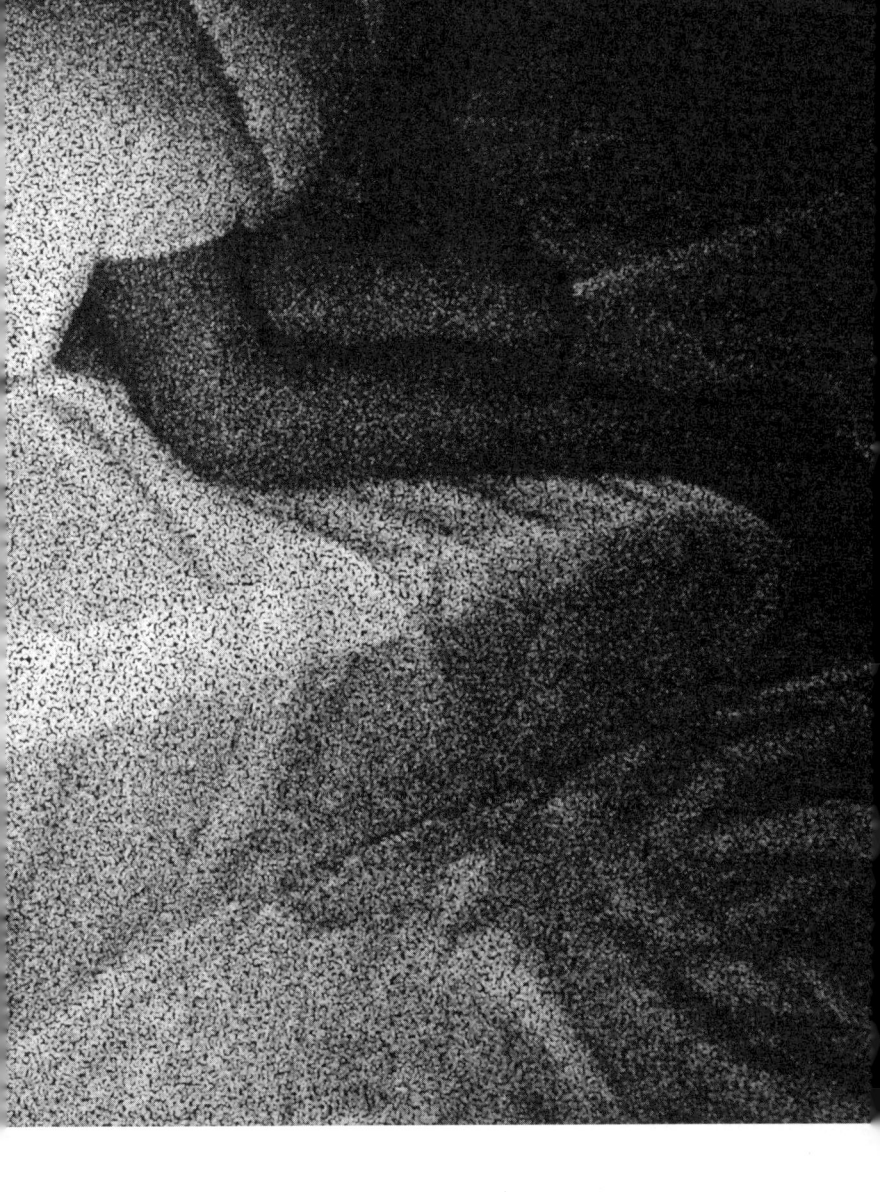

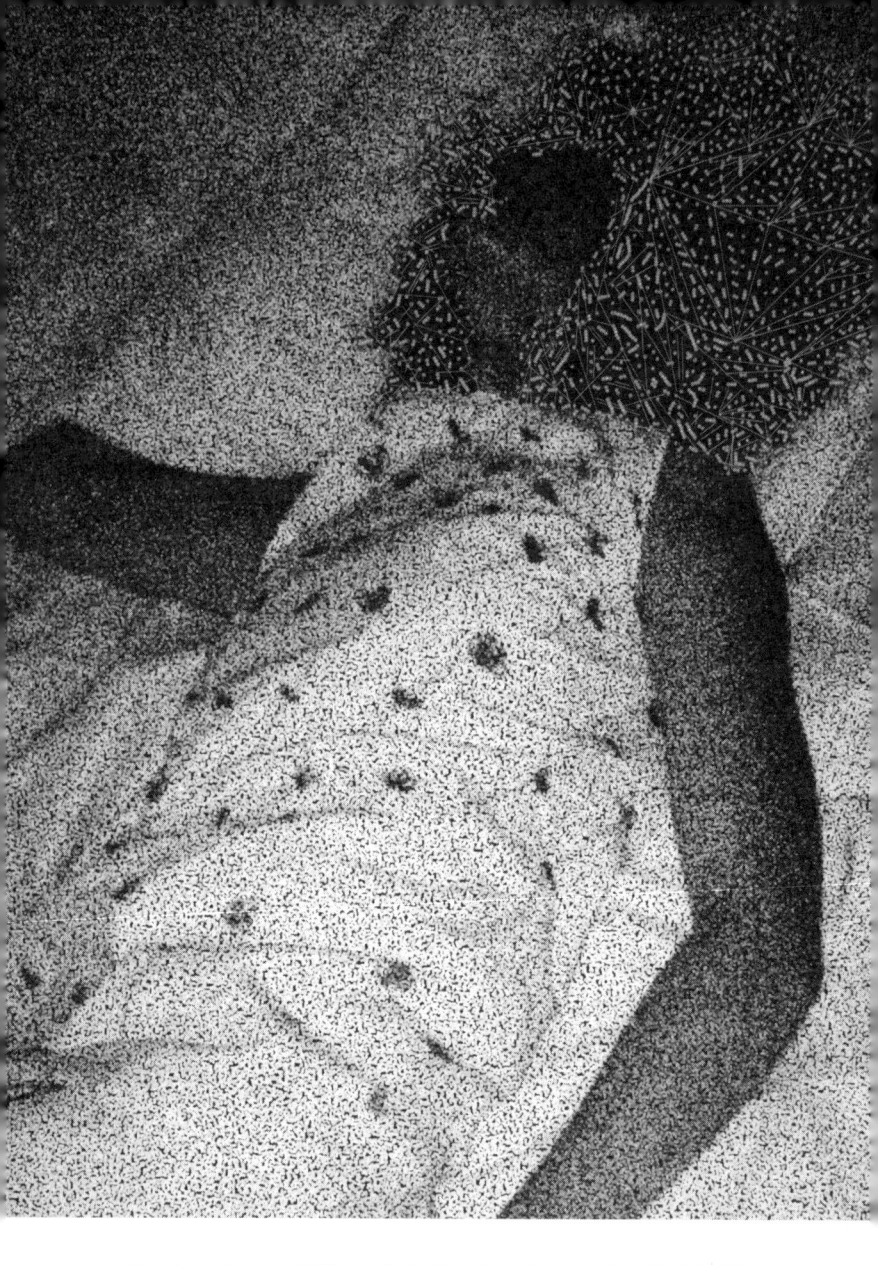

Matthias Nagry, *Pillow No.5 Cristina Bueno (detail)* (2003)
Digital print on canvas with embroidery, 104 × 63 cm.
Private collection, Brazil.

When I awoke again the woman from the night before was standing by the window. Exhaustion and sleep made me forget who she was and I waited for something to happen.

How are you? She asked in English.

Bad, I said, I feel bad.

She placed a glass of water beside my pillow, and from her pocket she produced two tablets and placed them down next to the water.

Take this. It will make you feel less pain. Do you speak French?

Un peu, I managed, setting myself up on one elbow and fumbling for the water, the two tablets. Merci.

De rien. It's nothing. Later I'll bring you a bowl of soup. For now rest and think less about the pain.

Yeah, I'll try.

Welcome to Paris, she said grimly from the door and was gone then with the words.

My collarbone ached dully. I lay back down and saw it as a piece of metal, radioactive, poisonous, sitting unhappily amongst the folds of my flesh. I thought of Paris, tried to think of all I knew about the city. Picasso arrived when he was eighteen. Giacometti had lived in Montparnasse. Christo blocked off rue Visconti which was somewhere near the river. Left bank. Right bank. Images of Vienna interfering. Trifke shouting or laughing, hard to tell which. Savić bringing me into the vaulted room where the seminars were held. His finger tapping me on the shoulder before the Derrida lecture. His old face telling me the philosopher had entered the room and to pay heed. His fingers continuing to tap my shoulder, tap, tap, tap across the three years until it ached and broke through the surface of my troubled sleep and I awoke, drenched in sweat.

Tottering on my feet I filled my lungs with air, expanding, and testing the tense knot of the stab wound near my shoulder. The pain of it was not as bad as the day before. I managed to hobble over to the window. The view was onto another building, darkened windows breaking the grey walls, far above a triangle of light. Loneliness passed through me, the loneliness of the sick man and I wondered where I was. The whereabouts of Gojković and Lubarda consisted of scrawled addresses on the front page of my German dictionary. I had no idea when I would see them again. As for you, Warmann, I had not spoken to you since that stop on the autobahn somewhere north of Munich. A day – or was that two days? – previously. The whole operation, or maybe transposition is a better word, seemed like a lifetime, a violent chaotic lifetime. I stood wondering if this violence made me somehow more European. I wondered when would you find me, how long it took to cross Paris by foot with a stiff erection the whole way.

There was nothing in the room save the mattress I had been sleeping and dreaming on. The walls dirty with years of cigarette smoke.

I managed to get myself out the door into a room with only a couch in it, the sparse furnishing giving the rooms their designated functions with minimal labels. Next to this again was an open room with the front door in its corner, an archway exposing half a kitchen and probably, I hoped, a jacks. I needed to piss badly but instead of investigating I sat down on the couch. At every moment of trouble, every adrenalin-filled strip-search at border crossings, the madness of Trifke's drug running, the horrible cramped pain of the days in the car, I had imagined my reward as Paris, a grand breakthrough into the streets of culture, freedom, the exalted past allowing me a future. Perhaps I had expected a champagne reception in honour of my arrival, I don't know, but right then I felt deflated, as if Paris had been just a lure, a trap, and I had walked straight into it.

The front door opened and the ladynurse came into the room. My jailor.

You are up, she said from the doorway, how do you feel?

Better. Not so tired.

She had in her hands a tray and this she placed on my lap.

Onion soup. I hope you like onions. And some bread if you can manage it.

That I could, there being nothing really the matter with me other than exhaustion, a split collarbone and a four day-old stab wound, all made worse by disorientation. I ate the food on the tray rapidly, trying hard not to be rude.

I'm glad to see you eat.

It's delicious. Thank you. What's your name?

My name? She seemed to hesitate, confused. Ella.

Thank you Ella. I'm Djordje.

Yes, she laughed a little girlishly, I know.

And you live here?

Yes, I'm the concierge. I look after the houses. I live in the first house across the courtyard.

And you come from Paris?

No. Well, yes. I grew up here. My father was Polish, but I grew up here. Mr Trifunović will be back tomorrow.

Something to look forward to.

We both smiled and I thanked her again.

You must rest now. As soon as you're better we can begin your French lessons.

French lessons? I asked bemusedly.

Why yes of course. French lessons. Mr Trifunović told me you're a philosopher and well, French is the true language of philosophy.

French? I could not help but laugh.

Absolument! She clapped her hands and stood up with the tray.

Perhaps you're right.

I know I'm right. Descartes, Rousseau, Sartre. Now rest.

She was on her way out.

Time for bed, rest. I'll see you in the morning.

And she was gone.

It did not feel like the time to be sleeping so I just sat there feeling out my pains and cursing Trifke and his drugs and his car. 'Mister Trifunović': that made me laugh.

I awoke to the sound of crashing bins and the dwndwndwn of plastic wheels being moved roughshod across a courtyard outside. French curses. The rising ire of unseen Indian souschefs. Noises that would in time sing of home but in my sleep befuddled mind my entire body only shook with disorientation. The need to urinate was overwhelming, making it hard to stand up. I raised myself up off the couch where I had fallen off to sleep for what I guessed to be a considerable time, the light a hue whiter than earlier. At the window I looked down and saw Ella my kindly jailor fight empty bins into order, a man and woman standing smoking at the back entrance to a restaurant whose kitchen I guessed was producing the intense, viscid smell of cheese. A Paris everyday evening.

***

Things grew complicated with Jovana when it came time to leave for basic training. Her mother somehow convinced my mother that we were made for each other because, and this I only found out some years later, we were both the same height. This makes Jovana a very tall girl, tall and skinny with a big nose and non-existent ass. You need to understand that I knew these people my whole life, had seen one of the family every day on the stairwell or in my kitchen talking to my mother. You do not think much about love at that age – sex yes, but not love or choosing someone, just like that, with whom to spend the rest of your days. But then they were simple people, our neighbours, utterly lacking in imagination, making up for this deficiency with a strong moral backbone. Just like my own family I guess.

She was shy, always looking at me sideways, barely stopping on the stairwell to say hello: what is a young man supposed to do with a girl like that? I had always defended her honour, so to say, when it came to comparing the looseness of the girls on the blok: the most made-up fantasies could be levelled against other girls for all I cared, and god knows I added my fair share of opinions and smut but with Jovana I never let a bad word be said about her. The fact that she was frigid and did not let any of us young guys fuck around with her I think made her only the more alluring. But not for me. Gojković and I had already, by the time we left school, become the kind of men for whom sex is a thwarted thing, made all-important to the detriment of other things we had no time in getting a hold of: companionship, intimacy, relationships. Gojković was a hardened onanist, the bullying of junior school having made him lose interest in people, as if he wanted to beat people to the starting line of mutual animosity. I do not know anymore what I wanted from sex back then: I think I just wanted to have fun. Jovana had always been the opposite of fun: serious and well meaning, I remember that from as early as when we played as toddlers. The evening before Lubarda and I were due to leave for training we walked around sharing beers, excited and bored, ignorant of the future as we were but still strolling along the same overgrown paths as we had done on countless other evenings. Walking from the apartments down toward the promenade by the Sava we heard my name rise out on the late summer air. A plaintive cry.

It was Jovana, walking tall and, so it seemed to Lubarda, ostrich-like.

Here's your wife. She looks like one of those wingless birds, an ostrich. Head in the sand…

Shut the fuck up, dickhead.

Coming up to us she stared hard at Lubarda: distrust and indecision coming from the innocent party.

Do you mind if we walk along for a bit Djorjde? I have something to give you before you leave.

Lubarda sighed, smiled, put his hands in his pockets and turned to face the flowing Sava. Then spoke:

I'll meet you outside Kod Sime, get us another beer. Don't use up all your energy on hump-hump or you'll be a dead duck training.

On our own she looked at my face but I just turned to walk and she followed.

Are you ready?

Ready as I'll ever be.

You're not scared?

Why would I be scared? It's training I'm going to, not straight to the frontline. I'm looking forward to it y'know. Get out of this shithole.

You think it's a shithole? I guess you're right.

Silence then for a moment.

Though I think I'd hate to leave it.

On the promenade we were not alone. Couples and young kids walked aimlessly along. The days of the barge bars and clubs had yet to fully take off but the few that were there I remember seemed terribly sad, empty and lifeless as they were, guests at a party without any friends.

So what do you have to give me?

I hope you don't think it's boring. It's just a book Papa said is good for a young Serbian soldier to read. And I know you like to read.

She produced from her coat pocket a small book wrapped loosely in brown paper. She stopped in her tracks as she handed it to me and I opened it there and then, quickly and dispassionately. It was a recent reissue of *Bosnian Chronicle* by Ivo Andrić. A book by a writer that was to become more and more popular with the nationalists and pacifists alike, a writer that could explain to each the necessity and inevitability of the horror of the wars.

Thanks very much Jovana.

I hope you like it.

I'm sure I will. Thanks.

Suddenly the thought of not going to the army, staying at home in New Belgrade and reading this novel, starting university in September (I wanted at the time to study German literature) passed through my mind. Even courting Jovana appeared in front of me, having a confidant. She touched my fingers as these thoughts took me away from the moment, just as she had learned to do from one of her mother's trash romance novels and my thoughts turned back to this girl, full of kindness and the will of others, and I kissed her then because that is what she wanted me to do. It was a bad idea: people's opinions, people's wishes became for Jovana her own opinions and her own wishes, and I was fooling her then by kissing her but the warmth and closeness of it repaid these doubts. It was like, in truth, kissing a brother, a sister, and it was an act of transgression, all these years of non-physical communion broken in a moment. It was what she wanted. Right then at least. As for me, I liked this sense of transgression, but what I didn't know was that this, my last stab at innocence, was to be tainted with a sense of wrongdoing.

Training was a lot of physical pain and meant putting up with some toughhead bastard treating you like shit. The whole time we were all of us cadets trading gossip about Titoists being given the sack and the likelihood of going to fight Croats, Slovenes, Bosnians in the name of unity. The infantry unit that was stationed in the dormitory next to ours enjoyed telling us that we were going to war as soon as we finished our basic training but they were as apprehensive as any of us, they had the same difficulty in trying to imagine war as us new cadets had. I went through the first day or two in a daze, induced from my farewell with Jovana, the thought of a quiet life back in Blok 64. Everything was changing – our camp trainer told us as much each day, yelled it into our ears.

This country is changing boys and you motherfuckers will be the ones changing it.

What we did not know was that change was tantamount to falling apart. A wide rip being slowly torn in the fabric of the Balkans, one more time, and we were going to be the first ones to topple over into it.

My body was extremely sore, the muscles filling out in protest, my shoulders getting wide. Every day was a challenge to keep up but after the third day I just switched my mind off and even enjoyed the prospect of getting stronger, harder. Vanity came into it: on the first day I noticed the others in the showers at the end of training and their tall, lean bodies struck me as beautiful. Gritting my teeth in exertion on the second day, climbing to where I did not know, just to the top and no further, just to the end and release from the strain, one hand over the other, one foot in front of the next, I said to myself: I want a body like those I saw the night before. Fooled myself even with images of pleasing Jovana with an Olympian body, muscular, perfect. The second evening I was glad I had wanked off two nights before, at home after my kiss with Jovana. So many wet naked bodies, all in sublime physical condition, some quite hairless, surprised me with their beauty and erotic power. That was the word for them: beautiful. By the third evening I finished my shower prematurely, horrified that my dick had twitched and blood had started to rush into it. I left the shower rooms immediately and later in my bunk bed, slowly, ridiculously looking back at it now, I wanked off under the cover of the coarse, heavy army blanket.

After it happened I told myself it was because they had seen my twitching dick semi-erect the evening before but perhaps it was just because they knew my only pal, Lubarda, wasn't going to stop them, or perhaps because they liked the look of me. Like I said, our company shared the barracks with an infantry unit, reservists called up into the standing army in the wake of Croatia's declaration of independence. Two troops from the reserves tried to rape me on my fourth night in the great Yugoslavian People's Army. Now, I am a reasonable guy, amiable, have always tried to be generous with everything and anything, including not least my fucked-up corpus. But I was not ready to let these two fuckheads from Niš rape my tender asshole and leave it in pieces, ruined and raw. I still hoped then that I would be a good soldier and Gojković had told me before at length and in detail the pain and disability brought about by sodomising somebody. He had convinced some girl or other who didn't want to get pregnant that it was the best option, though she lived to regret listening to him. As most people do with Aleksandar. I had to think of the next day's training.

The washrooms were grim places, fitting for the scene I guess. Lukić was the true homo. His accomplice Zoran was a toughhead idiot ready to put his dick in anywhere if he thought it would make him cum. It was Zoran blocking the entry making sure nobody came in, a lucky turn in a way, and Lukić was the one who tapped me on the shoulder and greeted me with a lockknife and an apologetic smile.

It's easier if you don't put up a fight.
What do you mean?

You're going to turn around and drop those boxers and let me put my dick up your sweet little ass. Any resistance and I slit your throat–

Ah man, fuck, listen–

I'll slit your throat and make it look like you had a fit while shaving. We've done it before with little Goran. Remember Goran, he said back to Zoran at the door.

Yeah: stupid fuck.

That's when he got his dick out and I decided to save the situation, to the extent that was possible. I could see from his eyes and his long, hard dick that this was not a joke, that he was wound up like a spring gun and he was not going to let anything stop him from going off.

Look, I said hesitantly, shock crashing over me that this should be actually happening, it doesn't have to be like this.

He stopped.

I've never had a guy fuck me before. But you don't have to fucking rape me with a knife to my throat.

What the fuck are you talking about? We don't have time for this. Turn around.

Let me loosen up and do it slowly. Better for both of us.

He coughed, cleared his throat, flexed his bushy eyebrows.

And then let me fuck your buddy there, I added.

Ha ha, he laughed, you hear this Zoran? We got ourselves a right little fuckbunny here.

Just hurry up, the dull brute spoke back from the door.

Ok, Lukić said, his dick in hand, get your dick out and start wanking. Then turn around and bend over the sink.

I did as he said, my whole perineum twitching in trepidation, the blood bursting throughout my body, my temples tight and throbbing. I heard him spit. Felt a finger slide down my ass, a fingertip slowly applying pressure on my hole.

There we go, Djordje boy.

I thought of shit, the absurdity of two men humping each other like dogs, all the silly thoughts that go through your brain the first time you have a bellend slowly pushing its way up into your anus.

I croaked, let a little cry out: it fucking hurt, and I knew then I had done the right thing, the idea of this being done by force was not worth even imagining. There was even pleasure to be gained. I closed my eyes and kept wanking myself like Lukić had told me to, diverting the pain into pleasure so that when he reached my prostate everything went off and I came before he did, leaving my virgin hole to contract and contract again around his dick and he bucked then and came and all of a sudden the whole thing was over. Both of us breathless with pleasure and shaky from our orgasms. We cleaned up and eyed each other.

You did well to let me do it like that. You let any fucker know about this and you'll be a dead man. Castrated and left to bleed to death in some remote boghole of the fields.

Sure.

And I don't even mean by Zoran and me. Homos aren't allowed in the army. They let us rape girls just to fucking prevent it. I ask you where the fucking decency is in that? They want us to be macho fuckheads.

I just nodded silently.

Something tells me you're not a paid-up queen, but you enjoy it and we'll help you through your training. No Zoran tonight though, it's too late and the washroom is back open now. But soon.

He shouted that the toilet was now open and turned to go, Zoran letting two guys from their unit pass him, toothbrushes in hand. Neither of them looked at me as if to say our being there was none of their business. I just turned and packed my washbag and walked out as normally and limp-free as I could manage.

Lubarda knew before long, I am not sure if someone told him or he just guessed with the clairvoyance of a childhood friend, but he knew I played ball with the other foot, that having learned to speak the foreign language in secret I had practised my accent with the natives. He let it slide: we only ever talked about fucking men when we got to Paris, when it was obvious you and I were sleeping together. He was caught up with hating the training and the whole army: the level of mindless obedience shocked both of us, but it was the violent nationalism that upset Lubarda the most. It was clear that some of the other units would be going to Slovenia and Croatia, that they were needed to fight against our own Jugo brethren.

Lubarda refused to even talk about it on our way back to Belgrade for leave. Our training completed, we were now fully gripped by cruel destiny, hardened and not a little desanitised, fighting fit and ready to be ruined by the forces of hatred and chauvinism. The army was falling apart at the same time as it was mobilising itself: our unit was sent home because in normal circumstances of how Yugoslavia worked it would have gone to Slovenia, only that was no longer possible. It was now another country. So they sent us home until they found out what to do with us.

I fucked Jovana a lot during that break in New Belgrade. We fucked like we had read they do before leaving for war in rosewater books, and she could fuck, was hungry for it and livened up by the impropriety of our sibling-like relationship. I was hungry for it after my time with Lukić and Zoran, confused from all the sodomy I had partaken in, topping and bottoming. I fucked Jovana to prove to myself that I could still do it, fuck women, and that I still enjoyed pussy. It was a surprise and a relief that I had equal pleasure in the long, female curves of Jovana's sweat-covered body and the roughened, hirsute asscheeks and testicles of Lukić and that of my own hardened body.

Our mothers consented to our cavorting and the charade soon grew too convincing, especially for me. Those weeks that were to grow into months, listening to all the changes on the radio and TV, following with anger the direction Bosnia was taking, they seem now like the calmest and most normal months I have perhaps ever known. My family all together, living in sleepy contiguity, Lubarda lending me books, talking as if the world was open for the taking, his talk continually turning to Europe, France, Paris, deluding himself and me along with him, that he could go there at any time and enrol at the Sorbonne just like that. Gojković turned up at the beginning of 1992, hyperactive and full of hate. He had briefly been to Croatia after his training and got to fire his gun and all that, become a real soldier in the defence of Yugoslavia. His suspicion and paranoia repeated, happily for us all, the hysteria of the media.

Before Gojković came back, throughout that December, I once again cultivated the idea of a quiet life. I thought about marrying Jovana and just envelope my experience in the army and fold it neatly into a trauma ready to be shredded and destroyed, forgotten about completely.

***

There was blood left behind on my sheets. The same sheets since boyhood. Red marks left by what should have been other people. We had always been more of a brother and sister: this was a crime against nature that was really only a crime against ourselves. Against Jovana. I was already set on a life of sexual nomadism; she had no interest in such things, her horizon was the course of the Sava and Danube, it didn't reach any further. I felt guilt, that too. I had not learned that it is okay, even advisable, to fuck multiple people at the same time, boys and girls, even perhaps in the same place. Such an education came only when I met you, and we excited ourselves in boring Vienna, only when I kept on going all the way to Paris and the Benoit's crowd got hold of my imagination, my body. Did I treat Jovana any different to how I treated you? Maybe she's dead too, but I know she is not: she is very much alive. Enjoying the life gained from a lucky escape from the likes of me. She went on to graduate as an architect and moved away from her claustrophobic family, her life bloomed basically only after I left her, and I've often wondered what kind of a person she has become.

***

It felt like I gained five years once I finally met you. Five years stuffed into the space? the time? of five glorious days. Nobody knew where I was for those five days, nobody save for you and the people I was introduced to along the way. After the army, anarchic as it was, the close-knit gossip-ridden world of Blok 64, Jovana, our mothers, the intense three years of university, even the excited cloyingness of Gojković as he harangued me about taking the avant-garde helm of European art: all these things had kept me in check, under observation.

Jovana forced me to go. I had received the latest letter from you and was looking forward to reading it in peace when she called at the door and my mother, despite me telling her not to, let the girl in.

We need to talk, she said without greeting.

Listen Jovana, I have stuff to do.

Djordje we need to talk, she said as sternly as she could. Beyond her weak voice a door closed somewhere within the apartment.

It was then I decided there was nothing stopping me from going.

Okay let's meet later. How about that? Then we can do all the fucking talking you like.

When?

Say at nine. At Café Penguin.

Okay.

She hesitated and I looked at her, just looking at her with that stare I had picked up in Bosnia was enough and she left and I was finally alone with your letter. It was the one in which you talked about the essays for the *Budapest/Belgrade* exhibition and how much you wanted to feel my hand in yours, to meet in person finally. I read it, then read it again, sitting there in my family kitchen, a dinner growing cold and me making up my mind. From the hook on the doorjamb I found the key to my father's old Škoda and got my coat in the hall and left, your letter hastily folded up and in my back pocket.

Driving is the only part of everyday life that approaches sex's facility to please. Not that I get to drive much these days, it's been a long time since I sat behind a steering wheel. I jumped into the Škoda and drove straight to the university. In Gojković's studio space in the department of fine art I lied: said I was on my way to meet Vuk Jovanović whose gallery we hoped to exhibit in and that I needed money. I took all the Dinars that he had on him, and Gojković always had a lot of money on him.

You trust me Aleksandar, don't you? I heard myself saying on my way out.

What do you mean?

You trust me when I say we're going to have this exhibition. That it's all going to be great.

Get the hell out of here, he yelled and slammed the door laughing.

I bombed it across the plain in the Škoda, pushing the poor thing to its limit. There was not a moment I stopped to think about the people left behind, uninformed, in Belgrade – I would ring my mother later. All I had to find you was the address marked on all your letters, bar one which was addressed from the Lettrist Café. Novi Sad was a city I barely knew only having passed through it once or twice. The evening sun was starting to set and the whole plain raised itself up to soak the tall buildings in a watery yellow sun. Outside the town I picked up a hitchhiker. Jons was his name, a chubby guy, Austrian I guessed, and he directed me to the house I hoped was yours. He had no problem ending his ride there, this Jons, even though I think it was the other side of town to where he was heading. I remember he said, 'I'll see you again', in such a sincere manner that I stopped a moment and wondered just how that would be possible. Every stranger was my friend at that moment, I felt the shackles of distrust loosen and the wide panorama of the possibility of others open up before me, all from this fat Austrian, so badly dressed in cheap denims and his belief that we may see each other again and he may then get to repay me with a favour, or I him.

So I was in Precani[21] country, standing outside your building with no idea in which flat you lived. I went up the stairwell, looking at each name plate, admiring the dappled sunlight dripping onto the steps, tracing out the summer evening and finally, at the top seeing your name scrawled on a card stuck above the doorbell.

---

21   Literally 'the other side' of the Sava and Danube, can often refer to Serbs living in old Habsburg territory. (Trans.)

You were living with Veselin and you know how impressive his apartment was, the black and white throughout, the gloom accentuated in a good way by Bartók, constantly set to warble through the smoke, the coffee fumes, the endless talk. This tall, slim Precani answered the door and I thought this gorgeous man was you.

You wouldn't happen to be Warmann?

Warmann? No. His boy's eyes grew wide. I'm a mere mortal. Come in, he ordered and disappeared. I followed and heard him telling me you were in the kitchen.

And so in I walked and there you were like a Helmut Newton composition, or a model in an advert selling the pen in your hand, your cigarette hanging off your lips, the sunlight still warming the tall casement window, your black cravat tied around your bare neck. We stared at each other for the briefest of moments, silent words passing between our gazes, the faces now taking the empty place at the head of all our correspondence.

Warmann?

Yes, yes, you said in Serbian, 'da da' the words you first spoke to me, without thinking, as you stood up and held forward your hand.

Sorry for arriving without a rendezvous. I'm Djordje –

Djordje!

– Bojić and well, hi –

Hello Djordje. So good to finally meet you man!

And you held my hand and our eyes stayed focused together, yours darker than anything I could have expected, your moustache a surprise, as was your age. All these things – unexpected. But at last after several months of letters, we were acquainted.

You won't believe me but I was just in the middle of writing you a missive asking you to come at once.

No, really? I laughed. We both laughed. That's what people do who are attracted to one another but cannot yet say so. They just laugh instead.

Yeah! It's funny. Sit down.

You found each other? Veselin entered breezily and you introduced us.

Djordje this is Veselin, Veselin, Djordje – the Belgrade connection!

Oh Djordje, you're here already?

Veselin is a fucking great photographer and will show with us in Budapest.

Oh good, I said sitting myself on the low stool on the other side of you.

Coffee Djordje? Help yourself. And if you're staying that's great – the sitting room is yours.

Get yourself to the shop Ves, you shouted after him, we're going to need wine!

Lots of talking, words, laughter, between the two of you, a carnival always in the making. I miss Veselin sometimes, a wave taking over the wave of missing you, and then the backwash, an everyday moment, and your absence rising up again, ready to break... He's in New York I believe – I do hope he is not in marketing or some such shit.

We talked non-stop from the start. There were the details of the *Budapest/Belgrade* exhibition – the artists showing in them – Nouveau Réalisme – Dada – the wars and the peace we foolishly thought had finally arrived – your background – dinner preparations – transport – my father – Škoda cars – Sweden – Strindberg – Edvard Munch – depression.

But there was no time then for depression.

You took me to the Lettrist Café and I met some of the artists you wanted to include in *Budapest/Belgrade* – Matthias Nagry, Vesna Jović, Zoran Živković. My mind was burning I remember with the names and faces and talk of mission statements, proposals, the need for a new manifesto, my body alive and high-wired by its proximity to you. It was like a dream or a fantasy and I remember even then worrying it might not last and all of it, the whole evening, the whole growing movement, would burst and fall asunder.

We had Gottschalk and Matthias back for dinner and Veselin sat in and joined us. Gottschalk went on picking my brains over Nouveau Réalisme and Andy Warhol or some such shit until he finally conceded I knew a thing or two. And so then he would not stop explaining to me what it meant to be *hochgebildet* and how I was myself *hochgebildet*, he was speaking nonstop bullshit and I couldn't shut him up, he was telling me that if I wanted I could call myself a *visoko učeni*[22] in my own language. I remember disliking this crazy Hungarian critic but I realised with shame that it was probably just xenophobia I was falling back on, not the man's personality. I remember looking around and realising that nationality, ethnicity, religion meant little to you people, that at root and in the terms of belief I had known all too well you all had reason enough to hate each other but did not. It is a difficult thing to shed your past, as difficult as losing your inhibitions and self-consciousness, donning a new way of living and thinking, ways of being you only ever considered possible for others.

What do I remember from that first night? Gottschalk was manic at the time, sweating profusely and talking non-stop, even when nobody was listening to him he would go on and on. I sat there amid this cacophony enjoying it all and more excited about the prospect of forming a group than I had ever been in Belgrade. We ended up dancing, completely drunk. Before passing out I remember seeing you dance with Matthias and wondering just what it was we had drunk. I remember laughter, laughter predicated on nothing more than our own selves.

The next morning I felt terrible. It was an ordeal to move my head from one side to another. I drank the coffee Veselin forced upon me and it just drained any remaining water from the inside of my skull. When you appeared in the kitchen doorway, showered, dressed, hair in place, I imagined only your naked body like a double exposure and then the image was gone and we were leaving.

I hope you're feeling okay Djordje, it's at least an eight hour drive to Budapest!

So we're going to Budapest then? I have no visa though. I said this because I hoped that we would delay the trip, stay one more day in Novi Sad.

---

22 'Highly educated, having graduated from many schools' (Trans.)

You don't need a visa. Hungary lets everybody in, just ask all those East Germans. But we need to go today. Elaine and Jan are expecting us. We're going to visit their studios this evening. And then in the morning the gallery is expecting us. I sorted it all yesterday evening.

And you already had your coat in your hand, a grin fixed on your face and I had no choice but to follow.

I never did find out where you got all your energy.

Ivan Veselin, *Empty* (2000)
Silk print photographs. Installation view.
Collection Lela and Milan Postolović, Belgrade.

The first time I managed to leave the apartment the sun came out in support. Walking was not easy and Ella was kind enough to give me an old walking cane. God alone the bastard knows what I looked like: my clothes were the same I had travelled in and even the shirt was the same one I wore when I was stabbed. Quite a figure to appear on the well-heeled rue Danielle Casanova at lunchtime on a sunny Thursday.

It was thrilling to see finally a little of Paris in the daytime. You know how it is when you first step out into Paris and hear and taste the dirty bitch of a city for the first time? It is like a first kiss or a long anticipated drink of beer in high summer. I am doing my best here to see Danielle Casanova and the entire city as I saw it that morning. This is not easy. Too much has come in between since then to obscure the view and cloud the emotions.

Has it really been almost a decade since that morning?

I crossed the street, getting beeped by a UPS delivery van, which I thought just a little rude considering my obvious bad shape and the narrow nature of the street. The back windows of Brentano's caught my attention and I stopped a moment looking in at all the book titles on display. Then I reached the avenue – I was not expecting it. That is what Paris streets do: they trick you into thinking that they just happen to be busy little village streets with just enough detail to keep you more than busy. Until you turn the corner.

Traversing in two goes, not fast enough to catch the light, I was forced to wait on the traffic island. I hoped that across the avenue was somewhere I could buy cigarettes. So it was that I stepped into, on my very first morning, the café run by my Japanese friends. Ever since they have called me 'the old man' because of the state of me those mornings when they first met me. And I can't hold it against them.

In Brentano's on the way back I bought paper, envelopes, some notebooks and copies of *ArtPress* and *Liberation*. I wrote Lubarda, Gojković and you all letters, outlining again the importance of the everyday, working together as artists and with the unsuspecting public. I was really worried that in Paris we would all devolve into the artworld and never think of normality again. *ArtPress* was full of ideas and recent exhibitions I wanted eagerly to go and see. I knew that we had come home and only needed to replicate what we had achieved up until then, without losing any momentum or confidence.

***

So many thoughts come back to me that I'm not sure I will ever manage to get them all down. Faces appear but then disappear again once I sit down with my pen and confront the white paper. Whenever I stop writing, alone in this fucking apartment, the sadness crowds itself around me. I lie awake and look at the walls and think, shit Djordje, none of this is fun anymore and there is nowhere else to go. I am supposed to be writing a fucking art history book but the faces keep appearing and stop any argument or unifying story I could possibly conjure up and I go out walking to Bastille and come home with a couple of bottles of Vranac or Kovačević chardonnay and sprawl out on the floor reading and get drunk until thoughts, good thoughts and bad thoughts, they're all the same, grab hold and all I can do is sit around and cry or sit down and write. And if that doesn't help I go downstairs and call on Ella and she will make some of her tarlike coffee and I will start all over again telling her about Bosnia and she will rationalise it all and lull me then with stories of Poland and war and suffering. If it was not for all those tales to be told, that need to be told, I would tell Ella's tales because they are true. The faces of Belgrade, of Bosnia, I have long ago convinced myself are not true. And all I want to do is tell the truth.

***

Of course Gojković had always been talented at art, all three of us were talented and intelligent. But especially Gojković. He was the finest painter and life drawer our art teacher Debeli, as we called him, ever had the fortune to teach. Or so he said. Looking back on it he may have been bent though, the fat old man looking to get a suck of Gojković's young cock, who knows? The funny thing is Aleksandar only ever painted reproductions or drew players before or after a game of basketball. I mean terribly poor imaginative work as if he fought his talent throughout his teenage years and submitted it to the role of a mechanical craft he only practised in order to pass the time. In 1995 or '96 Lubarda would tell me that he had done something similar with his poetry during his years at the gymnasium, composing formally difficult and intricate poems but avoiding all emotion or personal content. Like I said many times before: it was a miracle we became artists at all.

Aleksandar Gojković, *Hommage à Raymond Hains Orange* (1998)
Acrylique and aquarelle on canvas with matches, 24 × 30 cm each.
Courtesy the artist and Galerie Gojković

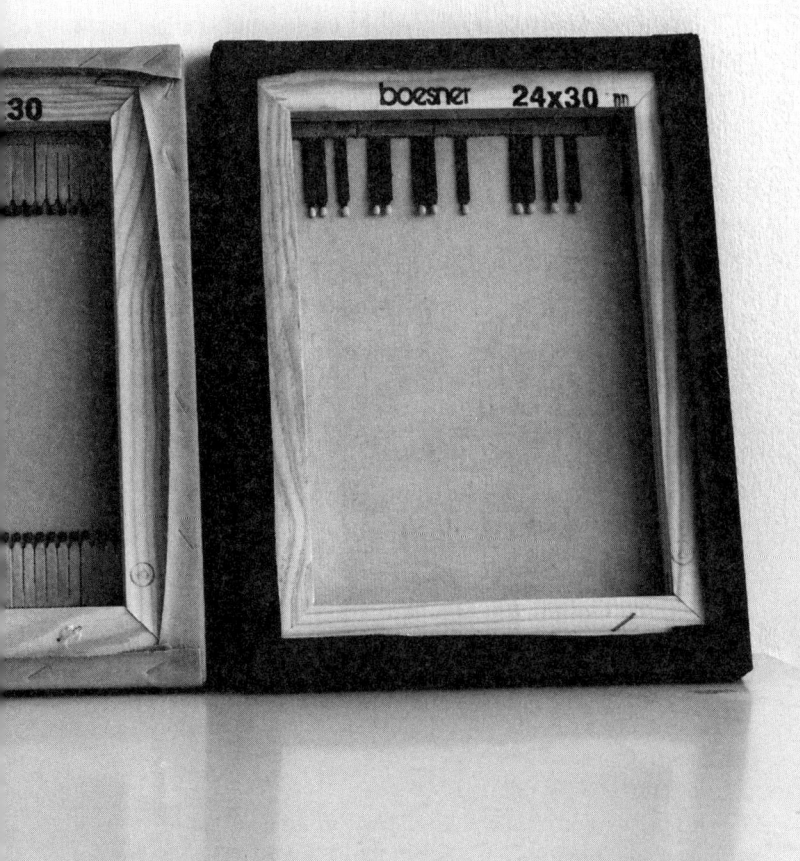

TO WARMANN

I got a letter today from Savić, and a very nice letter it is – the man is still strong and healthy and busier than he has ever been in his life. I must find the courage to write to him, but I need to find something appropriate to say first. What was the last book I have read properly? Can't remember. My plans for the future? Spontaneous licentiousness. Nothing I'd be proud to tell the old man. I'd only end up lying.

He asked me about this 'book' that I am writing. How did he find out I was writing a book? Immediately I thought of Lubarda and went around to the shitty little Chinese café he writes in, when he's not putting down bets that is on European soccer matches (yes, this is what we do now, a pathetic form of everyday art) and accused him of telling every Joe Soap from here to Albania that I'm writing a fucking book.

He smiled and said:

Ah, the man comes with blame.

Fuck you. Listen to me: what I am writing is an embarrassing series of ramblings, telling the truth. It takes the shine off each and every one of our names.

You think I care?

Gojković would care, trust me.

So who can we blame then?

What do you mean?

Who can we blame for your failed book?

It's not a failed book because it's not even a book! Besides, it's our lives that are failures.

Wow, now you're talking!

We both smiled then and knew we were going to play the game we have played many times before, the endless game of naming the blame. He started:

I blame of course Milošević, for these, our sorry lives.

I blame Tudjman, traitor.

What about the Slovenes?

No, no, the communists.

Organised crime.

I blame the West.

Western states? In general?

Yes: in general, I blame the fucking Western states.

What about the Vatican-Comintern conspiracy?

Conspiracy about what?

Serbian, Slovenian, American, Russian, Vatican interests: you choose.

No, no: it all happened because of horrible local traditions.

No: it was because of the economy, stupid.

Clinton the fucker.

The system was fucked to begin with. It was illegitimate.

Our grievances were legitimate.

No they were not, they were illegitimate.

What about 1389? You say that the Battle of Kosovo Polje is not grounds enough?

No, more like 1463.

1878.

1918 obviously.

1941.

1986.

1989.

Tsk-tsk: 1990.

Well we can agree at least dear brother that it was all inevitable.

No, we can agree it was avoidable, whence my tears.

And the bad guys? Milošević and Tudjman? Mladić and Karadžić.

You're saying we're the bad guys? The Serbs?

No, the Slovenes, naturally.

And the Croats.

The Croats and the Muslims.

All of us, Balkan people in general, that's what we're saying.

Don't forget Germany.

And the Great Powers.

All of them have to be held exclusively –

– jointly –

responsible for almost all the killing.

We know it all.

We just know it differently it seems.

And the two of us sit in silence, panting with the exercise of all these empty accusations we had been listening to for almost two decades, Lubarda not taking his eyes off the large, precariously hung Samsung TV in the corner, I just sitting with my melancholy, rolling the word *blame* around in my head. All I can do is blame myself for what I have done, the rest no longer matters.

Chelsea scores a goal, their third, and Lubarda sits back and gives me a big smile and thumbs up: it looks like he will win today.

And the rest no longer matters.

***

We raced across the Great Plain[23] and the sun on the poplars and wild flowers reminded me that I was heading only further away from Belgrade and I had yet to phone home. I would never really regain the routine of that apartment, or at least the semblance of a normal routine shared by most ordinary decent people. Another source of regret: having supposedly made the normal everyday the inspiration for all my art, I've only ever run away from it.

You sat driving, your grin fixed steady and talking and talking and making me laugh in delight at your tales of wine-soaked debauchery and foolishness. Your jokes involved people, people in places, and I wanted to meet these people, visit these places. You slowly erased my headache and the wind tunnel that the little Škoda became out on the exposed roads blew out the lethargy that the night before had instilled in me. We would form a group, you shouted over the noise of the wind rushing through the open windows, the whole lot of us from Budapest to Novi Sad to Belgrade and beyond, we would reinstate a Balkan neo-Dadaism the likes of which has not been seen since the days of Dragan Aleksić and *Yugo-Dada*.

---

23 Velika Plana (Trans.)

Djordje, what you managed to do in the LGB show changes everything. You understand that don't you?

Get out of it, I said and I can see myself blushing.

Not a single critic knew what to say about it and yet not one of the cocksuckers levelled a bad word at it. It's a done deal!

What is?

The course our art can follow. The turn we're taking. Now. Together!

I guess, yeah.

And what is Gojković doing? Is he still making his constructs?

(That is what Gojković called his canvas-combines at the time – constructs or constructions, later changing it to canvas-combines.)

Yeah. He's going down to Sarajevo I think. He wants to do a series of the everyday in wartime.

Sounds great.

Yeah, well. I'm sick of the war myself.

We all are Djordje, we all are. But things are looking good.

And you beeped the horn in a flurry of bursts and the farm truck behind us did likewise, flashing its lights and everything and you smiled and laughed and banged the door outside with your free hand. Letting out a great bellow:

War is over baby![24]

And I believed your optimism and that of the farmtruck driver's behind us even though I should have – we all should have – known better with the same people in power and Kosovo still unaccounted for and NATO only too ready to bomb the fuck out of us, the perpetrators of the latest act of genocide in Europe.

Europe. Were we entering it that morning in my father's little Škoda? We crossed the Ottoman frontier somewhere north of Novi Sad or when you and I swung out of the apartment and got into the car, Veselin and Matthias coming down to wish us bon voyage, Veselin still in his dressing gown, camera in hand and telling us to wave at the lens? Is that when we entered into something we

---

24 Appears in English in the original (Trans.)

could call Europe? We were off to get to know each other and form our alliance and tie our binds and enter the new age of expanding boundaries. Waving goodbye to the past. Onwards to Europe. How many borders were we to go on to cross together?

We were strangers that first morning, you bare-chested and giddy, hungover but turned on, pretending – or not – that we knew each other oh so well after the long months of correspondence. We stopped our laughing at each and every thing the other said (too inane for grown up men like us) but I was only getting more and more turned on by your proximity, your darkness lit up by the warmth of your smile, your laugh, the little lurch forward you made every time you changed gears.

At the border I wanted to get out and hide in the boot but you only laughed at me and drove straight up to the checkpoint and flashing your passport and slipping the grumpy looking border guard DM 50 you got us through without anyone as much as looking at my face. I imagine you mentioned your name, spoke the name of your father, but I will never know for sure now. That was border number one crossed: if only they were all as incident-free.

We pulled over for petrol and a piss and I heard you speak Hungarian for the first time to the old lady who ran the little pension behind the garage, ordering us two beers which we downed in the heat and which killed the last of my headache stone dead, leaving it for the little old lady to pick up and collect and store away with all her other ailments and fatigues.

Now it's your turn to drive.

What?

I've driven us most of the way. You drive.

But why didn't I drive in Serbia? What if we get pulled over?

We won't.

I can't even read the fucking signs.

Ha! I'll teach you what signs you need to know. Now drive.

Okay, okay. Give me the damn keys.

By then it was extremely hot and we both sat there half naked, sweating and smoking fags until finally we approached Budapest and you barked and laughed directions at me, infuriated and delighted it seemed in equal measure at my ability to drive like a blind person.

Djordje, you're far too cautious, you counselled not for the last time.

They're not expecting us for another two hours. Let's go to my favourite eaterie and have some goulash.

So you directed me down a number of streets in district two until finally you said: Let's park and get the fuck out of this little sweatbox.

We sat out in the beer garden of the little café whose name I couldn't read but whose sign, so ornate, the letters entwined with a flamboyant, thorny rose, I appreciated. You ordered goulash and beer and the young waitress, asking you to repeat the order and shaking her head, obviously thought we were mad ordering goulash in such heat.

Look, Djordje, I haven't been in town for ages, there are one or two faces I need to see. It's best if I go see them now rather than later on.

Okay, sure no problem. I'm happy here.

You don't mind?

No, of course not. Just don't forget to pick me up again.

You laughed at that and grabbed my hand as you made to get up. I shouldn't be more than an hour. This the first of your countless disappearances, mysterious Herr Warmann, always dodging off to meet god alone knew who, for reasons never to be known.

That hour on my own in some café whose name I do not know in some unknown corner of a city I had never been to before was an hour I composed my piece that I would later exhibit in Paris and Christian Klaus would buy for his collection. So I have to thank you for it. An hour when looking around me I marked down those strange symbols of a foreign language you later translated for me: enjoy Coca Cola, order a large burger and get a free plate of chips, not to park a car between the hours of 8:00 and 16:00 during the working week excluding Saturday and Sunday. I drew up poems that told of how border crossing No. 1 went okay with DM 50. How our trip had its destination where? In Europe, in Paris, in some masked gallery only to be revealed in time. How art was as much for the kitchen, toilet, bedroom as for the unmasked galleries of our growing cities. The suburbs, the vacant lots housing second-hand car dealers, the disused railway lines, the factories, the deserted commuter stations, logistical hangers, scrapyards, rubbish dumps: all of these our present and future museums to run through, naked like the happy children into the ruins of the future.

When finally you came back I was too happy and pleased with myself to notice any shift in your mood. You paid without listening to my reproaches and drove us over to the fifth district, pulling up outside the run-down building on Bajcsy-Zsilinszky that was at the time being used by many artists. Climbing the stairs I wondered what awaited us and whether I would like these people you were about to introduce to me. On the third floor you pushed open the door and strode straight along the uncarpeted, unpainted hallway to the back room where Jan Offe sat reading a copy of *Die Welt* cross-legged beside what at first seemed to be a pile of rubbish.

Warmann, brother! He shouted rising to his feet.

Jan. Alles gut?

Still in a half hug you introduced me.

This is Djordje. The new Tristan Tzara of Belgrade.

Holla Djordje. I've heard a lot about you and that show you put up.

Yes, it's good to meet you. Warmann has told me about your art on the way... here.

I spread out my arms and looked around the large, chaotic room, idiotically expanding my body to make up for my slow German.

Yes, yes. Please let's get a drink and then I'll show you my work.

The door adjoining onto the next room down opened then and a petite woman in her early thirties came through it. This was Elaine Pettifer.

Elaine, so good to see you. You hugged her and raised her up off her feet and we all laughed, Elaine included, at the spectacle of you engulfing the little woman.

This here Elaine, is Djordje Bojić.

Oh hi Djordje, her English surprising me, sounding as it did like it was straight out of an American movie, so good to meet you. I got to see the LGB show.

You did?

Yeah I went down. I have family there, my uncle, who's doing some work with the UN…

I saw her grow unsure and I was petrified I would sour the proceedings, my face probably clouding over in confusion.

Elaine is a true internationalist! Don't even ask her where she's from.

We all smiled and I nodded into the kindness of Elaine's face. I knew right away that these two people would become more than just mere co-exhibitors, that we would be joined as friends and as something more, participants in a relationship that transcends time and space and becomes a root in the worldtree by its very own objective authenticity.

Come, Jan threw up his hands. We need coffee.

And wine, you added.

And plum brandy, joined Elaine mischievously.

And plum brandy! You heard the girl!

So there we were, all four of us with a cup of coffee in one hand and a glass of plum brandy in the other. We commenced our studio visit with Jan slowly telling us in German about his past shows and where he went wrong. All of your artists were very eager to talk about past failures and wrong turns, always analysing and performing post-mortems of their past shows. And I never figured out where this came from, out of what need did they go on in this self-critical track? It was a habit somebody like Aleks Gojković would spit at. Jan was making installations in which the audience – a word he had big problems with, as he never tired of telling us – would not fully 'believe' to be artworks, installations 'that extended the normal world into the artworld'. It seemed like he was on the right track, but he was having problems incorporating the audience into the installation he was currently working on. He wanted to allow the audience to contribute somehow to the everyday clutter that would fill the space, transforming them into a participant.

Have a little kitchen space, you said, and let them toast sandwiches. Make coffee. A suggestion that would find itself, with slight modifications, in the final *Budapest/Belgrade* exhibition.

Next door in Elaine's studio we all four sat down on the ground and talked a bit more casually.

I have nothing to say to you both about my work. Right now it has to speak for itself.

On each available wall hung a single large canvas. Two seemed finished, the other only primed by the look of it. Junk mail brochures from new, garish commercial supermarkets and other throwaway ads were stuck on in lines on each of the finished canvasses, behind which, on the first canvas, was a scene of what looked like starving refugees but were, Elaine informed me when I asked, East German citizens on their way through a Hungarian processing office in a photograph she had taken herself in 1988 just before the Wall fell. On the other canvas football supporters fought with the police at the entrance to an underground train station. I stared at this canvas all that evening long, hung as it was over your shoulder.

All I want is to see movement coupled with expression. And don't think the junk mail is political: it's not. I just like the colours, she added smiling.

We talked about the show and what we hoped it would be: a *group* exhibition and you pushed on with the idea of the group, forming a group and how a manifesto could be written up, an Eastern challenge levelled at the international art world, how the avant-garde could ride high once again. Jan and Elaine were enthusiastic, at least it was obvious that Jan was, steeped as he was in theory and words. That talk faded out with the cooler air of evening. Jan ran out and came back with a couple of roasted chickens from the neighbouring butchers and we uncorked some German Liebfraumilch and ate and drank happily, our fingers slick with grease as we picked at the carcasses, talking all the while more about our personal lives, the histories that brought us to art and Elaine's studio. I did not say much as my German was too slow and broken, not being used then to speaking it. This suited me, I was happy to sit and listen, get drunk and look at you as you lay back joking and smoking, noticing I hoped, every now and then, my eyes resting on yours.

Drunkenness had settled on all four of us by the time Elaine started talking about Berlin from where she had just arrived a month before. We all listened to her attentively, her steady voice and clarity not inviting interruptions or distractions. She told us of the fall of the Wall and how she had moved to Berlin from Düsseldorf where she had been in a group show. She did not like Berlin, not as it was then just before the Wall fell. She found the West Berlin streets too wide and unnavigable, the bohemia of the '70s and '80s slowly burning out as the siege mentality grew out of fashion in a population getting too old and conservative to make an effort any longer. The Wall falling changed all that and she immediately joined the influx of drifters and artists occupying Mitte's and Prenzlauerberg's abandoned old buildings[25], setting up studio in a space she could never have afforded anywhere else in Europe, a huge space like a concert hall. Life was a party, a long, creative party. The look in her eyes alone made me believe it. Everyday spent drinking interminable mugs of coffee with her new neighbours from all over Germany, as well as Poles, Russians, Hungarians, Italians, her house on the Torstrasse a crossroads in a world all changing and on the move with the fall of the communist project. Then she would cycle to her studio near Gesundbrunnen and work on the series of canvasses she would later exhibit in the Malmö Konsthall, *Die Lebenslügen XX*, a breathtaking personal overview of the century that has remained one of my favourite bodies of work. And then the parties, the bars and squats springing up across the entire east of the city like spores on a Petri dish, every night a new face to meet and endless conversations in any number of languages. When the Wall fell Elaine, whose mother was Swiss and father American,

---

25 The German word *altbau* is used in original. (Trans.)

could speak German, French and English, but by the time I met her in Budapest she could also get by in Russian, Italian and Hungarian. No mean feat.

But what I'm getting at, she said shaking her head, is this one particular night and this one particular conversation I had with this guy. This was three years or so ago, and after a good day's work I went to meet my Russian friend Boris by Rosa Luxembourg Platz and he brought me along to this party in a bar or not a bar, not a real bar at least – whatever the hell that is – off Torstrasse somewhere, up the hill anyway. We had to step through a broken window in the front of an old *feinkost*, walk through what had once been the sad little shop to the back where, down a makeshift flight of steps a band was playing a sort of demented eastern folk music, Balkan turbo-folk I think they call it (she smiled and waved her hand at me) and where in the middle of the dark space there was a tower of several crates of Berliner Pilsner, around which were dozens of conversations in different languages, everyone sitting on upturned beer crates or old battered chairs, the only light was from a hundred flickering candles. The noise was frenetic, non-stop, chatter and laughter, manic music which eventually the most drunk danced along to. Boris and me sat down in a corner, and before long an acquaintance of Boris was sat near us and we were introduced but, and this is the annoying thing, I forget his name, this friend of Boris. He went off trying to convince a friend of one scheme or another and I was left with his acquaintance who started telling me about his art. He was a real skinny, dark-skinned Eurasian guy, his glasses thick and steaming up from the stuffy little bar. I asked him where he was from, out of curiosity, as we were both speaking our accented English, and he told me he came from Russia, from Astana in Kazakhstan to be precise and had just arrived in Berlin from Israel where he had worked for almost a year. Are you Jewish? I asked him. No, no, I'm Muslim as a matter of fact. So why did you go to Israel? I thought there would be good money, and the guys who smuggled me out had been two Jewish brothers, passport counterfeiters. So now I have very good Israeli papers, he laughed. But there was no money there so he left and came to Berlin. And you're an artist? Yes, ever since I had my vision. Your vision? My vision. And what was your vision? He had been on a bus packed with migrants all with old USSR passports, all Jewish and all heading to Berlin where, for another two years, they were entitled to residence permits and even possibly German citizenship. A bus that was part of an exodus, a stinking, crowded nexus of a strange Jewish resolution resulting from the failures of communism and the horrific debts of fascism, a unique fin de siècle pilgrimage. After two days of interrupted sleep, mere minutes of drowsy unconsciousness that were afforded him before being jolted back awake, he no longer knew when or if he was awake at all, his dreams and waking life blurring into one as the bus travelled out of the Ukraine and laboured north to Berlin. Suddenly he was no longer on a bus but on top of a roof, where he did not know, but a roof, and all around him were tower blocks, those markers of state planning and on one building across from him loomed a huge, terrifying mural of Lenin and Stalin, both white faced and grim looking, the red of the background putrid, nauseating. On a screen nearby ads for Coca Cola alternated with a little moving reel of Marx making his children perform Shakespeare to keep out the cold of Manchester. He ran from the roof into a stairwell that stank of piss and shit and descended into the most pitiful building you could imagine. A ruin, an on-going ruin full of loose mortar and peeling wallpaper, dust everywhere, each floor a further level of degeneration until finally he ran over the broken glass and spilt blood of the ground floor and out into the light of day and all he could see was a filthy street of some devastated suburb, rings of mushrooms sprouting up and wild plants growing menacingly, greedily, everywhere, the entire concrete and tarmacadam surface cracked and breaking apart. He ran then, ran and ran, covering his mouth with his shirt because of the rancid air, clotted with radiation and monoxide, he ran and ran and the only thing that caught his eye was a pack of wild dogs in what had been, before in the marked-for-death world, a children's playground. A pack of wild dogs the only creatures to bother with the pointless act of living. And they chased him and he knew then what it was all about. This abandoned world of old ruins and holocaust dogs. What was it about? I asked him. The world is going to die soon, he said, and all of us with it. We sat in silence, and for something to say I asked: And you're an artist? Yes ever since I had this vision. And you paint this vision? I paint it yes, what the hell else can I do?

This was just one of the conversations I'd have in Berlin then, she said laughing, breaking the spell and all of us sat up and blinked and shook ourselves out of this world of holocaust dogs and conquering mushrooms.

But has he ever exhibited these painting? I asked, needing to know.

Yes, once I think. In some little gallery in Mitte. I didn't see it though.

And what's ever become of him? asked Jan.

I asked Boris actually the last time I saw him. He said he was dead, that he had heard he was murdered but Boris seemed to think it was suicide.

Silence settled then and Elaine raised her eyebrows over the rim of her glass mischievously as she drained her wine.

Not quite an artist of the everyday then, you said, sounding dismissive.

No. Not quite.

***

Later, much later, that same night after we were both bedded down in Jan's living room and I had gotten up and joined you under your blanket, we made love like the sky was indeed already falling, that the film was over and there was nothing to do but fuck during the closing sequence, that it was a last chance and the moment was finite, the new world we found in each other's body was finite, our past over and done with, the present nothing but a full stop and the future the unwritten next line, an on-going blank space. Over and out. It smacks of hyperbole but I think loving you has always been tied up with the world apocalypse in my mind. Perhaps I have Elaine to thank for that. Or perhaps I have just you to thank for that. Who knows? You and me and the end of all things to come.

Jan Offe, Details from *3 Course Dinner* (2011)
Dinner performance. Courtesy the artist.

Jan Offe, *3 Course Dinner* (2011)
beetroot, carrot, apple, pesto, ricotta, spaghetti, mango,
strawberries, blue syrup, white wine, red wine, 220 × 180 cm.
Courtesy the artist.

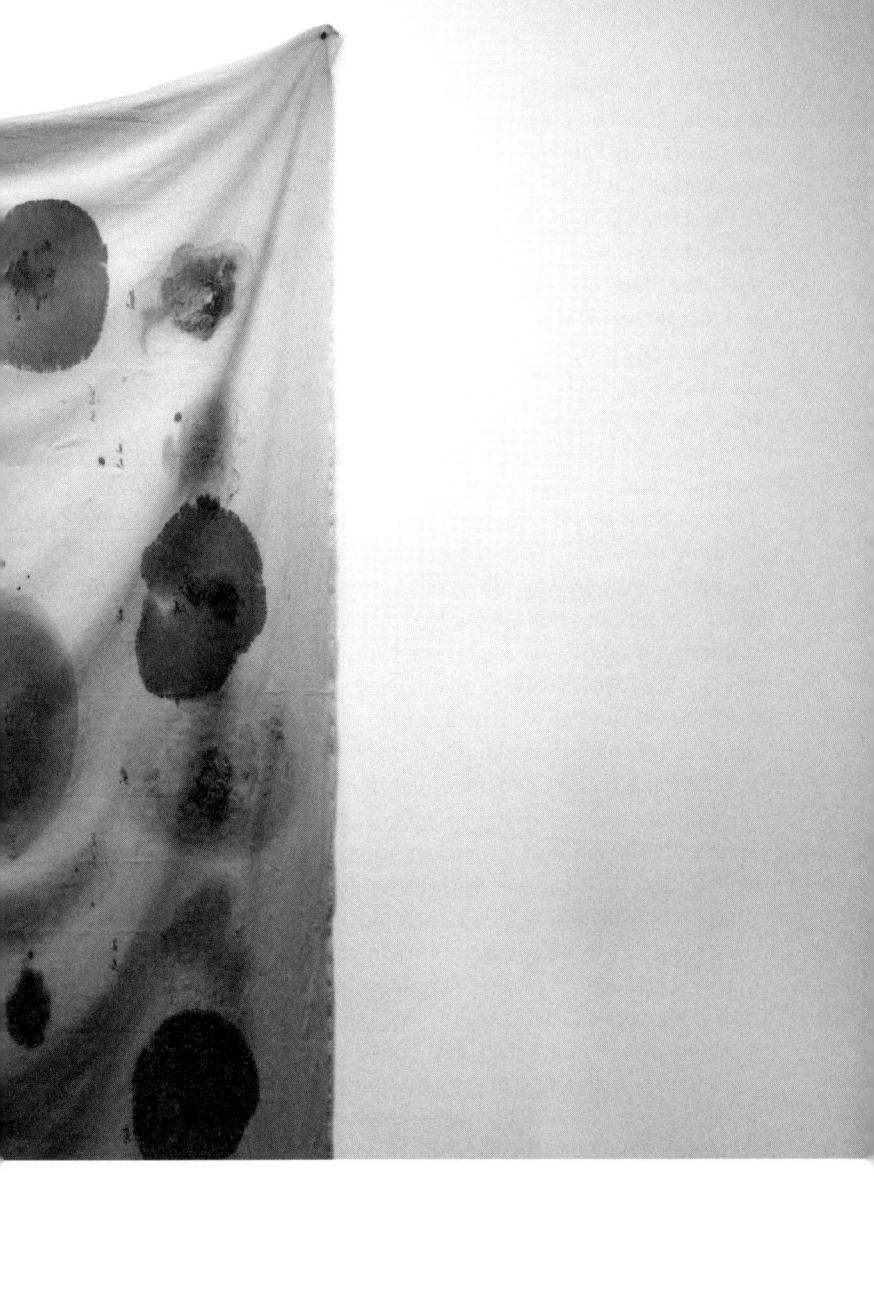

I need to remember the fun. I need to will to the forefront of my thoughts the remembrance of times when we laughed, because we most certainly laughed and that even in those crucial times when dissolution was ongoing we still joked and it still felt good. Getting to Paris for example: a long series of coincidences and mishaps that led to this new strange world of the city and all of them had, looking back, the illogical narrative turns of any good joke. Jörg Haider for instance, now that was a funny joke! The wars had presented Europe with so many problems, embarrassing problems because we were, the people of the Balkans, a mirror for them and their pasts – as was Jörg Haider. An embarrassing joke.

Jokes are based on some sort of reality and therefore some can be dangerous, but at the same time what better way of neutralising a threat than by joking about it? Floods of us immigrants were crashing upon Austria in those years: Croatians, Slovenes, Serbs, Bosnians. We were spreading out across the entire continent, up into Germany and France, anonymous in the big cities of these big countries, then further afield: the United Kingdom, Scandinavia, the US. The consequences of war have a surprising, bewildering reach. At the time we were really rather oblivious to it, like kids who don't notice that all the adults at the birthday party have stopped talking to each other and are only forcing smiles.

We were busy enjoying success. *Budapest/Belgrade* helped us financially and made us, how to say, more than just a little collective in Belgrade, a city at war with its neighbours. Gojković relished this new stature as it helped in turning us from being soldiers into something far more respectable, something beyond the lines of borders, ethnicity, religion; just as people pay counterfeiters for fake passports to their utopia, so Gojković pushed us on in our game of making networks and connections. He could start his process of re-visioning himself. So naturally we never once saw ourselves, at least not until France loomed on the horizon, as refugees from war – deserters maybe, but not desperate émigrés, those we imagined begging on the street or stealing fruit from market stalls in order to eat. No, we were proud, very proud, artistic young men who, having had our fill of war, now had moved on to our real vocations in life. We had sung the same song that they had bellowed in Zurich in 1916; we're talking here about Tzara, Ball, Hans Richter, Hans Arp, Joyce, Lenin and Zinoviev.

We would make things happen.

You called me up in the hotel room I had moved into in Budapest and announced that we were going to Vienna that same day, and because I trusted you I said okay, without giving it a moment's thought or asking a single question. The last sudden departure had worked out well; I had no reason to think this journey would be any different. We had exhibited sixteen artists in *Budapest/Belgrade* mostly from Hungary and Serbia with a few notable 'foreigners' like Elaine Pettifer who was Swiss, Jan Offe who was German and Maarten Varekamp who was Dutch. Going to Austria was a bid to carry the success beyond our immediate arena. Unlike myself, myopic and naïve, you saw that we were at the point of either making do with the Balkans, which was going to be difficult in any case due to the wars and the mutual suspicions, even within the artworld, or we could replicate our foray into Hungary and go further and further west. I remember putting down the receiver of the phone in the little, apersonal hotel room and looking around me, the sun making the room an obscene shade of bright brown, and I thought: how little I have in the world right now other than the potential of future achievement, future happiness, and the opportunity of my art. I packed my belongings, only clothes really and one or two books, a German dictionary I studied assiduously to help me get to know you better, all very battered, and left and went to meet you on Bajcsy-Zsilinszky.

How the West was won? A brief telephone call promising opportunity.

Vienna, well, a city I only remember so much of, and most of what I can recall is in darkness, fringed with an opaque, seedy quality of the winter-nights through which we traipsed around looking for fun. This was when our relationship took a turn, the signpost for which I do not remember reading, when we became more than co-curators of The LGB Group or lovers, but a team of two hunting for an expanse in ourselves found only through losing whole parts of those selves: we were trying to become perhaps nihilists, alcoholics, drug addicts, perverts. And all in the space of a couple of weeks. We crossed the border without any trouble and almost immediately things started to turn into a hardened, more personal, version of the war. You were thirty-four or something like that, I was twenty-five and I think what you realised was that I had somehow experienced more than you had, I had been to the far regions of where a man can go, and you suddenly wanted those experiences for yourself – death not least – if only for one moment, one moment or two of pure release – a very definite grab at this twisted creativity of which Gojković, Lubarda and I were such specialists.

We did not tell anyone that we were going to Vienna and to make up for it we talked non-stop about the group as if in an effort to make them present, each artist that had exhibited with us, the future programming of exhibitions, plans, hopes, dreams. We were going to meet a friend of your father's who would give us the keys to a shop where we could stay for a week or two. The shop belonged to this friend of your father's, Turgeman, and had been used as the local headquarters for a political party in the recent elections. You seemed embarrassed by Turgeman when you introduced me to him, your whole attitude was undergoing a transformation I can see now was due to your realising that I had a past before you received the first of my letters, before you read the words of a curious, intellectual young idiot aesthete, and that this past was one of hate and war and acts atrocious and inhumane. As is, perhaps, anti-Semitism. Or so you then worried as we followed this Elias Canetti lookalike from the U-Bahn station, a fierce Jewish man barely reaching to our shoulders with grey hedgehog hair in an ascendant wave back across his wide, intelligent face which was bursting between the arms of his tortoise shell glasses.

Have you bed linen? he wanted to know.

No we don't but we'll get some. We have sleeping bags.

I'll lend you some young Warmann, he said and he looked at me. You're both just passing through?

We're hopefully just going to organise an exhibition, and yes, then move on.

Well, here we are, he said reaching down to take the padlock off the shutter that covered the shopfront. It rattled up and he opened the door and let us pass him into the empty space. The election went well, I guess, as good as could be hoped. But things are changing in Austria. Like they're changing everywhere I guess, and he paused a moment with this and we both nodded silently taking in what he was not saying.

This will be perfect, I managed.

It's even got electric heating, you added. Thanks so much, Mr. Turgeman, it'll save us a small fortune in hotels.

Indeed it will. He seemed happy with us being there, passing the keys over and standing pointlessly for a minute or two looking about, taking in the room and us two, as if sizing the match up and finally deciding we suited the space well. Right gentlemen, I leave you be. The toilet is in the back, shower and all.

Thanks again, we chimed.

Be careful, he said then, and was gone.

It was a strange makeshift place to be staying but you soon made it halfway hospitable. You put me to sweeping the floor and cleaning the place up while you went out to buy some provisions and came back with candles and wine and some food.

What are we going to do now? I remember asking.

Have fun, you replied simply.

And we did just that. The strange setting gave events their cue and set them in motion: we sat on our sleeping bags and opened the bottle of wine and drank and ate cheese and crackers, talking desultorily. When the bottle was empty we went out into the city and got lost. The funny thing was that I had presumed you knew people in the city (other than your father's friends such as Turgeman) and was surprised when I realised you knew nobody and that you had barely any knowledge of the city whatsoever. Love:

the joy that you were at ease because you knew only me, that we were together, alone, at last. That first night I did not really stop to think about what it was we were actually doing in Austria. I did not have the chance to do so. By midnight we had found our way to a little bar that was all oak and Alps and served up Stiegl beer ceaselessly to the fat, bearded men at the bar. All the other men – for there were only men – drank vodka or sekt or Wachau white wine. The place was full, packed to the point where you wonder if it is actually possible to move (you're always surprised that, with a bit of determination and necessary rudeness, you can) and smoke hung low under lights that served illumination poorly and obscurity well. In the far side there was a pool table that seemed popular, men prowling around it brandishing cues and laughing at each other and what the next man had to say – the game in hand did not seem all that popular. How had we found this place? It seemed like a shithole, from the outside as well as from the inside, but somehow we had been directed there and had entered and never once suggested leaving. We got a bottle of wine and stood at an available tall table, resting our elbows and toasting our latest adventure together, turning our attention to the pool table to pretend, like everyone else, that we cared about it. It was not long until we picked up the forces of attention that are impossible to read upon first entering a bar like this, the direction of communication and the sign language it is spoken in: we were in a toilet cubicle with another man, he did not say much, but he knocked out three lines of cocaine, muttered something about the difficulty he had in getting good coke and snorted up his lot, before welcoming us to Vienna by passing over his rolled up banknote. Back outside by the pool table the place heaved, it swayed and rocked, and man after man came and went. It wasn't a gay bar that much was clear and soon it bored us, but there was a group of three or four men who we decided just had to be gay, the ones drinking glasses of sekt with their hands configured so delicately around their flutes it looked like they were acting at being queer, and these men eyed us thoughtfully from time to time. But we just finished our bottle and left the place, talking relentlessly to one another, flagging a passing taxi and getting home only to find that we were both of us impotent from the coke.

The next day we woke up late and prowled the city for art: we went to the big museums and it was leisurely, not at all the sort of fatigue-inducing endurance trip museums can be in a city like Vienna. We strolled through the Secession laughing, I remember us laughing, as you told jokes coloured by Hungarian dirty humour. That day we saw what Vienna has to offer with smiles not very far away: Schiele of course, and while I saw power and sex in his portraits you just smiled and continued on with dirty asides. Everything was slipping into the domain of the lewd, the inane, a target for fun, ridicule. We were becoming closed into ourselves like the very worst sort of couple, the type I dislike for their self-reliance, their horrible insignificant in-jokes.

It started slowly – the opening up to other men and women, comments about people's looks or bodies in passing and soon we had the chance to pick others up and that was what happened, the third, or was it the forth, night, we found ourselves in the company of a handsome man younger than me by what seemed like years, just listening to him talk made me feel melancholy for a youth that had passed me by somewhere between Jovana and the frontline. Adrian was his name. He smoked joints and was not overly interested in sex. However the next night he came with a friend, Jochum, and the little shop became a den of Mitteleuropean iniquity, with laughter spread on top and bodies spread below and in between our conversation, jokes.

The days passed and one melted into the other and I told myself that this was part of growing up, of becoming an artist: living a heightened everyday of your own making and pushing yourself in territory you've never seen mapped out before, not in books, or television or movies. You live it first, and then you go to the literature and you say, wearily but with empathy: Yes! That's what it's like, that is exactly what debauchery is like, though each artist represents their individual needs, their own drives pushing at the doors of the erotic, the acceptable, with colours and lines all their own. Each day I notched up the scores without realising what I was doing, on some invisible measure I would say okay, yesterday we did this or that, got that far, got that high, not bad, but can we go any further? Vienna, I mean it's not known for its craziness: it's not Berlin or Amsterdam, but I just need to remind myself of these weeks and I laugh at the filth you and I managed to drag out of its recesses.

My German had become more assured of itself, I would no longer spend anytime thinking about what I was saying, I would just bark it out and I was becoming cheeky, a rascal and would enjoy shouting at the old men we came across, all leathered up and pot-bellied and hard for no reason other than they looked it. Austrian society was so peaceful! I grew angry at this, this stillness: on the surface there was hardness and belligerent looks. We'd walk into a bar and everyone including the bar staff would give us these gruff, malevolent looks, the type of attitude in Serbia you reserved for people you were likely to kill. Only of course nobody killed anybody in Vienna. Rudeness is a lot different than hate, but it looked the same to me at first. But then there are many forms hate can take, are there not? You can institutionalise it and clean it up, make it bureaucratic and somehow make it more palatable, more acceptable. On the other hand, once the chips fell, you can pick up your guns and run into the next village, claiming it your own, and set about murdering and lighting the houses, smoking the enemy out. I would get into pointless arguments in those bars that were not overtly gay bars but were full of queers. I'd shout in my German, rasping it out, and then offer to take it outside onto the street. The old men would just shake their heads and go back to their beers. It infuriated me, this shaking of fat heads. There was the time I beat the shit out off a taxi driver who, taking a piss behind one of the few trees in that old city, a Linden tree, said after us: 'dirty faggots', to himself but loud enough to let us hear. Well I turned around and as he zipped up his fly all quick and nimble diving back into the open door of his shitmobile taxi I made a grab for the door and with my other hand snatched his collar and dragged his sorry ass out onto the pavement. It was dark there, shadows played about us, and with a terrible fury I laid into the motherfucker, with the anguish that is righteous, the anguish of the immigrant being misunderstood and forsaken on the fringes of the well-ordered, not-so-welcoming society. He was your age, a normal bloke, probably had a wife and kids waiting for him back in some boxy, eighth floor apartment. *U pičku materinu*[26]! I shouted this at him before realising abruptly that nobody would understand me. You had to stop me, there was blood and he was crying out, the scene shocking for anyone seeing it and no doubt the Polizei were already on their way. We moved on quickly, running I believe, and the relief out of me was tremendous, like an ejaculation of tension, as if since leaving the front all this violence had built up without an outlet and that taxi driver had given it vent.

You weren't shocked at all but just laughed about it. You made sure to bring some of that fury out when we made love that night, and it did come, you tickled me in every spot that made me thrash about, you teased me and frustrated me with fingers that felt like spiders running over my naked flesh. The electricity ran down my back and across my ass and under my balls and up into my prick and I forced you down underneath me to take the release of all this energy. And you soaked it up and it infected us and I do not think it ever really left us thereafter. We were smashing down walls with our pricks ever after, we were twisting the founts of violence in our lovemaking, opening up with each other and with impressed strangers, equating sex with death and vice versa as if we had a right to do so, as if we knew that in the depth of sex was the abolition of the self, the point where one is negated and made anew into something else, fleetingly, and that in finding this point we would dispel the absolute destructive nature of our own mortality. Gods only upset things. A god was no longer needed, no myth of origin and destination was needed, and I can't help but think, now that

---

26 'Your mother's cunt', or thereabouts (Trans.)

you went through completely and fought more violently than you should have, perhaps from the very beginning art was not needed either, that after Vienna we were nothing more than just conmen – perverted conmen – chasing death.

We met him before we heard about him. This shows two things: how cut off we were from normal functioning life in Austria and that, cut off as we were, we stationed ourselves underneath it: we were busy scratching the underbelly of the country when we came across Jörg Haider. The kind of man I never enjoy kissing or fucking – too old, too charming, too chiselled. Haider was the kind of man you expect crows to follow around like flies follow cows, a haunting character out of an Edgar Allen Poe story who had an entourage of young henchmen. It was in his smile, empty and sinister at once. Yes that is just it – a crow, then another, and out of the dark black of night he would appear with his group of young men, ready to bully the people of Europe into a government with fascists in it. Oh look Haider, and there's a black crow on that apartment's balcony. And another, and another, oh they're all over the street. How strange.

How long had we been in Vienna at that stage? I had talked to both Gojković and Lubarda that very day about possibly moving to Paris, the war with Kosovo was obvious and we knew that going back to Belgrade was out of the question, it would finish us. We left it undecided and with Gojković saying he would talk to our old friend Trifke about the possibility of getting us into France. I was talking to you about this in that bar on Heumühlgasse whose name I forget and you thought it was a good idea, if this guy Trifke could get us there and get us set up with visas, we should take the chance. Then the crows started to appear. First in the form of a very good looking young man, my age, with blond hair and leather gloves which he placed carefully on the counter next to us.

Hello gentlemen, he said smiling.
Hello.
Can I get you guys a drink?
And we let him buy us a round.
I'm from Hungary, you said darkly in response to his question.

And you? I noticed his smile had gone.

Serbia.

Ah Serbia! Like every other criminal in Vienna these days, though I shouldn't say that: you and I both know those would be smelly Bosnians.

And then some more crows appeared. The bar was warm, bright, the windows black with night, cold.

He let us be, this social Austrian and I calmed down and we went back to our conversation. It was not until much later we started talking to him again along with his group, and we all got on very well and due to my earlier anger the blond guy had created in me, I wanted then to take him home and fuck him, I wanted to come in his mouth and bite on his balls. And he wanted it too, that was obvious. We all of us, a group of ten or so, we all wanted it and the Jägermeister was on tap, I shit you not, and it came round after round and we all told jokes and laughed and it must have been six or eight weeks now that we had laughed like this, with men as bent as the next, in bars as warm and bright with their windows as black and cold as the next, our money all but gone, our plans interrupted by small talk at the bar.

Though the sequence of events is confused the endpoint stays clear even today, physically even. At one stage the blond guy gave me a blowjob in the toilet, I remember that: looking down at him I reassured myself that this was the way to deal with insults: get the bastards to suck your dick. There was a long story about the Second World War, the whole bar listening to it. It involved the storyteller, one of the crows, and his grandmother, travelling to Germany and into Bavaria, the heart of the Reich and getting to see Nazi officers fleeing ahead of the Allies. It ended in a joke, or at least a happy note, one which everyone could nod to, smiling, and turn back to their drinks and forget the whole story. Then there were more rounds. Rounds and rounds of beer and Jägermeister. Then I told my story and I told it straight, from the beginning to Vienna, quickly, and these fascist bastards actually listened. Then we were out on the street, walking through the night city as a group, this event the only one whose place in the sequence of which I can be sure. You and I and Jörg Haider and several of his jet-black crows. Where we were going I do not know, but we were all still laughing. And I ignored the Serbian jokes, and the Bosnian jokes and their confusing of the two, I told myself I would get every one of them to eat my balls later. And we were all friends, that I can remember, we were walking the streets in the dead of dark night, raucous and having fun – as friends would. Joining in the banter the most eloquent way left to me, drunk as I was, I thought it would be fun to trip Jörg up. It happened quickly. I tapped you on your shoulder, you turned around, I opened my eyes and mouth wide in jest and turned and, deftly, without a spare movement to it, I tripped happy Haider up and he went forward, fast and with quite a bit of acceleration, his leather gloved hands out in front of him to save his beautiful face. So it was we reached the endpoint of the evening. These guys were strong and they were mean and I was stupid not to see what would come from my moment of jest. You got away thankfully, and I know you were torn whether or not to call the Polizei, getting them involved would only have ended with my arrest and expulsion from the country. It was the natives' turn now and they let it all out, each getting their go and then three staying behind, the blond guy who gave a good blowjob among them, to really finish me off. For what felt like a long time they lay into me, their strength, their absolute hate for the likes of me, their righteous indignation that I should ever have even breathed one breath of Austrian air. The beating was on one of those clean streets, well organised and completely still, between a pharmacy and a shoe shop. My face was up against the squat bottom step of a raised doorway and when it did not end and I saw that they were working themselves up to greater and greater acts of sophisticated violence, the way three men let loose with each other and a silent, well deserving victim always end up doing, I summoned the energy to lash out in a final stand. Up I swung but I was too winded to be fast enough and they were too much the thugs, one instinctively drawing his knife, letting me have it in my right shoulder. That set me down again. I was no longer sure they were the same guys from the bar, I couldn't recognise them and with my cries of pain they took a last look at me and took off, leaving behind them a last few insults to me and my kind. Dirty Jugos the lot of us.

Thankfully the wound wasn't deep, nothing you couldn't fix at the shop. You somehow managed to drag me back there and tend to my fucked up body. Just breathing was difficult. You got in contact with Gojković first thing the next day and asked him to get us out of Vienna; he said he would be there by nightfall.

Of course we should have known who Jörg Haider was but we did not. When I awoke around midday, the shop space bright with winter sun, you said his name quietly to yourself, as if in disbelief: Jörg Haider. We looked at each other then before exploding into peels of laughter, laughter that brought me to tears with its searing pain across my front. Even that morning, so soon after being almost beaten to death, I could laugh about it, I could laugh about us two and our sojourn in Vienna and the whole mad, strange life we had been leading because it was all over, brought to an end by a couple of rightwing fascist thugs.

You went out and when you came back you had more info on this man and his Freedom Party. You had gone to visit Turgeman in his offices in the *Inneren Stadt* and he had told you all you needed to know and you in turn told it to me as I sat drinking plum brandy to dilute the pain. And I remember asking myself, after you told me about Haider and his *Österreich Zuerst* petition to change the face of Austrian politics, to maintain law and order and tradition and most of all keep out of the country what he saw as scum, people who had been burned and raped out of their homes in Bosnia, Slovenia, Croatia, Serbia: how many generations will it take for Serbian politicians to make up such a thing, such a petition, and not just pay some ignorant kids to go and kill and rape until the borders sat just right and the alien was expelled to somewhere else, god alone could care where? Turgeman sent a doctor as a reward for my having taken on the likes of Haider and his crows, and while he cleaned my wound and told me I'd survive with nothing more than a scar and a good story, I couldn't stop thinking about Haider and his sort of politics. Having left Serbia I saw him as a softie – he knew nothing about real xenophobia, he would never be able to kill a man for instance, that much I suspected. And then I thought: no Serbian politician could kill a man either, and nor will they ever have to, for it's the young men who do the killing for them. We call the politicians whores but really they are pimps, Sloba and Mira: nothing but first-rate pimps running a brothel. And the johns? The tricks turned are those abstract nouns people care so deeply about: Greater Serbia, justice, retribution, history, God. Ideas our writers started to propagate back in the 1980s, when they had been in the fold for so long, with greater freedom and respect than in any other communist country, they turned against self-management socialism and talked, in their resplendent national language and its literature, of parliamentary and national ideas, our terrible historical grievances. How can you be a dissident in a society that respects and accommodates you? It would seem you bite its dirty rotten hand when it comes to feed you!

All that afternoon I talked like this, half in and out of feverish dreams. You sat and read your book after you had cleaned the place up. I was barely conscious because of painkillers and plum brandy by the time Gojković, Lubarda and Trifke arrived. The latter was muscular and well dressed; I hadn't seen him for years, my saviour, my very own Charon. And there was laughter in my dreams as we left our little shop, and it slowly faded away and I went under, into sleep, into Trifke's huge Mercedes, and we were on our way, to Paris.

***

Let me try to be clear about some things, about how we travelled together: we were a happy ensemble much like a band of gypsies would be: full of secrets and arguments and reconciliations, relying only on ourselves and our cunning. The artists of The LGB Group were all at one time or another exiles starting as we did with war. We were a group slowly moving West but caught perennially on the barbed wire of the East and looking back perhaps we should never have tried to 'come over' at all. Venice proved the apogee in our travels together but both biennials of 2001 and 2003 get confused and gel together for me. It was a bazaar, where the artworld could watch on as salesmen like Jovanović traded between our old lives and our new existence waiting in France. It was like a border post that would process us and spit us out into the West, clean and part of the machinations of the whole dirty business. Looking back now, nothing seems to change between the two years: the art, the artists, certainly not the city with its canals and mazes and holy piazzas with their scorched churches. Unlike you I was never very good at remembering shows and the artists showing, where and when, dates, names, titles of artworks. I do know that it was 2003 when Gojković and Jovanović started to piss me off. That entire biennale come to think of it was a real endurance test, we were all out of control, lost to each of our wayward paths that were leading us away from the most important thing: our functioning as artists, as normal people. Whatever the fuck normal is.

I do not know what I am talking about today. I cannot think straight.

Let me see. What I do know is that each of these years accommodation was distinctly different. In 2001 I had not really thought about going to the Biennale. We were in Ljubljana meeting with Peter Tomc and Zoran Živković and arguing a lot but also staying up around the clock partying like it was our last chance to do so – I remember I had not slept for three whole days when we decided to go across the border to Venice. Yes, the difference was that in 2001 we slept rough wherever seemed good, I would sleep for many hours on the Lido where it was quiet and warm in the shade and then we spent a number of nights camping with Jan and his German friends out on Punta Sabbioni. I was also paranoid about getting stopped by the police and being asked for my passport and visa, a tension I think I have forgotten – the unbearable weight of being somewhere illegally pushes you to feel twice as present in the world than you would normally, and it gets to you after a while. It's a weight I have Trifke to thank for – just one more debt of gratitude. And I ask myself: what happened to me that I owe so much to Trifke the drug dealer?

The art that first year was endless and we saw it all together, every pavilion and the entire curated exhibition at the Arsenale: we were hungry for it and I needed the education. You pestered Gottschalk, the critic from Budapest (whose name I have not come across very often since then, come to think of it) to get us press passes. In 2003 of course we could get passes from many different sources – I think I got mine from Dejan Smetenović at the Serbian pavilion. I wrote a lot during that trip, four reviews got published and a whole notebook of my own thoughts for later – it was a constructive trip, edifying, educational, and how shall I say – fun.

Of course it is impossible to digest these big art spectacles properly anyway. All you can do is diagnose indigestion and proceed accordingly. I did not see as much art in 2003 as in 2001, for different reasons. There was a big show curated by Igor Zabel that I remember really affecting me and I studied it closely. It was called *Sistemi Individuali*. It was political, certainly more political than any dynamic I would like to see being set up with LGB, but its culminating power was something I admired, and I also liked how the exhibition included artists from the East seamlessly with those from the West. It included IRWIN – who I tried not to see as competitors but whom naturally I treated as a measure, and I was jealous of their inclusion in the biennale – Roman Opalka, whose work shows the course of the day over years and years, Art & Language, Luise Lambri, Collective Action Group, Florian Pumhöst whose work I knew from seeing it in Vienna and which I liked a lot, Mladen Stilinović, Nahum Tevet.

What else did I like from Venice? I have to try hard to recall the art. There was a show on painting, from Rauschenberg to Murakami, curated by Francesco Bonami that I went to see with Branko Savić and Maarten Varekamp. Buren, Ruscha, Kippenberger, Doig. Yes, they have a function these biennales come to think of it, almost more edifying than the big annual art fairs: I cannot recall a single artwork from this year's FIAC for instance. God what a waste of time! But the day-to-day timetable of the biennale can be distracting, all the parties in the evening, and 2003, with the unbearable heat creating an inferno and our splintering at the seams from the pressure of growing personalities and careers diverging, will be remembered for many things other than the art exhibited.

For by then Gojković had really started to lose his way with the gallery Jovanović was trying to set up in Paris. It had just become a distraction and he made no effort to try to cover this fact up, indeed Gojković gloried in it and made clear that this had become for him the meaning of success and not the paltry making of art. I will admit that I rode along happily with him and Jovanović however, we all did, but it seems in retrospect that it was the beginning of the dissolution. No, rather it was the peak, the crest. Jovanović, rich from his sell-out shows the year before and helped in no small part by you, rented that huge apartment not far from the Arsenale. We all crashed there at various times of the day and night and there were a lot of drugs and a lot of sex, that I can remember. It was one big celebratory reunion.

The difference between the two years is telling I guess. The first year it was just you and me and we were like fugitives running about sleeping wherever we could and surprised by the amount of art we could see, the names attached to it, the famous faces – that second year we did not care about anyone else, we were our own faces, our own names. I remember standing outside the Manchester Pavilion, that little bar overflowing with people night on night and the French critic Gilbert Klossowski coming up to me and asking me what I thought of such and such a pavilion and I had no idea what he was talking about or why anyone would want to ask me such a question. I was polite and did my best to indulge him but really he knew I was out of it. But what was clear, and this surprised me, was that this is what he expected to hear somehow because it was 2 a.m. and I was wasted and vapid opinions were available on tap in Venice. He was happy to stand nodding to my vague, inebriated and jaded indifference: all he wanted was to ask me a question, any question because I was an artist, a leader of a well known art group, an artworld *personality*, and so I tried to say something nice and accommodating so I spoke at length about Pierre Restany and the Nouveaux Réalistes and he enjoyed this immensely and nodded his head emphatically and the encounter left me a little surprised, suddenly it scared me that people like Klossowski should care what I have to say about anything at all. He became a friend back in Paris but I can never be at ease with him if I'm to be honest. That night walking back toward the Grand Canal with some loud, licentious Spaniards I knew that this space of respect, of listening to us and what we had to say, could have terrible consequences for someone like Gojković and I did not want to think about what they would entail.

So like I said, we were a big band back then in 2003, a band of travelling nomads. There was you, Gojković and Jovanović, Lubarda, Jan Offe and Elaine Pettifer and their friends from Berlin, all sleeping on the floor in the largest bedrooms. It was so nice to travel from all over, from Belgrade and Budapest, Berlin and Zurich even, where Vesna and Biljana were based then with their burgeoning theatre ensemble and for us all to meet in this huge apartment that seemed to me so acutely picturesque, exactly like a regal apartment should be, that it seemed to be straight out of a film set. This apartment was one difference between the years, and you, Elaine, Jan and I laughed about it, this difference between leaky, stuffy tents far off on the other side of the lagoon and the opulence of this palatial 19th century penthouse.

What is funny is that we all got into our routines so quickly, immediately made the apartment our home and went about the biennale as if it was a daily business we were well used to – I guess this is the way these things go, just like holidays when you arrive and immediately have your routine, it only feels exotic really once you leave and return home. Jan and Elaine would be up each morning and have rapid breakfasts of coffee and Italian biscotti, serious and diligent in all the art they had to see and the people they had to meet, they weren't at all interested in our sex and depravity but were well used to us by then. We needed them really, they gave us a weight to measure ourselves out with and the semblance of being grounded. And our routine? It consisted of sleeping late until the heat woke us and lazing around that aristocratic residence, waking each other up with lewd jokes and cigarettes, plotting the day ahead in a half-hearted kind of way, knowing that we were really only open to distractions, diversions, being led astray. If we had stayed any longer we would have set up our own homage to the OHO group and their exiting the artworld in 1970, right on the cusp of international fame, in favour of their Šempas Commune.

Yes, it was 2003 and Gojković had started to lose it, he had only time for meeting collectors and talked about these strange creatures so rich you could only imagine what life was like for them, what their struggles were, and he spoke not a word about the art itself. A typical conversation was at some little restaurant Veselin had found where we could all eat, close to twenty of us, for very cheap, antipasti that lasted for hours and huge bowls of pasta that would sit among the many bottles until we got ourselves together and hunted out the evenings' parties.

Gojković would turn up late, sit quietly at the end of the table until he couldn't restrain himself:

Who cares what the Italians or the Germans or the Americans are showing. We all know that Martin Kippenberger and Fred Wilson are great. We have the price tag to remind us for god's sake.

You cannot be serious?

I am serious.

Shut your mouth Gojković, we all know you hate Fred Wilson's work.

No, no I don't. I respect it actually.

And we would all laugh because each one of us knew right well that Gojković was letting bullshit through, even if he hid it with his hardman persona.

And who else do you respect? Jeff Koons?

Koons is a clever man—

And again twenty people would all start to laugh and cut Gojković off because it was so ridiculous all we could do was laugh. And of course Gojković would get angry as hell and lower his voice and address the people at his end of the table, not letting this group of poor eastern artists with 'their heads in the shitbrown past,' hear what he had to say in defence, probably because it would be even more risible than the last thing he'd come out with.

Today I was introduced to the Dutch Royal family in the Giardini – don't snigger you fucking cunt, shut up and listen – and I have to say these people know what they like. I am interested in people who not only know what they like – no please, don't interrupt, let me continue – but who also have the means to acquire it. This is something pure, for this is appreciation matched with the power to acquire it. You don't see snotnosed critics buy the work they like, do you? They don't even have the money to buy themselves the fucking catalogue – think about it: how does that let them think truly about the work?

And did you meet Queen Beatrix herself?

You're changing the subject, dickhead.

I just want to know who it was you met.

Maybe I did, maybe I even told her a joke. Like: how do you increase the value of a Serbian painting? You kill the painter and burn his house.

Do royal families allow jokes in their circle?

This isn't Tito we're talking about here.

And so it would go over dinner, spoiling the days with the dirty talk of money and power and influence until eventually Gojković got fed up with us and stopped joining our evening meals. I could blame Jovanović for this turn in my friend but that would not be honest as even Jovanović never went as far as Gojković, he would laugh with the rest of us at the excesses of our friend's belief in the money swamping the artworld and how it could not only better us financially, but in some misguided way, help our art. It was true that we didn't have much money left and that the future looked uncertain, but when does it look certain? I think it was definitely during Venice 2003 when Gojković decided to turn more to the dealing and selling of art than the creation of it. He was intoxicated by all the glamour and money surrounding the big London or

Parisian gallerists, and persuaded himself that because a Warhol was worth millions, any work that sells, and which sells for a lot of money, must in turn put the artist on the same level as Warhol. It is a form of logic so depraved and money-centred that I cannot understand where it comes from, from what deep instinct for survival it sprouts or why it hits some people and not others. Perhaps it is a legacy of a communist past, I do not know. Of knowing once what base materiality was and its counterpart – the non-existence of property – and hating the memory, and Gojković, goddamn him, has always hated so much. He is a connoisseur of hate.

But what about the Giardini, Jovanović would ask, trying to make up for this money-sugared conversation none of us wanted, what pavilions do you like?

The Icelandic pavilion isn't half bad, Lubarda would say.

I like Chris Offili, but then I'm doing the northern European version of Offili, Maarten would say, sheepish and earnest, waiting for the laugh, if such a version is possible. I don't know.

A load of shit, Gojković would guffaw, referring to the elephant dung in Offili's canvases.

Smelly shit. Smelliest pavilion award definitely goes to the Brits.

You were interested in seeing everything and I was at your side but there was a weariness creeping up on me that later I would recognise: it was the weariness of myself surrounded by people, all as talented as the next, and who needed guidance from me as the leader of The LGB Group that people took me to be. The heat didn't help either: the city was suffocating under the unbearable weight of a heatwave. I know that in probability these people needed nothing from me, I just imagined it, this need, because I wanted them to need me because I had no other family at that stage that would accept me without reservations. Even you I was in the process of losing: I went about surrounding myself with as many people as possible in the foolish hope that you would be there amongst them all.

I spent my last day in Venice in 2001 looking for a gift to give you on your birthday later that summer, a birthday present but also a gift of reconciliation. That was an hour or two during which the fact that Venice is of course a terrible city and that one could argue against its preservation rose up in front of me and actually made me jubilant. The happy scavenger amongst the rubble; the freedom of the ruins we all long for. Those miserable images of fat tourists in ponchos under a wall of rain, St. Mark's Square flooded below them as they file along on raised wooden gangways. What's the point of it all, I wondered as I followed the tourists along by the lagoon front, what is this fascination with the past, with beauty, with both of these things coupled with the irreplaceable and individual? All the tat for sale, and I wandered past it, eyeing the Africans and their fake Gucci bags and watches and had no idea what from all this I could buy for you, but I knew at least that it would not be art-related. I was going to buy you a Buren multiple I could not afford, but I thought that homeless as you were then, it would just get lost in some Paris apartment or other. I moved away from the large body of water and followed some alleys until I was lost, wholly and without the vaguest sense of direction, the type of lost that Venice offers, timeless and European, and I had to just go with it until I entered a shop that sold handmade Venetian masques and I thought to myself: I'm not one for ironic gifts but this could work well, these masques. An old woman made and sold them herself, from this narrow store somewhere in Venice. They were excitingly sinister, and could refer jokingly to our argument and at the same time draw a beautiful line underneath it. And I bought one, a very carnivalesque masque, demented eyes above a hooked nose the length of a large cock, and the old woman thanked me earnestly and wrapped her creation carefully, not knowing that it would hide terrible things and bear witness to acts her old mind could never in her lifetime imagine.

***

As soon as the pain was gone Paris really began, which is to say I started to abuse myself and try to obliterate reality with degeneracy.

Almost everything began at once: at last I had reached France, this huge country and its capital city growing older and more tame with each year, but for me it was all new and fresh and invigorating. The first weekend I could move with any kind of agility I walked out into the city. I met Gojković I remember and we sat by the Canal Saint-Martin and drank beer. It was like meeting someone you have heard a lot about but could now experience them yourself for the first time and see if everything you heard had been true. He was a different person, this Aleksandar, to the one I had known in Belgrade.

How long has it been since we had a drink together, Aleks?

A long time it feels like, brother Djordje. A year, maybe more.

And how have you been keeping?

Good, good. It's strange to be in Paris.

Strange?

In a good way.

I know what you mean.

It was a surprise to get that call from Warmann, and I was happy Trifke could sort us out. Just like that, no plans or nothing. I always knew we would leave and come to somewhere like Paris. I just thought we would plan and plan and plan. And I fucking hate plans! So I'm a happy boy.

Glad to hear it.

Have another beer.

Cheers.

Cheers.

Gojković. That happy boy. A man as complicated as they come, a man I have known my entire life but who only grows more complex in front of my eyes, each conversation between us as unique and distinct as the one before. He would hate to think that I am writing reports of us drinking beer by the Canal Saint-Martin; he would hate me writing anything about him, I know that. He would stop me if he knew that I am writing anything other than some sort of theoretical history of his art or an encomium for his gallery. One is not supposed to know who Aleksandar Gojković is, one just knows the art, the gallery, the list of artists he and Vuk Jovanović now look after, the logical addendum to the group formerly known as The LGB Group. How did the torch get passed onto this man, this volatile, dangerous man, this chameleon? How did I not stop to notice that he was taking over the fruit of a decade's cooperation between international artists spread across a Europe slowly growing over its age-old divisions? I guess I was busy with the degeneracy that started that night with those beers, the assault on my self that has yet to stop completely. With Gojković I only ever talked about the future – he may have hated plans but he wanted to know what the future held, that's why he was always egging me on to make them, he always wanted to know what I had planned. The past was out of bounds with Gojković, he would go a little crazy if we brought it up, tell us to shut the fuck up 'about all of that.'

That night we drank by the canal and then walked back across the city in the direction of my home, drinking in any bar or café that took our fancy. Gojković was living up in the 18th arrondissement with Lubarda in a building filled full of a huge extended Angolan family and where he had already made a number of connections to the world of logistics, drugs. Trifke kept us then as if we were his prize greyhounds, keeping us healthy for the Friday night he would need us at the tracks and where we would help him advance his business.

Gojković was always a pervert, a sort of sexually delinquent adolescent who has no shame when it comes to his dick and what he can do with it and indeed he only got worse the older he became. That night we never once stopped marvelling at the beauty Paris threw up, endless grace and sophistication. Gojković told dirty story after dirty story at each of the counters we stood at, getting distracted when a beautiful girl would walk in or out of the bars, perfumed, clean, sexually vibrant with their own self-assured power handed down to them from a couple of centuries of haute couture grooming.

The closer you go to the centre of Paris the quieter it becomes: starting out in the banlieux the danger to your person is probably highest, going inwards it gets proportionally safer, calmer, until you are by the banks of the river, snoring with boredom. When we got to rue Montmartre, Gojković had worked both of us up to a point where we were desperate for sex but certainly not willing to pay for it. Gojković was against this in general, for reasons as complicated and secret as his own personality, but which had something to do, I always inferred, with his mother and Biljana Pusić. We were in the bar that would become for us a sort of local, where we would meet and start our evenings and so it was here that we met the two girls for the first time. We were sharing the zinc with them, Gojković full of macho energy and me at one end, the two girls demure and giddy at the other. They looked little more than eighteen but that didn't stop Gojković from eyeing them up and when it became clear they were not all that adverse to his smiles, he sidled over to them and offered to get them a drink.

Hélène and Julia.

Their eyes grew wide when they heard we were artists and that we were refugees fleeing the wars that had ravaged and destroyed our country. From the very first instant I saw that they were not normal girls, I don't know what it was but something told me that they wanted probably more from us than we wanted from them, and not in a vulnerable, emotional sense, but rather in a ruthless, covetous manner. Gojković saw this too and it slowed him down, he suddenly wasn't sure what to do, how to proceed. We had a few drinks together and then I got it into my head that we should all go back to Danielle Casanova and have soup as I had made soup the day before, a potato and green bean soup that was creamy and tasty. The girls seemed unsure at first, they wanted to have more fun, tease and be teased, working up to any trip to an apartment. This worked, for both Gojković and I went into that idiotic mode where we gave all the good reasons, backed up by an orchestra of unsaid innuendo, why they should come back to eat green bean soup with us. Managing to finally persuade them, we walked back as a laughing group along rue des Petits-Champs, our crap French echoing down the quiet nighttime street. French was all we ever spoke to the girls, even though it was terrible, a horribly mispronounced, grammarless spew, but they said they liked it; after a short acquaintance, they even told us happily that it turned them on, our foreigner French, our émigré Gallic impersonations.

And Gojković and I were happy with ourselves, we were laughing because we had managed to get these two beautiful, blond girls to accompany us back to my place, and it was still our first night out on the town having drinks! Lubarda had a long speech in Trifke's car when we drove through Germany how we had to forget again the patriarchal ways of home, that we had to learn to treat people differently in France, men and women, if we wanted to enjoy any sort of success. I don't know where he gets this moral and etiquette bullshit, he is always explaining the way of the world to us as if we were his children, perhaps it's because he's a writer but we all listened silently all the same, even Gojković, and what is more even Trifke listened attentively, hoping to pick up some tips on how to deal with his clients. Or victims. So there we were walking with these two girls and we crossed the avenue de l'Opéra and we took in the Garnier and reached the start of rue Danielle Casanova and I went somnolently with my hands looking for the weight of my door keys, my trouser pockets, my jacket pockets. They were not there, I checked again and then again.

Oh shit, I said in Serbian.

What? Gojković switched into his battlefield seriousness, scared by the tone of my voice and the Serbian hissed in the dark of night.

You're not going to believe this: I left my keys at home.

What's going on? asked one of the girls.

You're joking right? Gojković switched back to French: he's having a joke with us girls. He's an idiot.

No, seriously. I don't have my keys.

The two girls looked at each other, unsure what to do, annoyance flickering across their faces. Gojković threw his arms up and rolled his head:

Look again dickhead, look in every pocket.

We had stalled as a group, the laughing was over but I had a strong urge to laugh, because it was true – I had forgotten my keys and it was almost three in the morning. It was so late that I couldn't wake up Ella. The only person with a set of keys was Trifke and he lived by Place de la République.

I'm so sorry, I said to the girls.

But you are just joking, no? Julia said.

He fucking better be, added Gojković.

I'm afraid not.

Let's just break in, Gojković had already started to move on down the street.

No, no, I can't just break fucking in. I'm sorry, but we'd have to break down three doors! I'd be evicted! No, I have to walk over to Place de la République to Trifke's place and get the spare set off him.

Last spring I shouldered both the door in the courtyard and my flat's door after having lost my keys when out drinking. I have woken up poor Ella so many times over the years. Back then though with Gojković, at the beginning, I was more considerate.

He came back shaking his head in anger: he would have hit me I think only the two girls were standing there, demure and confused.

Where do you live? Maybe we could go there for soup?

No, no, they both chimed: we don't bring men back.

Men have to bring us back.

I'm sorry girls, I turned to them and let out the laugh then that had been building up, I'm a real fucking idiot. Sorry. Let me take your number and we can meet up another time.

And they laughed then too. And then we all four of us laughed. Because we all knew that because of my forgetfulness we would miss out on a lot of fun, and you either laugh or cry, as they say. We had enjoyed each other's company up until then, had known we would go all the way together. And then I forgot my keys.

We'll get a taxi, boys.

Here's my number. 'Julia'.

Ring us and we'll see you again.

And with that they had flagged a taxi and were already clipclopping over to it, folding their legs into its back seat, waving briefly at us, standing like a couple of assholes on the corner of Danielle Casanova and the avenue. Gojković turned from the retreating taxi to face me, his face blank and I was ready to have to take him on in a fight, really, because I knew how he could be: he could be a real fucking angry bastard when people got in his way. But no, he just broke up into a huge grin and shook his heavy head.

You absolute fucking cocksucker, he shouted and slapped me on the back before moving off back across the avenue.

I'm sorry, I'm sorry. I ran after him.

I know you're a homo but I'm not – I need a good fuck and they were the girls for it.

Hey, hey, I wanted to fuck 'em too.

Then why did you forget your keys?

I didn't do it on purpose...

And so the argument went on, timeless and always the same: we could have been twelve again and it made us laugh. Why did you forget your keys? Classic Serbian dialectic to greet the dawn. We marched happily up the boulevards: des Italiens, Poissonnière, Bonne Nouvelle, Saint-Denis. We had just passed Porte Saint-Denis and were coming up to rue Sébastopol when two guys approached us, walking fast and shaking their jackets as if they were burning their backs.

Have. You. Cigarette? Asked the taller of the two, a twenty year old with ugly chains around his shoulders and fat silver earrings, speaking like an imbecile because he had heard us speaking Serbian. Stupid foreigners.

No, I said, and I didn't.

Here, Gojković said, offering forth the roll-up he had just finished making.

Then the guy with the metal all over him knocked the cigarette to the ground wordlessly and quickly slapped me on the back of my head, not hard or anything, just a little slap as if in jest. We both just looked at him, his little friend was not up for this and wanted to get away from us, he even tugged at his angry friend's sleeve. Gojković just silently turned around and went to pick up the roll-up on the ground and when he was doing so, slow with tiredness and the residue of our drinking, the metal covered guy daintily kicked Gojković's ass. He had to take a step or two forward but that was it, he had the roll-up in his hand and he turned back to face this random idiot looking for a fight. We both just looked at him as if confused as to what he wanted, his anger so bare and unprovoked that neither of us knew exactly how to react. Of course we could have just beat the living shit out of him but his antics, the little slap and the dainty kick up the bum – they were in fact comic moves, not aggressive ones. We both started to laugh, really bellow out great peals of laughter at this North African man so angry he would start a fight with us. His friend had managed to get him moving and they went on their way, shouting abuse back to us in a *verlan* we could not understand. He was lucky we were spent, all the violence emptied out of us – me because of my battlesore body and Gojković, well I don't know why Gojković didn't take him on. Maybe he was tired of violence too, maybe he had emptied himself of anger for a time, happy to be calm and clearheaded in his new home. Maybe it was because we could pretend we were twelve again, playing out in the fields. Or, maybe it was because of the comic absurdity of it all: we were really down on our luck, what with losing the girls and now this, the kick up the bum. All we needed were a couple of banana skins to round off the night.

***

Biljana came for a big performance as part of Nuit Blanche, an event which always unsettles me a bit. This night in October when everyone piles onto the streets and wanders for hours in great hordes, hunting for culture, art, theatre as if the world has turned to rot and the last reserves were to be found on Paris' streets. She had choreographed a piece that saw her sit in a shop window in the Marais for twelve hours, retro fitting the interior of the vitrine so it looked almost exactly like the kitchen of her childhood home in New Belgrade. Despite my insistence the knobs of the cupboards weren't painted red. Instead they were horrible metal handles. I was really happy for her to stay as I needed her strength and resilience. She dropped her bags in the hallway and wasted no time in giving her opinion of me and my life.

Djordje you're very close to turning out the little drug addict I always worried you would. You look like shit.

It's a state of grace.

Or catatonia.

You've always worried too much about us. I've never been better.

You mean you've never been more successful: better is another thing.

Another thing?

Success Djordje is something other people label for you, feeling better is all your own making.

We would go around and around in circles like this only to end up laughing at ourselves. She took no bullshit from anyone and really seemed to grow only more striking with each passing year. Her rapier sharp intellect grew only sharper just as her black hair seemed to grow only blacker. I had always respected Biljana, and even had been intimidated by her when we had been just kids.

What shall we do? She asked that first night.

I don't know. Aleksandar is going to an opening on rue Louise Weiss.

Where's that?

By the new national library. The 13th.

God, it sounds miles away.

We can take the number 14 line straight there. It's the automated line that's enclosed to prevent suicides.

Don't be so morbid Djordje. But please, let's not meet Aleks. I'm not in the mood for his childishness.

There was a knock at the door and I hopped three light jumps to open it, I remember feeling light, and it was Ella inviting me for dinner as she liked to do and I said she had answered two people's questioning of what to do in one fell swoop.

The three us went down right then and crossed the yard and

entered the boxy little concierge flat. I've always loved that flat because it was there that I started to learn French and the basic philosophy of the country I was to start calling home, at least as I saw it, which is a philosophy of existing in the world as fully as possible, as understanding this existence and the weight it holds for both the individual and the world they move through. I spent many of the first years worrying about us, Miloš and Aleks and I, looking for answers to questions that perhaps were not even there. I would sit in the parlour of Ella's flat and look at all the knickknacks she collected, vases and photoframes that housed countless family portraits, some of them looking so ancient you guessed they weren't from the previous century even but the one before that, and in my looking I'd think how I had studied philosophy in Belgrade with the guidance of Savić and some great teachers, only to abandon it quickly when I spent more and more time at the academy with Aleks. I remember reading about Conceptualism and devouring the work of Joseph Kosuth, Eva Hesse, Ed Ruscha. I think I started to put my 'philosophy' on walls and in galleries because I couldn't bear for it to be private, for it to be kept in the confines of academic essays nobody but my teachers would ever read.

Ella set Biljana to making an entrée and I poured us all gin and tonics. Ella lived on her own since her husband died and her apartment always had people in it, and it was the kind of apartment people immediately feel at home in, feel cosy and warm and in a mood for a gin and tonic.

Biljana, tell me about Djordje when he was just a boy.

There's not much to say Ella, other than I can't get over the fact that I'm here in Paris making hors d'oeuvres for him while he stirs me a gin and tonic!

Biljana always had an eye out for us three when we were in danger of ruining whatever small chances in life we had.

It's always strange to see young kids grow up and become adults, successful adults. It's strange.

C'est la vie.

Biljana laughed at this cliché, not sure if Ella meant it or not.

But tell me about your life Ella.

Life is life, and my life is much like any other.

But are you French, do you come from Paris?

Funny, that's the first thing Djordje asked me.

And what did you tell him?

That I'm from Paris, but my father was Polish.

And your mother?

She was French. From Paris.

And you?

Both my parents were Serbs. Both dead now.

I'm sorry to hear that.

That's life, and Biljana laughed, the first and only time I ever saw her laugh when talking about her parents.

How did your parents meet?

Well it's a long story. My father was a bull headed man by all accounts, I never knew him really. His family went back to Polish aristocracy in Galicia. A town called Buchach.

Bukack?

Buchach. Or Buczacz. Ukrainians, Poles and Jews lived there. The Soviets attacked them all at the start of the war, then the Jews were eliminated when the Nazis arrived, then the Poles were attacked by the Ukranians. Then when the Soviets returned they killed anyone speaking a word about independence.

My god, Biljana managed.

I don't even think I could locate Galicia on a map, I admitted.

My grandparents were killed, probably by Ukranians resentful at their wealth. Which was not much in any case. My father left on foot at the age of nine. I don't know how he managed it, but he left the Soviets behind.

On his own?

No, no, with his sister. They thought to go to Warsaw but that was a ruin, completely, worse than Berlin. So they traipsed across the continent to France where they had an aunt who had gone into exile with the Soviet revolution years before.

And he grew up here?

He travelled a lot, even back to Poland which wasn't easy. Then he met my mother. She's amazing, still going strong. Lives nearby in the apartment I grew up in.

Wow, I'd like to meet her, Biljana said transfixed.

Yes that would be nice. She often comes around for dinner. She likes Djorjde.

And I like her, I laughed, I'm nothing without the strong women in my life and she's definitely one of them.

This was true, this was exactly how I saw it: I had tried too hard to be independent and strong after the army, but Ella and her mother, Elaine or Biljana whenever they visited, they were the balance against Aleks' myopic manliness, and your aloofness. I could even say insensitivity. Ella knew that you loved me less than I loved you, she was the first to spell that out for me once you left Paris that first time.

The funny thing about me I fear is that I still know so little in my hard shell, for all the extremes I've been through, for all I've seen and all I've done. Ella showed me this, this ignorance of the world's width: right from the very beginning she knew more about me than I knew about her and somehow I feel it remained the case – she never really needed to tell me about her life until that night, thanks to the presence of Biljana. And since that time I've talked to her endlessly about Poland and the Poles and their tragic history.

Her strength, like Elaine, lies in the frankness that she views the world, its horror and injustice, the stupidity and weakness of the people in it. She is also patient. I lock myself out all the time and recently have started to knock the doors through with my shoulder, or ring her bell in the dawn, out of my mind on drink or drugs, and she just calmly lets me in without any great fuss. She never really judges me, no matter what I tell her or what I do to upset her. C'est la vie, is all she says. And this platitude seems to sum up her own morality: life is life and there's not much we can do about it. Solace, even grace, can come in the shape of a good hot pot, her meals blow my head with their spiciness but in their own way show how simple the solutions to life's problems can, potentially, be.

Trupa Blokovi, *Kool Kat Walk I* (2004)
16mm b&w, 10′04.
Courtesy Trupa Blokovi and Galerie Pflugfelder, Zurich.

Trupa Blokovi, *Kool Kat Walk II* (2004)
16mm b&w, 10'04.
Courtesy Trupa Blokovi and Galerie Pflugfelder, Zurich

Trupa Blokovi, *Berlin Performance* (2004)
Colour photograph.
Courtesy Trupa Blokovi and Galerie Pflugfelder, Zurich.

Now then, the fate of those who are destined to love each other is often – not always of course, I'm not saying it is inevitable – that they will cause each other pain of a greater magnitude than anybody else they will ever know. Which leads me again to wonder how well I knew you. A question I hate, but one that comes around and around almost daily now it seems. What are facts: you were a dark man, older by a decade, wise, generous, caring. We met each other first through the careful words of letters, an epistolary acquaintance that broached so many topics, so many points of personality that I wonder if we ever got back to all of them once we met in person. My experience in the war for instance, this remained a shadowy part of my make-up, a point that we only broached with the most extreme caution, I because of shame, and you, well I think you were partly jealous, but also partly scared, it was my darkness that threatened to transform the person you had come to know into an agent of greater things, of evil forces, someone you could never leave alone for fear that they will pass the time as a professional assassin passes his, sharpening his knife and plotting his next kill. And also your father, his history and story: you never once told me or anyone else in our group that your father was an important man and that this weighed heavy on both him and his son. In those letters, so carefully crafted and written with great care, both of us expressing ourselves to a stranger in a language not our own, we built up portraits of ourselves but they were oblique, theoretical, somehow dry and impersonal, not in relief. But then once I got to Novi Sad and entered your world in person we had both softened immediately and how good it had felt! It was like a homecoming, a return to a place so obviously mine because of the warmth and naturalness of it, the feeling of being in your company, but which I had never before known. And it never ceased, this getting to know each other, this enjoyment of each other's company, it was endless like the amount of knowledge one can acquire in life, stretching out infinitely.

But something did creep into our relationship. I envision it as a dark sleuth who set himself the mission of testing our love, and in the deep dark of night he set to work. When this started I do not know: 2001 maybe, early in the year when we were housebound due to the cold and waiting to organise more shows, when we had nothing to do but stretch out in each other's presence now that we had it, now that we knew each other – the testing time was over, we had become fully operational. Looking back now from this barren present I complain so much about, I think that from that cold winter onwards I realised that you did not need me. I always want to include people, include the disadvantaged, the marginalised, the lonely. I want to take people in from the cold and let them feel warmth. That's why I always went in for the sex, why I paraded around the streets of Paris in search of those whose eyes betrayed them as artists of an everyday that at first appears to be just another unit of morning, noon and night, but which can hold so often nothing more than pain and grief. You never had this, at least not on the surface where I would be able to read it: this empathy, if it existed, was deep down in some part of you I never got to see. It is the same old story: you love a person and in your love is the seed of the thing that allows you to abuse them and their love; you start to take them for granted. We never pretended to read each other completely, I with my war wounds and you with your Hungarian past I knew nothing about, but we did get to know the infinitesimal ticks and habits of each other, and we let them grow out of proportion in our minds: the annoying way the other left milk out to turn sour in the heat, the wet puddles in the bathroom after you shower, the disgusting click of your tongue as you masticate in your sleep. You moved in with me in Danielle Casanova casually, piecemeal over time, much the same way as you would move out of our Parisian network in 2006, and is it not ironic how the two of us, great proponents of the everyday and how it is an art form in itself, how it makes the world we live in endless with grace and creative potential, that we of all people should have allowed the everyday and its ticks and currents to annoy us, to come between us and lead us to quarrel, give the dark sleuth the clues he needs to do his dirty work.

You did not like this. A dark mood would descend on you and your face would grow even darker than it normally was, you would declare sombrely that you had no room for hypocrisy in your life.

You had learned to hate if from your proximity to the cutthroat world of politics, from your father. Every time I said something to you about the apartment, some little thing like using the shower curtain or taking the rubbish out as soon as the bag was full, your mood changed and you would say vehemently for me not to be so pertinacious and we would both be silently angry and depressed then, hearing ourselves go on like this was terrible and not at all what we wanted to be like together. You talked about moving out but we knew it would hardly happen: the apartment was so well situated, and quite large with its three rooms and Trifke was not interested in doing any more favours for us.

So when the big argument came neither of us was surprised but perhaps the intensity caused not a little shock. Out of nowhere one day we went crazy at each other and from deep down somewhere we grabbed insults we never knew we had, things so terrible I wondered when I had formulated them or did they just arise in the moment? I called you an Ugric bastard faggot who had no manners, no class! That would make us laugh later upon reconciliation but at the time it just let you fire your guns. Because of course, I was the one with no manners, I was just a son of lowly, ignorant workers, growing up in some socialist shithole in a country bent on war and hate, who had killed and raped – this is what you shouted at me: 'You dirty fucking rapist, you dirty fucking killer' – and who had pretended with the greediness of my kind to wipe myself clean with the hubris of art, an art I didn't even believe in because of my mania about how fucking clean the bathroom sink is! How did this equate with my glorious bullshit words championing the dirty kitchen textures of Jan Offe's installations? You fucking hypocrite! And we enjoyed this, as people often do in fights of this kind, they are a sort of purging of the entwined soul – of course it is nice to be in love, to be together and live as one, but each of us is born alone and the matrix that makes up an individual gets grumpy with too much communion, too much meshing of the self. The slate needs to be cleaned every once in a while. We roared at each other for what seemed like hours, our shouts louder than the Indian chefs in Fuxia's kitchens, so loud Ella came out into the courtyard to cock her head and listen to see if she should be really concerned. We screamed, we cursed, we let all the pent up grievances of the five years we had known each other explode in a volcano of invective. And as you packed a suitcase with your clothes I stood over you shouting, my voice trembling with the realisation that you were leaving but on a roll that neither you nor I could stop. Well you could stop it, you could leave and that is what you decided was the best course to take; you didn't want to become an old queen living with your manic, obsessive-compulsive boyfriend like a couple of pathetic bitches for the rest of your life, oh no, you would travel, you would be free again. Fuck off then, I shouted, get the fuck out of my life. And you did. Out you went through the door and you closed it gently, and I was left in the studio room with my arms on my hips and tears threatening but I was still too angry for tears so I just went to the window, shaking and watched you pass out through the courtyard and I looked up to the sky and felt, I was glad to realise, the slightest stirring of relief.

I don't know if this episode, dramatic as it was and which constituted a new development in our relationship, was part of a course that ended with your death. I tell myself it is not. Well I tell myself I don't know how the end was reached, why you died. That is the problem. Why? It is a mystery, but at the same time there is no fucking mystery about it, it is the opposite of a mystery, it is clear and self-evident. This fight we got over, of course we did, it was even healthy. By the time we went to Venice three months later we were talking again, and spent most of the biennale in each other's company, and indeed the time apart led to a more intense time together. You did not move back in and that was also healthy to begin with, but I wonder now if you had stayed with me in rue Danielle Casanova would I have been able to observe you more closely, to see how close to the edge you were going, how you danced like a lunatic on the precipice and that nobody saw this dance, so self absorbed had we all become. Perhaps, but it is hard to know: people living together can have greater secrets between each other than those who live far apart, indeed the proximity can lead to a virtuoso performance in concealment.

I never told you my secret because it wasn't mine to share: it belonged to Aleksandar and Miloš equally, we were all culpable.

So many things I never told you, never having had the opportunity or the courage. That I always thought you were younger than me for instance, that your body put mine to shame with its youthful litheness, that I was jealous of your life in Hungary that you told me nothing about. I never showed you that I kept myself open to others not just to network and make our circle grow. I wanted to please you by finding new talent. You never understood that I would fuck anything if I thought it would make them happy, girl or boy. Other people have always given me my cue, most of all you, and now that you're gone I don't know how I can go on. I never told you how the three moles at the base of your back, which perhaps you had never seen, reminded me of the three stars that made up the belt of Orion in the night sky. Most of all I never told you my greatest secret, my collusion. That's the word. For the war, for my time with you, everything: collusion. I had the Union of Pioneers, Marama and Titovka, but it just as easily could have been incense and prayerbooks and the church that the kids go in so readily for these days. Yes and we had the army of Yugoslavia in its dying days. Republika Srpska. If I've left Dada, Zenitism, Nouveau Réalisme behind in these notes, it's because I decided to try to write about the readymades of my life, the acts of collusion, of baseness, the secrets of war that have determined everything but which I've only to date passed over in silence.

***

When I woke up the other morning in Benoit's apartment in Nation the only other body awake was Hélène, the taller one, all the others were still passed out all over the bedroom, naked and sleeping, and in the morning, still and calm, they all seemed vulnerable, terribly open to attack due to the slight curls of the hands, their bent knees rising toward their stomachs. We nodded to each other from across the width of the bed; she smiled at my morning erection but I ignored her. I moved my mouth, forced it open, pursed my lips, swallowed several times, exercising it awake and free of all the fluids from the night before. I felt alone, as I always do. The girl with her smirk and dirty blonde hair only deepened this feeling. She was propped up with several pillows, the white sheets brought up to her chin, an arm appearing from her side to play with the wisps of her fringe. After some time like this, the only sounds those of a hum coming from somewhere in the building's walls and the heavy breathing of everyone asleep, she jumped out of the bed and walked out of the room: I followed her naked body, compact and beautiful, and listened as she went to the toilet, urinated, and came back into the bedroom, ignoring me while she went through Benoit's wardrobes until she found a dressing gown, obviously a girl's robe made from a dark, shiny ersatz silk. She slipped into this, leaving it open to hang loose from her thin frame, and turned and left the room, nodding at me boyishly in an early morning, wordless invitation.

In the kitchen she was cleaning out the coffee pot when I entered.

Good morning Georgie, how are you today?

Oh, you know, the same as ever.

Fun last night, no?

Oh, you know, the same as ever.

She looked at me out of the corner of her eyes, fixing me with a stern grin as if to tell me to stop the playacting and talk normally. I sat down at the little table and looked at her from behind as she busied herself between the empty bottles and champagne flutes, piss-yellow liquid clinging to one or two of them, she got the coffee out of the fridge, tapping out a small heap of the brown powder into the glass pot, wiping the dirty surfaces clean, rinsing out the dishcloth, fetching bowls, sugar, teaspoons. When the water came to the boil she poured it into the cafetiere in a big rush of steaming water, some of it escaping and hitting her exposed flesh somewhere for she let out a cat's *Merde!* Then she stirred the contents once, twice, put the plunger on top and set the pot down in between the two of us. We sat watching it swirl and settle and after a minute or two of silence she finally plunged as if unable to sit and do nothing for any longer.

We smoked in silence.

Then she started to talk, about this and that, and I listened: I never really ask them questions, the two girls, because their answers always scare me, or rather they always set me thinking in lines of thought that end up in shadowy, inexplicable paranoia. I think it's because I never know who it is exactly I am talking to, Hélène or Julia, Seita or Saffa, innocence or experience. She started to talk and I listened, letting out grunts of approval or disapproval as I knew she liked: both of them love men grunting, both of them hate men shrugging their shoulders. Strange the things we know about people. She was talking about her exercise regime, how she kept fit and her ass tight.

Everyday Georgie, I go to the swimming pool, the one behind the Panthéon. I go there because first I jog across the river and up the hill and then swim and there are all the students you know, and I like them, I like looking at them because so much is going on in their heads and their lives lived in the real world are so small I wonder what it would be like to be one of them. And she giggled then, talking about how she dreamed about fucking some young boy straight out of the Lycée Henri-IV in the changing rooms and opening up his world like only dreams could. Then she spoke of one morning during the last week: I go very, very early, she said, because I like to have the pool to myself when there is nobody else in it, this only lasts maybe five or ten minutes or so, depends on the morning, but every day I jog over there and I'm waiting at the door when they open at seven. That's very early, no? And it's always me and another woman, a large, middle aged, or even I could call her old, yes she is old, who I think is a poet, I saw her reading in Colette's when I passed on Nuit Blanche. Anyway, she just seems like a poet too, you know how they seem? It's always just me and her for half an hour or so, though it depends, and anyway, what I'm getting at is that this week, it was very funny, both of us were there swimming, the whole big pool to ourselves, and we were both doing the back stroke. Here Hélène leaned her head back and threw her arms above and around her body, her chest open and exposed and she laughed before going on: and do you know what happened Georgie? We both managed to swim straight into each other! To collide in this big empty pool that we had all to ourselves, we swam blind and bam, we hit each other. Not badly or anything, I don't think we were even all that surprised. We just clung to each other, this older woman and me, and laughed and said 'excuse me' and then went on swimming. So funny and strange.

Suddenly I had to ask her: Why do you have this sex with all of us? I asked her when she had paused to smoke and drink her coffee. Why do you go to these sex parties with Julia and lose yourself with us old ones?

She looked quizzically at me through her cigarette smoke, as if puzzled not by my question, but by my very being there.

Ehmmm, she said cocking her head to the side, because it's all going to end Georgie, you know that. With Julia? The same reason you and your love-of-your-life, dark mister Warmann come: to lose myself through the body of another.

We blinked at each other; she was challenging me.

Then with the morning light and the coffee and the intimacy that sleeping naked bodies in the other room created I rose to her challenge:

Tell me the truth Hélène. No bullshit. I need to know what we're all doing.

Me? I fuck because it makes me the same as every other human being in the history of humanity. I fuck like this, and she swept the kitchen then with her arm, cigarette ash falling to the floor, because it promises to make my life better than most. I don't want to spend my time now being conservative with life. My future after all…my future. Here she paused and drank from her cup. Some day I am going to grow up, some day I will get a job in a big architecture firm, get married, buy a house, have a kid or three, watch 14.5 hours of TV per week. Allow myself to grow old. To grow frustrated. Is this not reason enough?

***

We're falling
Central planning
~~War slogans~~
The time
has come
to admit
try to tell
a story.
No.

George Cup. No police have come knocking.[27] Some unpleasant speculation in the daily newspapers, then the same hagiography from some friends in the art press. Nobody really cares, not even my friends can mention your name. To tell the story as a lover's feud?

Shame is all my day has to offer when I awaken and I don't know if I can stand its undulating, never-ending hours any more. I should fill them blackmailing Gojković for the secret to not caring anymore, for the secret recipe he has concocted in order to forget completely.

Shame? That lies somewhere else: in self-obliteration; it is also everywhere.

Everywhere and nowhere.

For nothing, a long rummage in a shop where the shopkeeper smells only of sweat, he sells junk, rubbish, plates and glasses and some coats, vinyl records, pots, pans, toasters, kettles, posters, clothes hooks, plugs, electrical items, all sorts of crap that nobody wants but never throws out properly. Things that end up in such a place as this, the proprietor stinking of sweat and black tobacco. Filled to the ceiling, a plenum of everyday goods, second hand.

There's a swimming pool somewhere with two women in it, each a reflection of the other and they are doing the backstroke, one rushing into her past and the other into her future. And it follows, naturally, that they should only go closer and closer together, as if

---

[27] Refers to the artist couple George Cup and Steve Elliott, the former being convicted in 1986 for the murder of Elliot, his romantic and artistic partner, in New York. (Editor)

attracted to each other, a crease in the pool where the page is being turned and they move into each other. They go home. Where is my home of childhood gone? Who is turning my page?

For a morning sky cut with the flight of an unknown bird, a bird simply, when innocence stands face to face with experience. When god becomes man and man becomes animal. When shame appears.

Let us
say: now
for then.
Let me
say: I
am go
ing to
die soon
and that
is the
way of
it, and
that is
okay
by me.

I won't
go home
again,
be it said,
I won't
go home
again,
across
mountain
snow or
riverbed.
The show
is over.

Deluge
of rain
& snow.
Seasons
change.
Like the
size of
cocks
from one
instant
to the next.
Blowjobs.
I like
blowjobs.
Tell your
self this:
I like
giving
blowjobs
and I like
the end
of things
because
ends stop
the deluge.

TO WARMANN

I knew you were back in town and that there was a possibility you would come out to play. I also knew it was cold, a biting, raw cold like the type I remember from home, a chill that would disinfect you of any unclean warmth lingering on your bones, polish your insides until you felt them rawly, rattling around on your hurried way through the streets. And it made me want you, to have you by my side ready to laugh at my jokes or me to laugh at yours, for the easiness of us together but I think I knew that it was not to be, that when you left the year before you had left not just in person but in spirit, that you were no longer connected to the way we thought, to the way we acted in the world. And because you just slipped away, stepped out of our network like a lover does from bed in the early morning trying not to rouse those sleeping, nothing would stay together much longer. For two years now I have been chasing release, drinking more and more and acting more and more like an absolute fetishist, which I know in my soul I am not: I was just lost, I am just lost, and through this damned city and its streets I chase a distraction which is total, a distraction of both mind and body. And I can find it, it's right there, night on night. Your slow desertion was the starting point for this mission and your death its axis, the world I have rotated through during the last year more intense than is bearable, like the cold of that ill-fated weekend, an endurance test sent from gods that aren't even generous enough to exist. Attempting to write a history of The LGB Group was the last blow on the fire to rekindle it for warmth – and look how spectacularly the fire has gone out! Our history together and what I make of it: what a sorry tale we have all become, I go on writing it feels, just in order to find a way out, an end, an explicit.

And that weekend when you returned played itself out without me, I was there alright but so empty in my soul and full of drink and amphetamines in my body that I was a blind spectator, an empty participant. Julia of all people told me you were visiting from Vojvodina and it hurt, it really cut the skin and went deep, that you would come to Paris and I wouldn't know anything about it, but only hear about it second hand from some schizophrenic nymphomaniac. Ella invited me for dinner with her mother which was a rather polite beginning to the proceedings; I remember she cooked a chilli-con-carne, a really hot pot that blew our heads off but did us good against the cold. The dinner put me in a mood close to one that wasn't black, somewhere above ground at least, which is what I needed after hearing you were in town. At the time I was sleeping through the daylight hours, only waking up in the evening, having coffee, strong and black and lots of it, about the time people were going home from work. I think the lack of photons affected me, of course it would, seeing nothing but the Paris night is enough to drive one crazy after a couple of weeks, or even a couple of days come to think of it. So the chilli-con-carne was a hot breakfast and after dinner ended I went to the Franprix in the square and bought a bottle of red wine and brandy to take back to the flat. I sat listening to Miles Davis records waiting for Lubarda to call around, which he did presently, accompanied by Gojković, which was a surprise but which was also nice, to see them together again like the old friends that they were. And they didn't mention you even though they must have known you were in town, maybe they had even met you I contemplated. They had talked to the girls the night before at Gojković's place where they had all snorted a couple grammes of coke dancing to Turbo folk, a scene the idea of which depressed me greatly. Lubarda caught my eye, and silently apologised. We went about getting hammered and talked about frivolous, pointless stuff and I was on the point of making excuses and going back to bed but Gojković ordered up a huge take-out of sushi from the Japanese restaurant below and it revived me, its coolness brought me out of my lethargy and I managed to get us talking about things that still seemed to make sense, to have a weight in the world.

Our talk may have grown heavier but we were drinking to lose weight, to rise ourselves up above the earth. Gojković went out and brought back very expensive bottles of wine from the little wine shop next to Fuxia – he had by then entered the realm of money, by-passing the realm of taste, and demanded the quality that only money can afford. Such perfect material for the trappings of the nouveau riche, Gojković, he is the best example of a peasant parvenu I have ever known, only of course his origins are not obscure to me: I know how he got to be where he is today. This should make me only more impressed but it doesn't, it just makes me sad. Paris is a city that rewards handsomely the successful parvenu – indeed everyone who arrives in Paris is nothing more than a peasant parvenu as far as the city is concerned. A peasant from the campagne trying to fit in as inconspicuously as they can. It had been a long time since I was face to face with Gojković like this, drinking together, acting as if equals, as if brothers and in my very thinking of this I knew that somewhere along the way we had gone so far in opposite directions there was no coming back.

So you're going to write a book about us? Gojković asked, opening his fifty euro bottle of wine.

I guess I am. Everyone in the whole of fucking Europe seems to know I plan to write a book. I guess I must thank you for that, Miloš?

People ask me what the great Bojić is doing, Lubarda put up his hands in defence, and I have an obligation to tell them.

But tell me, Gojković said seriously, how are you going to write about us exactly?

I don't know, I don't know, and I meant it for I had no idea how to proceed. It seems somehow terminal, you know, to write a history of the group as if we were already dead.

Perhaps we are, Lubarda said mirthlessly to himself.

But since the shows in Novi Sad and Dublin things have, how should I say, splintered somehow? And it seems like a good way of trying to figure out where we have come to. But I don't know.

So would it be about, like, how it started, us three running around New Belgrade with our trousers falling down or would it be about the big group shows, the dynamic together, or what?

Gojković wanted to know what I would and would not say about him, personally.

I would like to write about LGB objectively I guess, I was even thinking about making a big joke out of it and write a sort of fake history or a history so sterile and dry that it puts us into the museum.

I like that idea, said Gojković flatly, I don't want you writing about the war.

This request stopped all three of us and we looked at each other without looking, we felt each other and what we were thinking respectively.

Nobody mentioned anything about the war, I said simply.

I know, he said sounding angry despite himself, I was here in the room just like you were: I just don't want you writing some long tear-jerking saga about me and my personal life. In fact, if you could hold back any words on me, my art, I'd be most obliged.

Ah Gojković, take it easy. Lubarda didn't go any further, just sat back in his chair and stared at the two of us.

I have barely begun, I protested, so don't worry I haven't mentioned your name yet. I don't even know if I'll go on. It's too hard, it reduces things down and makes them seem futile.

Ah, futility!

And with this Gojković visibly lightened and knocked back his glass and then emptied the bottle into our three glasses. The conversation was over for the time being and I was glad as my routine apathy toward the world reappeared with force just then in the face of this bickering, and I swallowed my wine greedily, cutting the anchors, setting myself forth. And we did what we did best: the three of us stopped being artists, stopped being professionals and became old friends again, friends who had grown up together and who knew each other's darkest, dirtiest secrets, who knew jokes that cut right through our tastes and humoured us directly. We became bored men on a Friday night.

We left my flat when the wine was finished and wrapped ourselves up and trudged out into the city night and we walked to rue Montmartre but the quiet street was closed up so we walked on to Saint Denis where a favourite bar of Gojković's sat open all night, the very worst of the city passing through its doors. This was all part of the routine: on Monday morning I would awake early after twenty or so hours of sound sleep. Coffee, walk, reading. I might visit libraries across town, see exhibitions, meet the occasional acquaintance, though admittedly less and less. Then I would spend hours on the Internet, emailing back and forth with whoever, pretending to organise shows with artists whose work I no longer really knew or understood very much. I would buy in bottles of wine, boxes of the stuff and go around my flat in a drunken daze, listening to records, rereading books. I would go to bed later and later each day of the week so that by Thursday I was having my morning coffee in the afternoon, by Friday at dinnertime, Saturday at the zinc on rue Montmartre, ten or eleven o clock at night. And this cycle works well once you are in it, trust me, it may even work better than a nine-to-five, five-days-a-week routine. My body wants something, I let it have it; it wants something more and more and I stay around until it gets its fill. Of course it is full of loneliness and ennui, and the days are soaked in an emptiness the type of which I can only define by how out of it I get, how strange my sexual desires are, how late I brew my coffee. It had been like that for a year since you moved, and was a routine so set I hardly noticed it, the way all good routines should be noticed that is – not at all. It was only ever broken by the seasons or by Trifke needing me to do some work for him, although even he soon disappeared and moved his operations from Paris to Oslo, or indeed by you, when you would reappear in Paris on business and we got to meet each other.

And that weekend I did not know if we would get to meet each other and that was painful, or at least now I think it was painful but at the time, when we reached the nightclub on rue Saint-Denis, I think I felt more trepidation, the familiar emptiness about to be overtaken by sex and drugs. I had only ever been to that club drunk and busy getting drunker and that night was no different.

Let's get ourselves some fun, Gojković declared at the bar.

We set about drinking but soon I was in the need to come up on some amphetamines, whatever Gojković had to give me. I hate that club because it's always the same, guys blowing shit loads of money on drinks and some whores hanging around the fringes to deal the final blow just when these guys' dicks are too limp with booze for it to be worthwhile to anyone, man or whore. The only thing it had going was that it wasn't chauvinistically hetero, it wasn't really anything and this was its saving grace, this shitty sleaze-infested club, it didn't really care about anything: fashion, orientation, wealth. I just know that when I am cocooned in its whorehouse-red, I'm on to a late one. That night I saw that Gojković was out for violence, loosened from his good behaviour when he was in the suit of the up-and-coming gallerist, when all the blind angst of the world, the madness of the soldier, was present in him. We were talking to two huge men who both wore fat turtlenecks that their squat heads exploded out of, their pates bald and shining under the cerise lighting. We were all of us telling dirty jokes, Gojković trying to impart to these two men something of the kind of world we moved in, a world where sex was carried out in a group and champagne was used as lubricant. Lubarda rang the girls to see if they were out and up for meeting but they weren't and how I wish they had been out somewhere so we could have gone and fucked each other that night and not the night after. Because the night after you would be there and you'd go too far. Fate has its way. The bar area was quite small and our group stood just back from it, up against a railing that separated the sunken little dancefloor and the few seats and tables by the way out. Mirrors at the back of the room gave the sense of the shithole being three times the size of its actual boxy layout. All the time there was this little moustachioed man bumping into us, his hair long and curly down past his shoulders, his glasses little round steel frames that looked cold surrounded by all the red of the club. I think I recognised him from the Connetable, or from some other all night watering hole; a jumpy character who never stopped going on about all the injustice the world was levelling at him. Not in a general, abstract way, those people stay quiet at the bar with their hard lives sealed up tightly in the drink in front of them; no, this guy talked about current injustice, as in the mugging he had suffered earlier in the day or the short change the waitress did him out of so that he was always pointing his finger. I didn't notice it but Gojković and the two big guys were getting a bit pissed with this crazy guy, and then of course he knocks into them and Gojković gives him an innocent shove, resulting in half the man's drink sloshing onto his tatty blue shirt. This sets him going, over and back between the bored waitress and Gojković, manic and indignant, wanting another drink, either paid for by Gojković or on the house. With Gojković he pointed his finger at the bar, telling him in his garbled language to go over and buy him a drink, then with the waitress he pointed his finger to Gojković telling her he is paying for the next drink. The place fills up and Lubarda and I try chatting up some people and the crazy guy fades into the background. Then out of nowhere, when the place is really quite full, bodies packed shoulder to shoulder around the little bar, the crazy gives one of the two big guys a kick or something and he lets out a girlish little whimper, while his mate decides that's enough and pushes the crazy guy backwards and of course he manages to fall, practically jumps to the ground and I just see the angrier of the two guy's half empty bottle of Kronenbourg 1664 coming down on his nest of curly hair and beer foam and blood shooting up everywhere and the guy has his hands over his head and Gojković cannot help himself and lands a kick straight into the guy's stomach and everything tilts up and the Algerian bouncers are on the two big guys as well as some customers, a mass of bodies going to earth. I just lightly tap Gojković on the shoulder as if warning him of the impending collapse and all three of us, Lubarda, Gojković and I step back and watch as the little floorspace of the bar clears and the two guys, wide and small are held to the ground and told to calm down, while the crazy guy is helped to his feet and told politely to shut the fuck up. I cannot really see properly in the red light, everything turns and I realise I am completely drunk, to the point where I can barely talk. All these men move out of my sight, away towards the door to disperse into the dawn before the police come and we all three just laugh and I'm happy because Gojković is happy because he got to kick a crazy man prone on the floor defenceless and this is the type of men we have become. And I'm ready for one of the whores to rob me of all the money left to me, money that is really Gojković's money, but they don't materialise.

Things just intensify because this is the routine: it is just after lunchtime for us night-people and the floor has been cleaned and the music is turned up and more people pile into the tiny club, the sleaziest club on the sleaziest street and Gojković treats us to the house's best vin mousseux and on it goes and suddenly we're back in the city fresh from Mitteleuropa and I have just been beaten up by Haider's friends and Gojković and Trifke have just masterminded our refugee status, our crossing of the border and we're angry and happy depending on who you are and what you can do for us. Gojković does the talking, fast and smooth and just a little charming, I stand tall and intimidate or encourage, depending on who you are and what you can do for us, and Lubarda hangs back silent, offering a seriousness and intelligence that makes you believe in these strange Serbs running from the wars, from themselves, into the arms of the West, of Paris, already successful in what they do but desperately in need to prove it to you. This is how we took Paris, this is how Gojković first sold his overpriced 'Eastern European art', how we fucked our way through countless beautiful bodies, kept Trifke on our side and him keeping us well kept and well fed, how we got our work into countless galleries and institutions, how we made a name for ourselves that people could recognise, The LGB Group, and how good, talented people lent themselves to it, how it became more than just this smooth, scary and silent triumvirate of ex-soldiers.

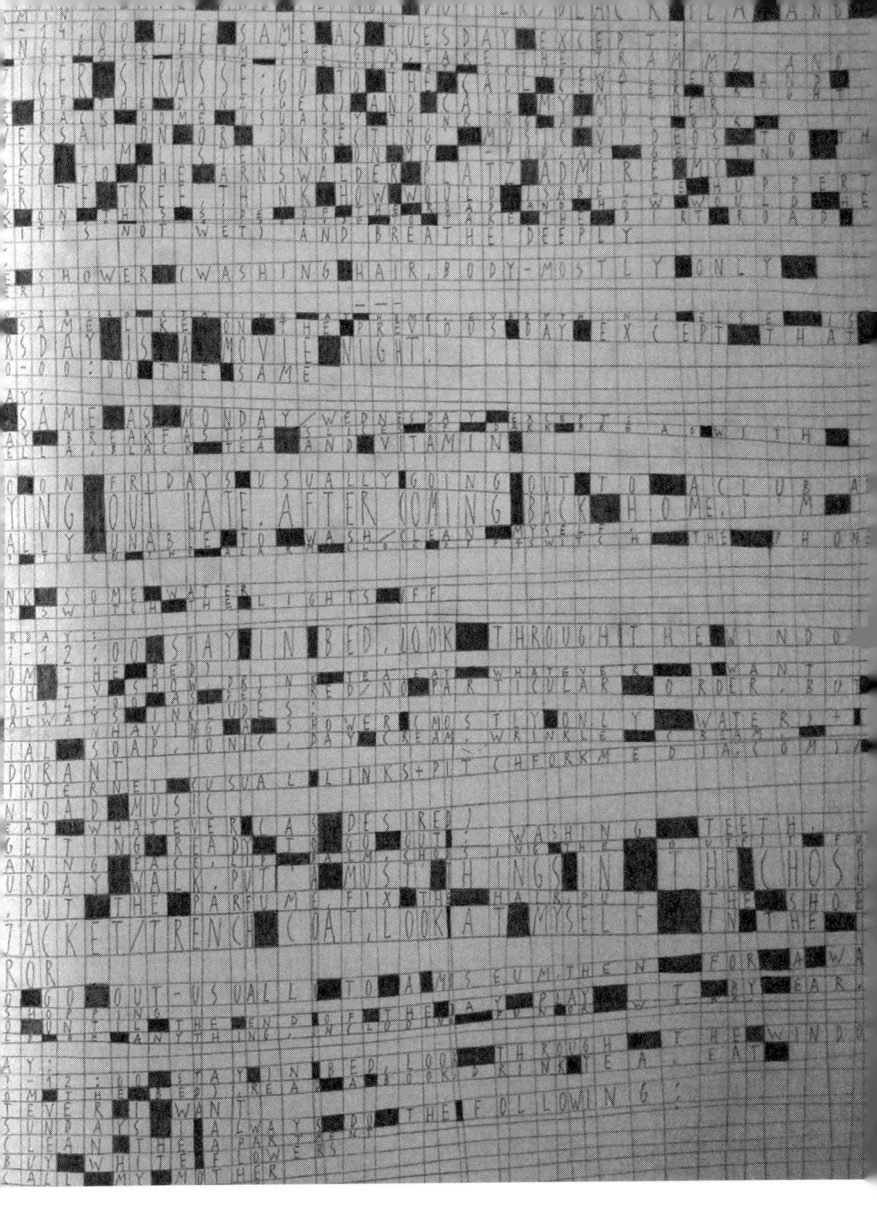

Djordje Bojić, *Ideal Week III* (2007)
Pencil, egg tempera and ink on paper, 28 × 35.5 cm
Courtesy the estate of Djordje Bojić and Galerie Gojković.

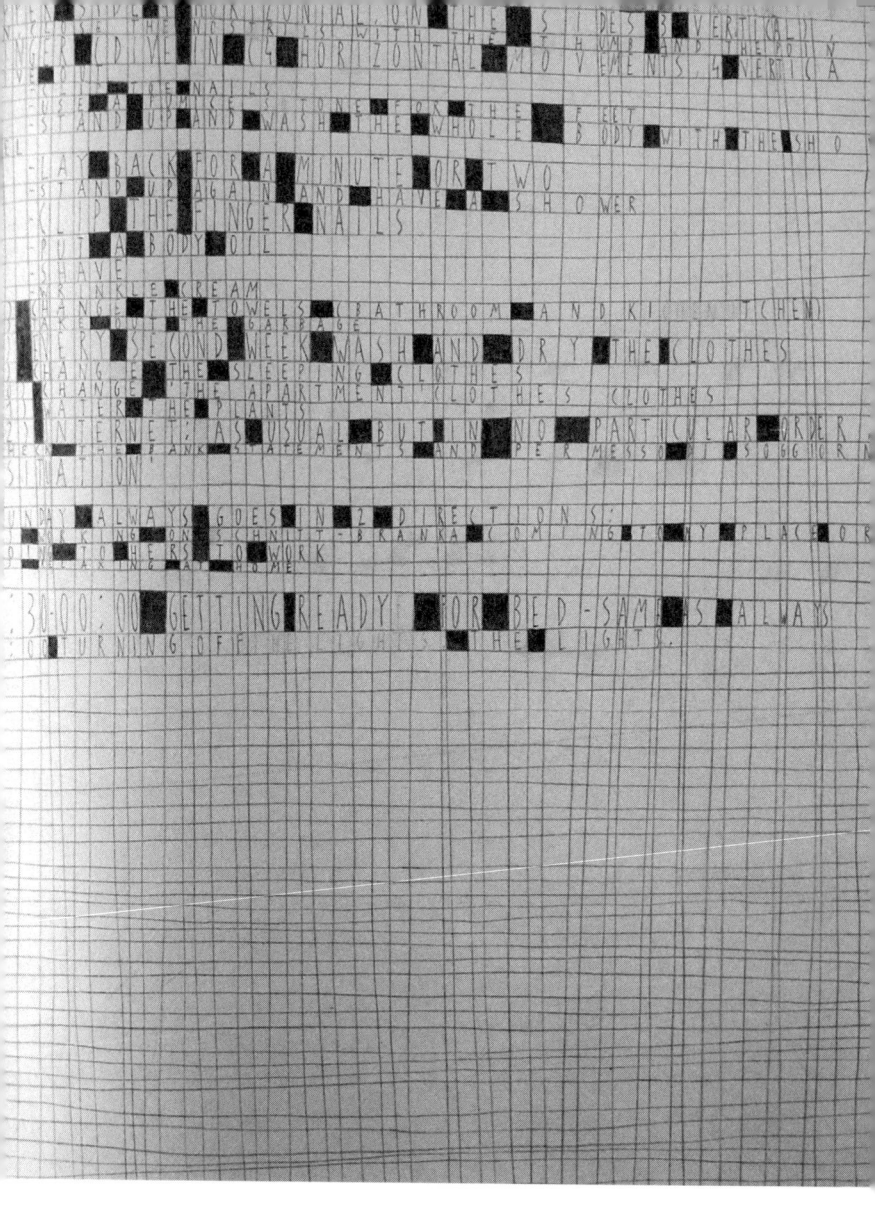

Djordje Bojić, *Ideal Week IV* (2007)
Pencil, egg tempera and ink on paper, 28×35.5 cm
Courtesy the estate of Djordje Bojić and Galerie Gojković.

Getting mugged seemed to be a common occurrence in Belgrade, I think it was all the boredom, loosened from the fact of frontlines not 100 kilometres away in a war that did not officially exist, where the kids could do as they pleased when their parents felt it permissible to delude themselves so much. But then, getting mugged is common everywhere, at all times, at least it is once you get mugged yourself and put up with the randomness of it, the sudden fuck with your sense of security, right there in front of your eyes. Lubarda seemed to lose his wallet to thugs perennially, once a month or so it seemed. But Gojković, I've never heard of him being mugged. What crimes are perpetuated on the criminal? That's what I would like to know.

Violence follows me around, so I know that getting mugged can happen anywhere: I'm the living proof that if you are open enough to it, haunting the ugliest streets of Europe's cities during those hours when soulless men are the sole occupants of these ill-bred thoroughfares, they'll come right up to you, at a rush and a push and a shove and with pieces of cheap abuse barely thought about but just uttered, instinctively. Boulevard des Italiens, three or four in the morning and two dark men come running at me, all teeth and hate in their eyes – assailants are always more aggressive than you, they must be for their attack to succeed, their hate stronger than yours, their ruthlessness having no bounds. Two motherfuckers trying to get what I don't have and sheer rage overtakes me and strength comes from where I don't know but I crash their heads together right in the instant when all I want to do is sit down with them and share a drink and our cigarettes and share our war stories, our wounds left from mothers who loved us too much, our regret at hating the world so much that we no longer respect it: all I want to do is put my arms around them and laugh at the natives, the bourgeois all around us, the soft ones – but no I knock the wind out of them and knock them about, cut the chase right out of them and they know they have lost and so they run off, quick only as thieves can be when caught in the act. These people who could understand me and my past, my trouble with the world, they flee and do not look back. In self-preservation I find only a sort of thug's vulgarity. And this has happened so many times now, in one iteration or another, that I am losing heart in petty crime, my possible brothers fear me and I fear myself, I fear self-protection because it is just one more barrier between the world and I and with this I know I'm in trouble: I am a man running out of options.

Djordje Bojić, *Prazno V* (2006)
Pencil on paper, 28 × 35.5 cm.
Courtesy the estate of Djordje Bojić and Galerie Gojković.

But we wake up, head down in the pillow, trousers still on, half dressed, and that is exactly our natural state, us trio of emptiness with nothing left to prove. This is just how I woke up, like so many other mornings, on that fateful, arctic cold Saturday. It was already threatening darkness and I lurched out of bed, telling myself that I had to rehabilitate myself for you because you had, after everything, rang me around the time the crazy guy got beaten up, and we had agreed to meet the next night. I searched for my clothes in the half-light and put them on, my head feeling sore and stiff, the dark carmine of the bar coming back to taint my day, and out I went into the cold to the little market on the Place Marché Saint-Honoré. I never stopped being impressed by the tall, monumental glass building they placed in the middle of this little Parisian square, like a postmodern effort of a market hall it towered up narrowly between the old Hausmannian buildings around it, selling only furniture and expensive cars and nothing really at all. Everyday I walked around its gleaming reflective windows and searched for my reflection in this tower of glass but all I saw were cars, furniture, offices, all anonymous and useless to me. Out on the street in front of this evanescent glass was a diluted market a couple of times a week, there not being all that many residents living in the area. Jean-Pierre was a fishmonger and something of a friend, he came to sell his wares with his daughter (secretly, I wanted to marry this girl who reminded me a little of Jovana and live the quiet life with her ever after) and I would religiously go and buy fish from him and hang around and talk. In New Belgrade I never missed the market either, I would go with my mother and we would buy almost everything there, vegetables, cheese, bread, meat, and we would pass and say hello to everyone we knew in the entire world because that was back when people only concerned themselves with living, eating, saying a friendly hello. Before things changed. But I can hope it still goes on and I can smell that market right now if I try, can see its colours, hear its bustle, but this little market here in Paris is what I am left with, barely any sense of community and no faces to say hello and goodbye. Save Jean-Pierre and his beautiful daughter.

George, you look like shit, look like you just woke up!

I have.

Oh la la, George, some day you'll sleep all day.

That's the idea.

He shook his head because for him the day started at five or six in the morning, just about when I was going to bed: we were each other's antipodes and our exchange at his little trailer stall, the equator.

Give me the cheapest, best piece of Atlantic animal you have.

I have some salmon left mon vieux. How about that?

I didn't stay long at all, just bought the salmon that I could not afford and went back to my flat, put it in the fridge and went and got back into bed still fully clothed, my teeth chattering right up to the point where I fell back asleep. By the time I awoke I was shivering, this time with the familiar need of a cigarette and a drink: lucky for me it was aperitif hour! I showered and brewed some strong coffee and tried generally to clear my head. Then I put on a DVD, what I can't remember, and poured myself a large brandy, or in fact if I remember correctly I just drank from the bottle. Then I fried the fish and ate it without any ceremony. I was nervous about meeting you, our conversation the night before, or rather that morning, just after the altercation with the two huge guys, must have taken place toward six in the morning and I had been in no fit state to talk, but you were clear I could recall and seemed to have yourself tied together in a sober knot. And I was very happy when you said you would give me a call the next night, it was a free pass and I could go home on it, and that is just what I did: I walked through the silent streets just waking up and I was happy.

Now it was getting on time to go back out into the city and my blood was moving again. Protection against the cold. The fact that it had not managed to get above zero during the daylight hours should have warned me, like the end of the things in mythology when birds disappear and their singing stops or the sun goes dark and dogs run wild.

What a strange night it quickly became! The strangest of them all, no doubt, but also uniform and much like all the rest. It was strange that Gojković should appear again but I thought nothing of it, I guess he just wanted to fuck seeing as we all got too limp with drink and drugs the night before and his moment of violence probably released too many endorphins that were still flowing inside him and which saw their endpoint in orgasm. Of course he also wanted more information from me and he got it: he knew I wouldn't be shocked to discover that he would use violence against me and my book if it in any way tarnished his growing name. I knew what he was capable of more than he himself did. But I brushed it aside, I no longer cared. Because I also knew that I was going to make you an offer, that I was going to suggest leaving Paris and returning to Budapest with you to start over. I had talked to Guido and there was a curatorial position open for me if I wanted it, all I had to do was make the decision and apply. The future. It was a crazy night full of the future but bound up in the present, and what a dangerous admixture that is, one that leaves you using up in the present what belongs to the future until in no time at all you are left with a future of penury, indigence.

This night collapses in on itself with its own weight and I hate it, I really hate this evening of penurious future and dead pasts. We got completely smashed as if we knew it was a valediction. There were the three of us, the two girls, you, that band of burlesque girls, Benoit joined in too – all the old faces out for a last gangbang. There was nothing holding us together so it wasn't surprising that the rivets would burst: this was after all what we had always been chasing: physical release, pure eroticism in the form of killing ourselves. Gojković hated all of us, the two girls most of all because they used us for the sex, for our murderous pasts and he wasn't used to this order, this inverted hierarchy, he remained too much the rapist in his make up; the girls hated us in turn because we had failed as artists and could barely keep ourselves together. You hated all of us too because we were full of a history you weren't part of, because we were younger and less serious and foolish, because we hurt you. Lubarda was too caught up in himself and his gambling and this made him unloveable. Like me I guess. Shame stalked our souls and we couldn't stand our own reflections. We wanted to be shadowless men in a world of perpetual noon.

So there is plenty of hate but we all give each other kisses and touch lightly our arms and smile and joke and pretend like we are having fun. A tremendous nervousness overtook me when I reached the rue Montmartre bar, I was nervous about meeting you and my plan to move to Budapest – I wasn't sure I wanted it myself so how could I expect you to want it in turn? Gojković and Lubarda came in and wasted no time in letting me know what Gojković was after:

I want to read what you have already written.

Which totals ten pages of complete shit, Aleksandar.

I don't care. I want to read them. What are they about?

A load of shit, that's what. Dada, Zenitism. Some words on Elaine.

Elaine Pettifer? What do you say about her?

Ah man, what do you think I say? Do you think I'm putting us all on trial, writing this book I'm never going to finish? Is that it: do you think I want to play the role of judge for our shitty lives?

I don't think you should write anything about us.

It's about the art.

Well I don't want you talking about my art. Give me what you've written.

No. There's nothing been written.

You just said you have ten pages down. Give them to me.

Fuck you Aleks. You can't just demand shit from me.

I can and I will.

This kind of talk went on until the girls distracted him and they were good at that. Little did I realise that this would continue. After you died he laid off a bit but he quickly picked up his assault again, becoming apoplectic when he heard I had almost a hundred pages written. I will never show that bastard a single page; he'll just have to wait for it to be published and who knows how long that wait will be.

At least Gojković always had the very best quality cocaine: his links with Trifke and his network meant that for very small favours and handling services Gojković had an almost endless supply of white powder. Many of his clients found this out the nice way and it sweetened them up to know that they could buy some art and snort some fine cocaine while they were at it. Of course over the last months he has used this to frustrate me to the point where I almost threw the fucking pages with all their stupid fucking words in his face, just to have a line or two. Once he even convinced Lubarda that he would publish the manuscript! And then not so long ago he sent Miloš around to get it from me. What it is they think I'm writing I do not know, but they have ganged up together, that much is sure and I'm becoming paranoid about them and their schemes to get their hands on this manuscript. We know too much about ourselves, we look in each other's eyes and see ourselves reflected back, slightly distorted and disfigured, but our own damaged lives nonetheless. Like Narcissus and his pool of gelid water, only the ripples are caused by a dead body being thrown down the far bank, going plop, breaking our masks up with the dead weight of murder.

That night Gojković made sure we were all filled up with Columbian fine powder, the two girls were especially high and twisted with their own power. By the time I finally met you in the green room of that seedy shithole theatre I was coked up and far gone on champagne. Gojković had Benoit flood the place with Veuve Cliquot as if he could wash out the prudent and unwilling and leave the swingers behind for us to cling onto. I don't know why he was so bent on a gangbang that night but he so very clearly was, he so very clearly put all the resources he had into cocaine and champagne and taxis and all the other fucking paraphernalia he enjoyed so much. And since that night I have thought many times about this expenditure by Gojković, and in my deep paranoia I see perfidy and duplicity. You arrived with a big smile on your face and nodded to one and all and you made sure to put me at ease.

Quickly you got fucked up yourself.

And we were all laughing, I remember clearly.

Dark taxi rides rushing through the night and cigarettes gaily lit and allowed by drivers who were as shadowy as the streets obscured out of the taxi windows along all the boulevards, hiding rooms full with rich and well-fed bodies. This is not an end. It is a beginning. Of a mystery we don't know the name of: where had you been living those last months? What had you been doing? The night before, what did you do? We haven't got a single source left to tell us. We're not talking about Jean-Michel Basquiat here: you weren't twenty-seven, you were thirty-seven. Resembling, and not for the first time, Yves Klein, if anybody at all.

We rode through the barrier of our physical selves, those people connected to decent minds and the inhibitions that come with them, we collided with each other and pushed harder in order to gel and exchange particles. We undressed casually, smoothly, using another's hand to slide between flesh and elastic, to follow curve and outline, to slide down crevices and up small mounds, to go inside dark red caves and stand guard on promontories marked with the depression of fantastic aureola. Small murmurings behind loud laughter and affected accents, the delightful invite of moist pussy and loosened assholes. Not a single moment of it belonged to you or I or anyone else for that matter, we were no longer people and had no say in what we felt or what we did.

Who, became a word devoid of interrogation.

I, a forgotten taboo of another race not our own.

Euphoria has its way of playing with you, creating the pretence that in fact you do not exist, the subjective a simulation of the real which is in fact a shared fusion of people: sex is not of two, a man and woman, but of many, of neither man nor woman but a blend of both, a many headed Shiva of multiple cocks and pussy, of a darkness under the hotel lights that obstructs caring who – and the word is useless remember – it is fucking you from behind.

Our last words together were in the taxi on our way to the hotel. They were flippant words and I did most of the talking, trying to apologise and make up even though there was nothing to atone for in particular. You just smiled and didn't say much, in fact I can't remember you saying anything at all. So much of that night I keep secluded and neglected, a willed disuse taking over my memories so that they can lie to degenerate on their own. The future is not of us, no, not of me. But what about our past? My memories can go somewhere else, rest hidden.

But today I woke up and it hit me like an avalanche of shame, powerful and strong because this is all my day was going to have. We just went on fucking! This is what makes the whole thing so stupid and foolish – you died for fuck's sake, and all I can use are the words stupid and foolish – because it was obviously bad enough that you would get a belt out and go ahead and try to orgasm on the cusp of oxygen depravation, and die, so idiotic-looking, like a fetishistic Swiss German, but we had to go and fuck in the presence of your death. Now how evil does that make me? Or how stupid: the fine line between ignorance and evil is exactly that border deserted by all our craven gods and empty ideologies, and which tenuously keeps out the animal. And has it been crossed, this border? Has it fuck.

And this is all there is to my day because the image of you at the time was just a spur on to lower depths, we were so far gone in our sex and inebriation we just left Benoit's giggling as the only comment until we erased all emotion or sensible thought with the whiteness of orgasm. Then what, then what did we do? Too many drugs, the girls argued, for us to call the police straightaway and I just stumbled around with tears in my eyes shouting what was I supposed to do, what was I supposed to do. Some didn't care and just went on snorting lines of coke or drinking from bottles. There was laughter still, the reckless laughter of the high. Mocking. I hate these memories bottomlessly – of those rooms, that fucking decadent suite where all I can see is me blubbering, out of my mind, turning around and around in a pathetic circle inconsolable, attracted to a last look at your dead body but petrified of it at the same time. Repulsed. This now a scene of primal shame for me. And for loss to be shameful is a monumental tragedy because loss should be beyond reproach.

***

It is about talking to someone and saying to yourself: what's the point? We're all going to die. This is all pointless, this is all utter nonsense dressed up as civilisation. We are killing ourselves. We are shooting each other and raping our neighbours, and when we aren't doing that we're buying an SUV or a fridge or clothes made by slaves and these things give us pleasure. We have made a fetish out of the end of things. All things. We will not stop until we have wiped the slate clean completely, until not one of us is left to wipe any longer; this is what my life has taught me, this is the end point in any history of our art that I once started to write. The great artistic unit of the day – well the day must end, that we can be sure of. We are killers, some less sophisticated than others. And, we're all going to die. Now then, you know how bad things have got when you think like this, when this is the alleyway you have backed up into. The question is: what am I going to do to get out?

Djordje Bojić, *Shame* (2006)
Pencil, oil and varnish on canvas, 100 × 90 cm.
Courtesy the estate of Djordje Bojić and Galerie Gojković.

Djordje Bojić, *Zukunft I (Future I)* (2007)
oil and varnish on canvas, 3 × 1.5 m.
Private collection.

We stepped out onto the dusty ground and felt the muscles soften in our legs; it had been a long journey. The army car had grown stuffy and the air thin during the last hour of driving. Crossing the river Drina into Bosnia the mood among us grew grim and the talking stopped. At this base there was a great deal of activity and all the tyres and army boots ground the dust into a fine red layer that swirled up in the morning wind. We were part of a large-scale movement of JNA soldiers and equipment into Bosnia. There was a lot of confusion and not one of the four of us had known how long our time would be on the other side of the Drina. We knew that the JNA was going to spilt officially by May 19 and that the VRS was already strong and fully operational. Just looking around us showed as much. It was a nice morning, one with a wetness on the ground that was busy burning itself into the ether of the spring day. Goran, our driver, ran off immediately in search of somewhere he could piss, his need almost killing him during the last couple of kilometres. He had been extremely tired to begin with and the drive through the night had been hard on him. Miloš and I went to report to our commanding officer who nobody we asked had ever heard of, the Bosnian Serb commanders all thought we belonged to JNA Novi Sad Corps or the forces under Arkan or Šešelj. This made Miloš panic slightly, like a child who loses his mother at the market, but I calmed him down and told him it was a good thing: neither of us knew what was in store for us, but both of us were certain we did not want to be part of anything bad, and we knew that there was a lot of badness going on in Bosnia. Shelling had been carried out over the last few days on a number of towns and villages, the goal to reduce to rubble those areas with a Muslim majority, to set a people in motion and get them to leave, simply, and not come back. We were expected to follow through on the ground and conduct street fighting and clear any last people holding out: the tactics of this flushing out was to induce fear, by any means necessary. Darkness had overtaken and we saw only the light. We picked up our guns and our kitbags and started out knowing full well it would take us a good part of the morning to get there, if not longer, and we liked the idea because we were like recalcitrant schoolboys and would do anything at all to skive off the work the teacher gave us. There were no teachers though, so I guess I should take that observation back. Just merchants in death and darkness. But we enjoyed being together and talking and joking but none of that is going to be reported here. That's not what I want to do, that would be too easy. I never saw Goran again and I think he was killed that spring, tortured and then killed. The image coming to mind one of a dank and smelly room, the kind where we had heard they would rape you only to humiliate but I am not sure about that, they would rape old women maybe yes, but not someone like Goran. They found other ways to wipe the dignity from your body and soul. It was a spring morning and really the air was wet with dew and the countryside was rushed with it. To the left lay low undulating fields with a brook cutting through them, low bushes growing here and there and out then in front of us were lank, stunted trees thwarted by the hardness of the winter here. Some irregulars turn up and we get a lift and the car is humming with five men and their accoutrement and the terror ahead. There are orders everywhere but we duck through them. This is now. Apocalypse then. I saw him come out of the room and Gojković grabbing at his coat to tell him to hurry the fuck up and my intelligence, fallow though it was, knew what the fucker had been up to. He went off, distracted the fat idiot, and Gojković went straight back the way he came and slammed the door shut. Later we moved out. No. What a sorry career in the sorriest of armies. The last days of existence and kids like us hiking through open country to get lost and escape the fighting. General Vuk Obradović may have promised our mothers we would be home in Belgrade by May 19, but when are such promises ever fulfilled? Promises such as that are always needed to get the war started. No. We had no money, no family willing to pay for our flight from the draft. Some of our classmates had gone to Italy, others still to the U.S. But we had open country and Gojković who just dragged us across it. I remember thinking in the car back to the Drina how it wouldn't be such a bad thing if we crashed, like a clairvoyant. The guy not braking once or so it seemed, he just drove like a maniac and we all felt the car rise up off the ground as he took the bends and the hedgerows were closer than they ever had been before. I wonder now what those three women thought then: that they were rescued? That the war was over for them? That safety was just a bus ride away? If it was we didn't let them find out, we just took them to the river, to that hotel. A holding pen. We were all leaving the war behind before it even started. Thoughts are not in line with what the world gives you. I find an art form like Dada and I think of it and agree with it and on we go and then it slowly crumbles and the reality is a whole lot different and these thoughts hold the seeds of my destruction but I don't notice. I will never know. And why can't I write about this clearly? We were three of us walking. No.

***

Cut my hair and want to kill myself. Funny the things which reflect back at you from mirrors, not just noses and eyes and ears and scars and wounds, but something more. Cut your hair and begin again, that's what we all do every time, each as vain as the next. I went out today for a coffee and to get out of the apartment. The Japanese they speak at the café always gets into my head, this bramble of noise and sound and I think, for the hundredth time, what my life could have been if I was born in another place – not another time, just another place. Like Japan or Norway or Germany. The café did not bring me out of myself at all, which is why I went in the first place. I just sat there and watched people come and go buying cigarettes and drinking rapid espressos, thinking of the films of Yasujirō Ozu and feeling like I was starring in one, with one of the many trains that appear in his movies coming to take me away out of my little apartment and routine and sadness. A train journey could solve everything. I've always been fascinated by Japan ever since that first day when I hobbled into the café, the high speed trains and all that technology. Even the nuclear bombs and the scorched streets of a raised Hiroshima, that other end point in supposed progress. The suicide cults and their mania over the end of the world, the inevitable yet ever receding apocalypse.

I paid and left the sound of Japanese chatter behind and as I walked across the avenue I caught my reflection in the window of a 29 bus and thought to myself: I should cut my hair, long and greasy and lank about my whole face as it was. And as soon as I got in I went to the bathroom and hacked it off in great, ugly cuts until it fell stupidly around my ears, then up more and more, until all that is left now are some fluffy islands of hair around my dome of bone, square and bumpy. I look like a younger man alright, but a fucking idiot young man.

Somehow I just want an end to things, go to a Japan or a Norway built of the bones of gods I know don't exist. A messianic banquet of famine, a banquet of meaninglessness. The tears surprised me at first but they make sense; a younger man staring at himself and hating what he sees – why would he not have tears in his eyes?

Trips to the outside world no longer bring relief. The last week I had walked from here over along the river as far as the Institut du Monde Arabe and sat and read by the Quai Saint-Bernard and the walk and the different atmosphere of that part of Paris managed briefly to transport me away and above the present, to the cities I've walked in, by all those rivers I've sat. What is the Seine other than an acolyte of every other river I've swam out in: the Sava and the Danube and their inky silk waters. And us kids running and jumping, old shoes sucked onto our feet and skinny arms bolted to our sides and little cries ringing out as we crash into the water. Jumping in timelessness. Now we could never watch on as innocently as we followed one after the other into the swirling dark waters of rivers we've always known.

That is why I am sending this manuscript to Peter Tomc in Ljubljana and dedicating it to you: I've realised that the key to this airless dark room I sit in is one you gave me over a year ago but whose use I never realised until now. They're not going to stop this persistent nagging campaign to get me to hand over a year's work. Their fear is pathetic, especially when you consider the state of this miserable manuscript and how it lounges over itself to fit me and my misery in, the art shuffled to the back like the way in Belgrade the waters of the Sava must meet the intemperate Danube and pour themselves into it, erasing themselves in the process.

I can hear and feel the water. Many have jumped before me, and many more will follow; some others have been pushed, others still coerced. All into the water. The rivers of Europe flowing with blood, meandering with bad conscience and sad memories. Levees built with evil. Water flowing over the honest man, his course awash with an ebb and flow it must be wonderful to be part of, nothing less than a sublime release.

***

We three of us were walking. We were lost, completely, and we did not want to be found. We were supposed to be in the village of Brusna. To do there whatever it was we were to do. But at Dragočava we lagged behind. Absconded. We could hear shelling, low and dull and lazy sounding and plumes of smoke going up from the other side of a small knoll. But none of this spoke of action. The whole enterprise seemed intensely slothful. Words were few between us. A jeep could be seen on the other side of two large fields that had a farmhouse centred along their median. Three buildings. Miloš guessed that Brusna was not far away. We rested and put down everything we had. Hands on hips. A strong indolence in us and in all the world around us. This obscene action going on, the whispers of heavy artillery and the susurrus of automatic weapons firing. Into the darkness. Houses being emptied. There was a bird in the sky above. Swirling and diving. An occasional scrawk. An eagle perhaps, who knew? We knew nothing about nature. Or about the Bosnian landscape. There was a fight: was it an eagle or just a bird? But all three of us failed to muster real passion and the argument died away with nobody knowing anything. What constituted 'just a bird'? That is what I wanted to know. Anything that wasn't an eagle. More gunfire from the village. It was getting warm. Let's go to the house down where that jeep went. Could be Bosnians. Then we will fight. There are no Bosnians left between here and Foča willing to fight. Do you think? Well, I don't know. We put our stuff back on our shoulders and entered the field. Over an ancient-looking stile. The field had grass in it, and it looked fresh. It looked strong. And green. There was dew on it but not much. No animals or trees save some of the deformed trees bent from the wind of winters innumerable. The jeep was nowhere to be seen. From the direction we approached, we saw only one gable of the biggest house and the front of one of the outhouses. It looked like a sheep farm, or so Gojković thought. I would have loved some sheep's cheese. Strange cravings and stranger concerns. The land ran down in a gentle incline. The others got their guns off their shoulders and held them out when we were within three hundred metres or so of the house. I had learned to read distances at the camp. The image of Lukić entered my head and I was busy thinking of him so didn't notice the others drawing their guns. Gojković of course ready to fire. I was thinking fondly I have to say, of Lukić and the strange rites I went through with him. His idea of helping me through training was not exactly a great favour. More like some fatherly advice. I forgave him completely his initial attempt at rape. The knife not an inch from my neck. We even laughed about it. He knew he had done wrong and that was enough. Was it enough between me and you, homme de guerre[28]? I had done wrong walking down that field, reaching that house. But I never told you. It was my knife that I sharpened by myself in the dark of night in this dark apartment on the rue Danielle Casanova, so very far away from that sorry land of Bosnia. When I was a boy. When I was still growing. Still yet to learn an iota of the world. We never laughed about it. My victims faceless. My atonement unspoken. Suddenly the two guys separated at a run, down on their hunches and guns stuck out and Gojković was up against the gable and Lubarda to his left behind a wall that ran around to the first of the outhouses.

---

28   Appears in French in original: a play on the English: War + Man. (Trans.)

And me just standing there looking at them playing at being soldiers. It was funny because it could have been New Belgrade and we could have been eight years old again, that sloping field like any one of the fields full of rubbish that had been our first playground. Who did they think they were about to attack, I wanted to know? And off they went, Gojković first with Lubarda covering him, shouting that it was Serb forces and demanding to know who was present. I never for a second thought there would be violence. A shout went out from the second outhouse, which was behind the first and which neither of us three could see, even Gojković who was out in the farmyard, crabwalking like he was Martin Sheen, darting his gun, perpendicular from his body, in all directions. Welcome, could be heard. A perfectly warm salute on a fine spring day. Lubarda put down his gun. Relieved, he smiled at me. I shrugged my shoulders. He appeared: a tall fat man, around fifty years old I guessed. A shock of white hair on top of his concave face. In army fatigues, but not those of the JNA. Gojković and he were immediately the best of friends, shook hands, introduced each other. Lubarda handed me a cigarette and we moved out into the farmyard and put our gear on the ground, lighting our cigarettes and frowning at this fat man. He was visiting the farm, it belonged to his brother-in-law who had gone to Sarajevo to help his family move to a safer place in the north. Where he also had family. The man talked at length and it was clear he was a bore. He had in his hands a small tin bucket half full of water for no reason I could deduce, and as he emptied this up against the wall which Lubarda had protected himself behind from an enemy never there, he offered us a lift to wherever we were going. The village? Which village, he laughed? Brusna? Foča? Of course Gojković didn't want this fat, pedantic seeming man to know that we were lost. He became vague, elliptical, until the older man looked closely, almost with suspicion, at all three of us, young and wholly indifferent to being soldiers. Lubarda looked like a field doctor, a scientist. I think he came to the conclusion we were pulling off some special operation, what the hell else could we have been doing, lost and disorientated without any officer or set of orders that we were willing to impart to him, scouting out pointlessly his deserted brother-in-law's farm? It had not been a jeep we had seen, but a small hatchback. We all climbed in and our bags and guns were stuffed in the back alongside Miloš and I. Off we went and the guy would not stop talking to Gojković, telling jokes about the first campaigns they had carried out against his village's Muslims. How it went like clockwork. He was a bit manic as if he'd already started drinking for the day. He thought himself to be a good joker, able to tell a joke just right. And I saw it all as a joke: us in his car, going AWOL in the middle of a war that was being carried out by an army that was not supposed to be there in a country we Yugoslavians did not recognise. And this was when I saw the hedgerow pass by and saw it closely like I had never seen the countryside before. It was real, it may have all been a joke, but it was real. He was taking corners like he was a formula one driver and Miloš stopped smiling and I could sense his panic. It was obvious we were going to crash. We both of us in the back just knew. Things sped up, the punch line was near and reality was about to get twisted and turned until it made us, forced us, to look at it anew, like an unveiled window in a prison that held its captives for years without an end: there it is, the new country, a vision of sights so wonderful in its mundanity you could love this world again and the fat white-haired man went on laughing, even after he had lost control of the little fucking car, and we moved with the swiftness of an eagle or bird, just a bird, and why is it that fat people drive small cars, and how will this end, how will we be when we reach the impact point, the place of conjunction absolute between man and machine and peasant country? Questions and thoughts crowded my mind. Why do so many great people die in car crashes or from drugs? Because there should be nothing natural about their death I guessed, it should be a step above the natural laws of the world. Belts for example, cowhides leathered and cut and buckled. Why evil people silence their friends who tell the truth? Aleksandar Gojković, Miloš Lubarda. Playing in the fields together and I out with them, escaping the watch of my mother. I can still recall after all these years the sudden electricity of these things filling my head in an instant. As it turned out the crash was less spectacular than I had instinctively imagined it would be: he had lost control, this fat stupid bastard, going around a bend in the middle of the road and the mere sight of a small truck coming the opposite way, five hundred metres away, set him turning wildly on the steering wheel and the back of the car went out from behind us and he braked right when he shouldn't have and the car's end went out into the verge and this slowed us thankfully as my side went flying into a tree. Our impact point. The hedgerow had fought its way right up against the car and the frame scrunched down toward me and I was suddenly wedged on top of Miloš and a kitbag. It felt like something was attacking the car from below, all four of us flew up and hit our heads on the roof before being dropped back down on our seats that felt horribly deformed, all of us cursing as roughly as we could. Then silence. Then the truck flew by and beeped its horn happily and went on, not even slowing down to see if a fellow human had met their end. This set our incompetent chauffeur cursing his enemies, whom he felt just had to have been driving the indifferent truck. Who else but Muslims? This was war! Probably fucking Serbs, Miloš grunted, extracting himself out from underneath me and contorting his wiry body out of the busted car. We all got out and looked at each other, shocked and surprised at what had happened, that we were alive, none of us even hurt. The car was in a pretty bad way. The fat man looked at it with bewilderment, shaking his head, and then suddenly he turned from it and looked up and down the deserted country road. Okay men, we must walk the rest of the way. He had already forgotten about his poor little car. This was war, after all. He got the hunting rifle out from the front passenger seat that he carried like a peasant and we all four of us took one last look at the wreck, cosied up against the tree, and went on our way. He said then that there was good to it, for most of the Muslim community were camping out in the surrounding woods, had fled there since the shelling started and the first units passed through. We walked this interminable road and it was lonely. And pointless, listening to this fat idiot go on about his childhood and how he had grown up in these fields. But I could hear in the sound of his voice that his childhood was a lie to him, his view of the world when he was a child was a morally superior one and the adult in him was embarrassed by this and so he lied to himself. He was pigheaded. It didn't matter because I stopped listening. Gojković kept him entertained by asking the odd question and laughing at his terrible gags. More important was that right then something akin to the appreciation of the artwork, or rather of everyday life's alignment into the category of the artwork, the surprising readymade, grew up in me that morning while walking along that deserted road. I looked around the open country at the hills that rose up to the south and then at the thick blanket of forest to the east. Up until then we had done nothing, seen nothing, the three of us knew nothing of the world nor of the weight our lives carried in it. There was a long moment of silence I remember when we were just walking with each of our thoughts when the fat man had finally shut up with the exertion of the walk. Last moments of innocence. Then finally the fat man spoke again: What's this we have? I told you so. They've been hiding out in the woods. Ahead of us in the near distance, three figures came out from the woods to the east. They were women of different ages, and despite the stretch of land between us, I felt they were unmistakably Bosniak Muslims. I looked across at the other men and Miloš was frowning, he knew that this was bad news. Aleksandar looked blank and opaque, ready for anything. Much like the way his face would look later at that horrible motel by the river. Friendship is seeing people you recognise disfigured and mutated again and again, becoming disgusting or loveable in turn and that which you always have a name for. We watched them step carefully over the heavy, matted grass and thread their way up a low embankment onto the road.

[The typescript ends here]

APPENDIX 6:
DOCUMENTATION OF DJORDJE BOJIĆ AND THE LGB GROUP

15 rue Danielle Casanova, Paris in the present day

From the series, Everyday, Everyday, Venice intervention, 2001

Galerie Gojković, which manages the estate of Djordje Bojić
and many other LGB artists, in its present day location
on rue Turenne, Paris

APPENDIX 6

From the series, Everyday, Everyday, Venice intervention, 2001

The original folio of 'To Warmann' as it came into the editor's possession. The title page was missing and no address was indicated on the envelope.

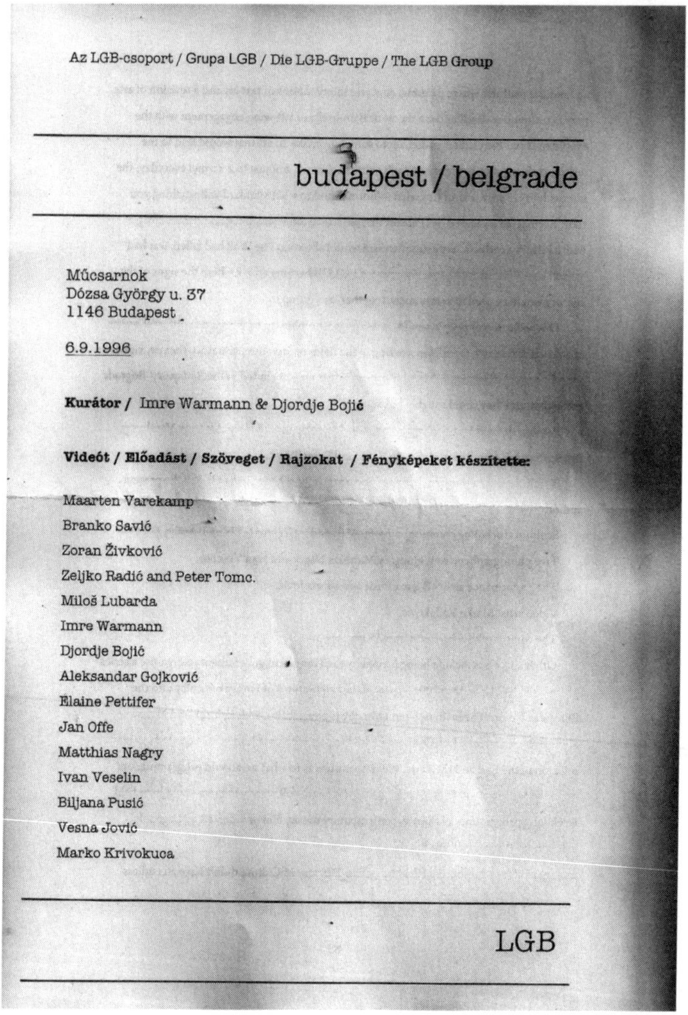

Az LGB-csoport / Grupa LGB / Die LGB-Gruppe / The LGB Group

---

budapest / belgrade

Műcsarnok
Dózsa György u. 37
1146 Budapest

6.9.1996

Kurátor / Imre Warmann & Djordje Bojić

Videót / Előadást / Szöveget / Rajzokat / Fényképeket készítette:

Maarten Varekamp
Branko Savić
Zoran Živković
Zeljko Radić and Peter Tomc.
Miloš Lubarda
Imre Warmann
Djordje Bojić
Aleksandar Gojković
Elaine Pettifer
Jan Offe
Matthias Nagry
Ivan Veselin
Biljana Pusić
Vesna Jović
Marko Krivokuca

LGB

'Budapest/Belgrade', 6 October – 28 October, 1996.
Cover of exhibition calalogue, courtesy the archive of
Kunsthalle Budapest.

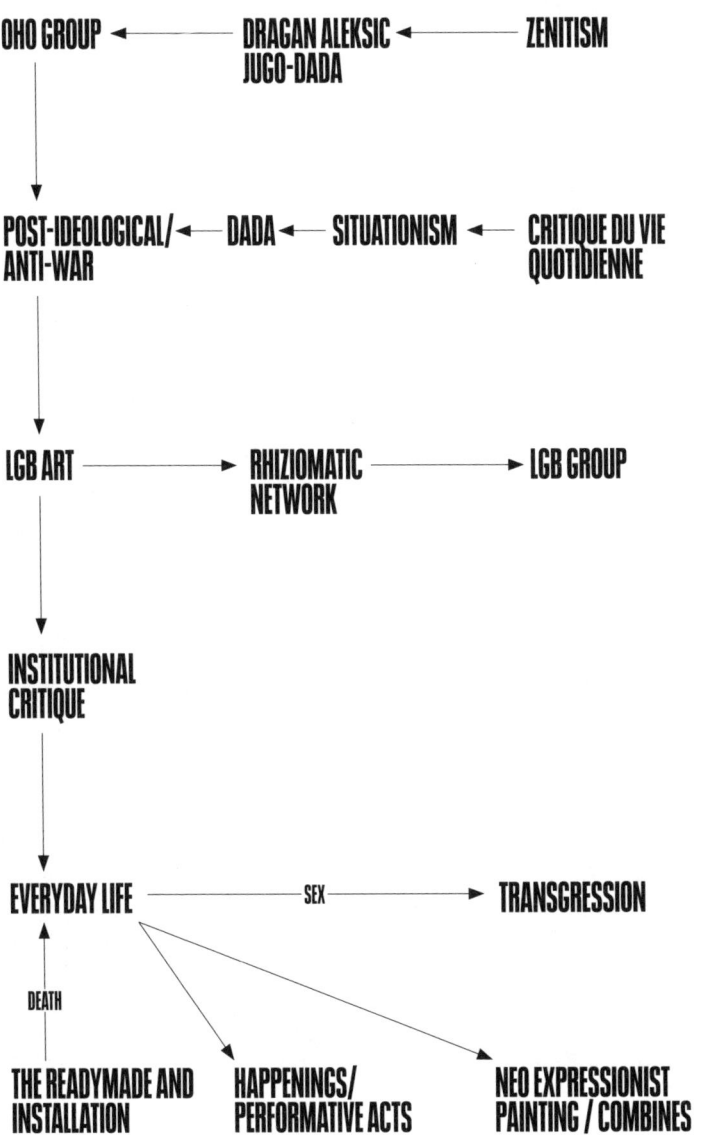

LGB Documentation conceived by Imre Warmann, c. 1999

Opening of the retrospective exhibition 'Seven Years: LGB',
Museum of Contemporary Art, Belgrade (6 October, 2002).
Photo: Vuk Jovanović

The LGB Group reached their international apotheosis in Dublin in May 2004 during the celebration of ten member states' accession into the European Union, marking a new era in east/west relations. Courtesy Biljana Pusić.

Today I haven't been satysfied
and I think that I might ri
and even start cutting myself

the final result. This empty
and I truly don't know
I do not know who I am
sleep with or work with
I just want to do so

Even my hands are not whe
Where is this going
I'm afraid for my endi

> Today I haven't been satisfied
> and I think that I might in
> and even about cutting myself
>
> the final result. This empty
> and I truly don't know
> I do not know who I am
> sleep with or work with
> I just want to do so
>
> Even my hands are not like
> Where is this going
> I'm afraid for my arti

Note in one of Bojić's last notebooks, quoted by Andrew Bradshaw in the catalogue of the retrospective in the Museum of Contemporary Art, Belgrade (25 February - 20 March, 2008) in which he makes the case for Bojić's suicide.

ARTWORKS BY DARKO DRAGIČEVIĆ

inside cover:	Belgrade, 2011 [from the series The Readymades]
p. 112:	TISCH, 2011, courtesy of the artist and Jelena Pančevac.
p. 113:	Autechre, video No.7, 2008 [from the series Taste of Life]
p. 121:	Miloš Lubarda: Карађорђе, 2011 [from the series The Readymades]
pp. 122 – 123:	Miloš Lubarda: Другови и другарице I, II, III, IV, 2011 [from the series The Readymades]
pp. 124 – 125:	Miloš Lubarda: Биће боље, 2011 [from the series The Readymades]
pp. 128 – 129:	L.A. A&D, 2008
pp. 130 – 131:	L.A. III, 2008
pp. 141 – 143:	Elaine Pettifer: Down Shall Kill The Bull Up Shall Fly A Kite (After Lawrence Weiner), 2011 [from the series The Readymades] (photos by Milica Lopičić)
pp. 144 – 145:	Elaine Pettifer: Each Moment Depends Upon A Perception A (After Lawrence Weiner), 2011 [from the series The Readymades] (photos by Milica Lopičić)
pp. 148 – 151:	Elaine Pettifer: Each Moment Depends Upon A Perception B (After Lawrence Weiner), 2011 [from the series The Readymades] (photos by Milica Lopičić)
pp. 178 – 179:	Pillow No.1 Ann-Marie Johansen, 2003 [from the series Pillow]
pp. 180 – 181:	Pillow No.5 Cristina Bueno (detail), 2003 [from the series Pillow]
pp. 199 – 203:	Empty, 2009 [from the series Empty] (photos by Saana Inari)
pp. 208 – 209:	Aleksandar Gojković: Hommage à Raymond Hains Orange, Jaune, Rouge, 2011 [from the series The Readymades], private collection.
pp. 224 – 227:	Jan Offe: 3 Course Dinner, 2011 [from the series The Readymades]
pp. 260 – 263:	Kool Kat Walk, 2004
p. 264:	Berlin Performance, 2009
pp. 283 – 284:	Ideal Week, 2009 [from the series Empty]
p. 287:	Prazno V, 2009 [from the series Empty]
pp. 296 – 297:	Djordje Bojić: Shame, 2011 [from the series The Readymades]
pp. 298 – 299:	Djordje Bojić: Zukunft I, 2011 [from the series The Readymades]
p. 320:	Vernissage "When The Air Gets Thin", Circus Gallery SKC, Belgrade, 2002
p. 318:	Untitled, 2009 [from the series Empty]

The Readymades
John Holten
A Broken Dimanche Press publication,
Berlin 2019
www.brokendimanche.eu

Ragnarok I

ISBN: 978-3-943196-78-8

Second edition

© John Holten 2011, 2019

Artwork © Darko Dragicevic, 2011, 2019

Assistant editor second edition: Ross Fraser-Smith
Book design and layout: Form und Konzept

This is a work of fiction, all characters, situations, conversations, scenarios, art and cultural occurrences are the invention of the author with the exception of those belonging to factual history.

Broken Dimanche Press
Büro BDP